PARIS IMPERFECT

Recent Titles by Susie Vereker

AN OLD-FASHIONED ARRANGEMENT
POND LANE AND PARIS

PARIS IMPERFECT

Susie Vereker

severn
House

This first world edition published 2008
in Great Britain and in 2009 in the USA by
SEVERN HOUSE PUBLISHERS LTD of
9–15 High Street, Sutton, Surrey, England, SM1 1DF.
Trade paperback edition published
in Great Britain and the USA 2009 by
SEVERN HOUSE PUBLISHERS LTD

British Library Cataloguing in Publication Data

Vereker, Susie
  Paris imperfect
  1. English - France - Paris - Fiction 2. Love stories
  I. Title
  823.9'2[F]

ISBN-13: 978-0-7278-6725-4   (cased)
ISBN-13: 978-1-84751-106-5   (trade paper)

All Severn House titles are printed on acid-free paper.

Typeset by Palimpsest Book Production Ltd.,
Grangemouth, Stirlingshire, Scotland.
Printed and bound in Great Britain by
MPG Books Ltd., Bodmin, Cornwall.

For my family

One

My mother doesn't believe in spoiling her daughters, but she set aside her principles to phone on my birthday. Calls to Paris are a little cheaper these days, she told me.

Finally she asked, 'Is he going to marry you, that Frenchman of yours?' She never refers to Philippe by name.

'These days marriage isn't that fashionable,' I began, 'and since I've already tried it . . .'

'Twice,' she reminded me helpfully.

'Exactly. Twice bitten.'

She cleared her throat. 'Well, if he asks you, you'd better accept. You're not much of a catch and you're not getting any younger.' She was entirely serious.

'Gee, thanks, Ma. Always nice to know there's someone on my side.'

Ignoring this heavy-handed irony, she ploughed on. 'You may've thought I don't approve, but I've come round to the idea of a Frenchman and I'd like to feel you're settled before I die.'

When she comes out with that kind of stuff, I never know whether she's had a bad chit from the doctor or if she's making a general philosophical point about the Grim Reaper's eventual harvest. Probably the latter because, like many Northerners, she's a tough old bat.

All the same, weakly I asked her if she'd had a check-up lately. She snapped no, she was as fit as a fiddle, but as for her friends . . . She then began to tell me about the ailments of the old biddy next door in the genteel retirement village where she lives.

The good-hearted people of this world probably think I should take care of my mother if she's too old to be on her own, but actually she's relatively spry. She's plonked herself in the oldies' farmstead because she likes to plan ahead. Anyway, whatever she says, she hates France – and Philippe, for that matter. He and she would never, ever see eye to eye about anything if she lived here, so the chances of her not-getting-any-younger daughter becoming a respectable married woman again would be even more remote.

She and I don't see eye to eye much either.

One thing that bugs me is the question of the photos. She has several of my sister in her sitting room. 'Rosalind meeting the Queen' has been enlarged and sits in pride of place on top of the television. Roz is in mid-curtsy, and the Queen, radiant despite a curious beige dress, is beaming down on her. Roz's husband, a senior civil servant, with emphasis on the 'senior', is looking proudly on.

They have three quiet, academic children who've passed oodles of exams and done all the right things at the right time. I've observed, though, that my niece has a twinkle in her eye so she may do something wicked one day. Hope so. I'm tired of being the only scarlet woman in the family.

There's just one adult photo of me in my mother's so-called luxury bungalow. I'm holding Alexander, my son, who's then about two and looks like a cherub on Slim-Fast. He always was a thin child – I underfed him, Ma thought.

She's packed away the pictures of both my weddings. Two weddings does sound bad, I know. It's an old story, but what happened was that when I was young and foolish I fell madly in love with a gorgeous man – truly irresistible, film-star good looks – who, I eventually discovered, had begun to stray soon after we returned from the honeymoon. After several dodgy years I decided I really couldn't hack it, so there was a divorce. On the rebound, I married portly but seemingly kind Dr Jekyll, who then metamorphosed into Mr Hyde on a permanent basis. Gerald/Mr Hyde turned out to have a hefty right hook, which he used to break my nose – no permanent damage actually, except to my soul and, since there was another divorce, my status. Not everyone around here takes a twice-divorced woman seriously.

Certainly not Philippe, though he thinks I'm a good lay, if nothing else, or so he says. Big deal. He doesn't like my stomach, which is not flat enough. Flat stomachs are de rigueur in Paris. Legs? OK below the knee, but the jodhpur thighs are a problem as far as he's concerned. Bosom passable if on the small side – better than droopy, he thinks – but he's worried that soon my stomach will stick out further than my boobs. He quite likes my eyes – navy blue – but my thick mousy hair is too curly. Parisiennes must have smooth hair. My face is just about pretty enough, but chic and presentation are more important than mere prettiness, and someone rather messy-looking like me needs someone like him, a man of impeccable taste, to keep me up to the mark. I've improved enormously since he took me in hand, he says. One advantage I have over the French women is my height – they're mostly midgets and I'm 5 foot 7. Philippe likes this. My excessive flesh would be *insupportable* if it were not spread out over a long frame.

Why do I put up with these backhanders? Beggars can't be choosers, as my mother would say. I have vowed to stick with this relationship and make it work, and I've evolved a new way of dealing with him. I said, 'How about if we keep it to Monday evenings? You can save up all my black marks, write down my faults as and when, and then dish them out on a Monday between seven o'clock and eight. Then I can have the rest of the week off.'

One thing about Philippe: he does have an intermittent sense of humour, and he took the point.

He's not the only nag-bag, according to the network of foreign spouses and girlfriends. It's the way the French are brought up. Their parents and schoolteachers give them hell: sit down, shut up, do this, don't do that – especially don't do that – so they think it's natural to criticize. We Anglo-Saxons are wimps if we get upset.

I won't allow him to bully my son Alexander, though, and to be fair Philippe treats him well. Luckily Alex is sporty and Philippe is patient about teaching him tennis and taking him to the Stade de France to watch *le football* or *le rugby*. Philippe only has to play the father role in small doses as Alex is not around all the time. He goes to school in England, paid for by his dad.

I was dead against the idea of sending him away, but Alex begged and pleaded to go to boarding school, partly to emulate Harry Potter and partly because, when I tried sending him to the local *lycée*, he couldn't take the flak the teachers dished out. Then, of course, his best English friend in Paris was going away to school, so Alex just had to do the same.

I have joint custody with Harry, my first gorgeous, treacherous husband – we still get on pretty well, thank God – and he didn't want Alex to turn into a French boy, and frankly nor do I. So when he, the ex, offered to pay the boarding-school fees, it seemed like a great opportunity for my precious son, and probably good for an only child to get away from his sometimes obsessive, possessive mum.

I miss Alex dreadfully, but he doesn't miss me. I work flat out during term-time so I can spend every moment of the holidays with him, and it works a treat. He's a happy, well-adjusted boy. A credit to me, kind people sometimes say, not without a smidgen of surprise that Clio the Black Sheep has produced such an angelic little lamb. Big lamb now, I should say, as he's twelve and growing by the minute. He must be about to transmute into a teenage horror. I've told him I'm steeling myself.

In case Philippe throws me out one day, I'm building up a nest egg. I'm a tour guide, which he thinks is downmarket. He prefers to talk about my other job, restaurant correspondent, he calls it, food being the top serious subject in the Gallic world. Actually, I write about France, restaurants, hotels and touro-cultural stuff, for a one-horse magazine published in America. You can hardly call it journalism, but Philippe does when he's trying to boost my standing with his friends. Sometimes he comes with me when I travel around France researching places, but mostly he stays in Paris on his own. This is a big mistake, according to my mother. One should never leave a man alone, for fear of what he might get up to.

I don't know if he strays or not, but he's always touchingly pleased to see me when I get back and these absences seem to make his heart, or his desire, grow fonder. I'm pleased to see him too, and to be home in the apartment. Like Elizabeth Bennet, I was convinced I really fancied my man when I first saw his pad. Not that I'm a gold-digger – he doesn't have much dosh to dig for – but Philippe's apartment is so imaginative and so original that I thought, as he'd chosen it, he must be imaginative and original too.

We live in the sixteenth arrondissement, a staid, residential part of Paris. Most of the flats here are vast and elegant, but dark and gloomy. Philippe has something quite different. The building looks conventional enough from the outside, and the sombre entrance hall is unremarkable. Nervously you take a tiny two-person lift – you can't believe its flimsy swing doors are made from basket-ware, and why is it making that sinister rickety noise?

If you're still alive six long floors up, you open our front door. Then there's a magical room with giant windows that run from ceiling to floor, the height of two storeys. Minimalist modern furniture, faintly oriental in style, creates a quasi-Japanese ambience, not unusual in London but totally different from the overstuffed formal Parisian decor. There isn't any colour in the apartment, just beige, white and the soft chestnut browns of the wooden parquet. And Philippe likes it to be tidy.

This sitting room, or salon, takes up the whole of one floor. The kitchen and bedrooms upstairs are tiny and inconvenient, but who cares? The best part, as far as I'm concerned, is the little roof garden, where you can see the Eiffel Tower looming close by, with the Bois de Boulogne on the other side and the rest of the city sprawling out below. Philippe has allowed me to plant a white wisteria and even some red geraniums – he doesn't mind colour on the roof, as long as it isn't pink. We had quite a few problems finding sufficiently refined garden chairs, though. He sometimes suggests I should sunbathe naked in summer, so I'll be uniformly tanned and more tasteful to look at, but I'm a modest person and there are other blocks the same height.

Mostly everything is pretty uniform here – the buildings, the size of the trees, the chic-conservative people – and it all adds up to a cohesive, elegant whole. The world-famous Paris landmarks and the various outcrops of modern architecture appear all the more dramatic and different against this well-ordered classical background.

As for Philippe himself, he's a little younger than I am – two years, actually – tallish, very thin and intellectual-looking, with black, black hair, a serious bony nose and amazing cheekbones. He wears designer glasses and, of course, carefully chosen, well-fitting designer clothes, which look good on his lean frame. But I've concluded that he is chic-conservative French, rather than the dramatic-different variety.

Two

I call my boss Miss Piggy. Not to her face of course. Her name is Elaine and she's a tall, Amazonian bottle-blonde of mixed European ancestry – Scandinavian/Slav/Russian, I'm not sure what, but she speaks English well with a vaguely transatlantic accent.

'I have an assignment for you, Clio,' she drawled over the phone. She has given up smoking, but her voice is full of ash.

Elaine has decreed that assignments have to be discussed in person at the office. Mary was there too when I arrived. She is the nicest person in the world, somewhat cowed by her man, who is Very Big at the British Embassy, as Elaine is always telling everyone. She gets a real kick out of mentioning that one of her employees, her tour guides, is a diplomatic spouse.

Plump and demure, Mary grinned at me as, notebooks in hand, we sat down opposite Elaine who was staring importantly at her computer screen. She dished out our assignments. Mary gets nothing until next week, explained Elaine, as right now she has some VIP colleagues from London staying. Mary and I do this job because, though Miss Piggy pays peanuts, she is willing to be flexible about hours.

Today Elaine seemed uptight and edgy, more so than usual. She even complained that my skirt was too short. I said it's the same length as it was last week, but she was not amused. It's not as if she's a fashion queen herself. Despite her age and her porcine figure, she dresses in leather and flutters her long false eyelashes like a drag queen.

I was instructed to pick up an American couple and a Canadian guy from separate hotels and take them on a tour of battlefields from World War One and Two, with the Bayeux Tapestry thrown in for good measure. Should be profitable, as Americans are kind and enthusiastic, and sometimes even give me tips. I accept gratuities unblushingly, both for my nest egg and for my numerous trips to England to see Alex. Most of the rest of my salary is allocated to my share of the household expenses, which Philippe carefully calculates. When I was young and had money, I thought it was a vulgar subject of little interest. Now I have none, I find I think quite hard about it.

It wasn't a good start to the trip. I was stuck in one of those solid, horn-blaring Paris traffic jams and consequently late in picking up the Americans. The arrangement was that I'd phone on my mobile when I arrived near their hotel, but they'd jumped the gun and were waiting in the street. The guy wasn't happy as I loaded their luggage into the boot. He was small and plump with a red face and a beard like Father Christmas, but without the ho, ho, ho. Was there no one punctual in this goddamn town? he enquired.

His wife twittered anxiously, 'Now, dear, never mind. She's here now. I'm Kay, and this is Melvin.'

I smiled gratefully at her. Tiny, white-haired and bespectacled like her husband, she was wearing the regular tourist's uniform of beige anorak, cream trousers and tennis shoes. Melvin wasn't pleased to hear we still had to pick up the Canadian. A private tour was what they had booked, he grumbled.

'Now, dear,' said Kay soothingly, 'the nice lady at the agency explained all that and she's making a discount.'

Melvin fumed on about how it had better be a pretty darn good discount and for God's sake watch out for that car and these Frenchman don't have the first idea how to drive.

I made confident remarks, like 'It's not as bad as it looks' – untrue, it's worse – as I nudged my way along in the Renault. Not the most up-to-date model, I admit, but it goes and it's comfortable, and anyway, North American clients don't usually know or care what's fashionable in Europe.

'You speak English well, dear,' said Kay.

'Jesus, that's because she *is* English, Momma,' said Melvin with what was almost a chuckle.

'No way! That's just so interesting. Did you know, dear, that my Melvin was born in England too, but he was raised in the US? He's American now, of course, but he still has his cute British ways.'

'Really?' I said.

I had to stop talking because we'd arrived at the Etoile, the most terrifying roundabout in the world, six lanes swirling round the Arc de Triomphe. Foreign drivers have been known to circle it for hours, unable to break free once they're in the middle of its mad whirlpool. Sometimes I wimp out and avoid the area, but today it was necessary to be brave/bite the bullet/grasp the nettle/take the bull by the horns.

Glancing back, I could see Kay's white face as I nudged my way through the melee. You have to glare at the drivers bearing down from the right, who have priority, and force them to give way without actually hitting them. Even Melvin was silent apart from an occasional 'Shit, would ya believe it?' Finally, as I managed to fight my way out, he muttered, 'Not bad. You've got balls, young lady, I'll give ya that.'

I laughed politely, faintly flattered by 'young lady', and turned into the slip road beside Avenue de la Grande-Armée, where I was due to collect the Canadian. Melvin was gazing at my knees. Now the danger of being killed by a mad French driver had receded, he couldn't seem to make up his mind which he preferred to study, my anatomy or his map of Paris.

'That crazy Arc de Triomphe circus has to be just about the worst piece of town planning I ever saw,' he said. 'Eleven roads meeting together, most of them major routes out of the city. Jesus!'

'I don't think Baron Haussmann envisaged twenty-first-century traffic,' I said, and then went into my Haussmann spiel about how, in the mid-1800s, this imaginative but draconian urban planner had the grotty narrow streets of central Paris pulled down. He then revamped the city with all these wonderful wide boulevards and great golden stone buildings, not forgetting the remarkable 1,300-mile network of sewers.

While Melvin was getting out his guidebook, probably to check figures on the diameter of the sewer pipes, I double-parked and was about to call the Canadian when a pleasant-looking specimen of mature manhood swam into view. Judging by his untidy clothes, he wasn't local, so optimistically I opened the window.

'Mr Dryden?' I gushed.

'Insider Tours? Clio Forrester? Hi! Great to meet you.'

I sighed with relief. I don't know what TV stereotype I'd been expecting – lumberjack or Mountie, with touches of Jim

Carey? What I saw was a crumpled-looking king-sized bloke, with wavy iron-grey hair, an intelligent weather-beaten face and deep brown eyes. I don't go for this large outdoor type at all, and yet, as he smiled at me, I recognized that unmistakable jolt of mutual attraction.

Always a good way to go. A mild flirtation helps the touring business, though any kind of serious fraternization with clients is against Miss Piggy's rules. As she says, this is not a dating agency. Of course not. I explain to the occasional lone male client who may think a hot date is nevertheless on the cards that I am spoken for. My heart belongs to Philippe, I tell them. And it's true. My conscience is clear. Maybe I'm too prim for my own good, but I don't play away.

I made the introductions, and Joe Dryden settled amicably in the back of the car with a pink-faced Kay. It was clear even she couldn't help responding to his hunky attractions. I peeked in the mirror. There seemed to be an awful lot of him folded into the rear seat.

With more gasps of horror from Kay and oaths from Melvin, I edged my way into the kamikaze traffic of the Boulevard Périphérique, the Paris ring road, another of hell's highways. Apparently a French anthropologist said his countrymen use their cars to demonstrate their own superiority and contempt for their fellows. I believe him.

Melvin studied his map. 'I guess you need to take the A1. That should get us there.'

'Yes,' I said politely.

'On second thoughts, you might be held up by airport traffic if you take that route.'

'I'll risk it.'

'I'll yell out the turns for you,' he said, rustling the map.

I gripped the steering wheel and braked to avoid a 2CV that had suddenly pulled out in front of us. 'So kind, but I have lived here a while, you see, and I know the way.' The car behind blared its horn.

'Yeah, yeah, all you gals say that, but I never met a woman who could read a map or find her own backyard without a couple of wrong turns.'

I bit back a retort.

'Hey, Melvin, in Canada you could be thrown in jail for that kind of sexist remark,' said Joe comfortably.

Kay giggled.

'Have you two been to France before, then?' asked Joe.

Kay chirruped, 'No, this is our first time.'

Melvin rustled the map again without speaking.

'Must get the traffic news,' I said, turning on the radio to calm my nerves. Then I stole another glance at Joe, who caught my eye in the mirror. Hastily I concentrated on the road ahead.

Yes, he was nice, that Joe, but what was it with this Melvin creature? Americans were normally the most friendly and appreciative tourists, so I guess Melv must have inherited his tendency to complain and crab from his British parents. Not that we are as hard to please as the French, but in their case I have to admit that high standards do pay dividends.

The French announcer on the radio was babbling about a jam on the A1. I was only half listening, and in a sudden unwise swoop took a last-minute decision to change my route for a cunning short cut I thought I knew.

Argh, not so cunning – roadworks and a long queue. Even on the best of days it's no fun being in a traffic jam going in the wrong direction when you're already behind schedule, but with Melvin at your side, it was purgatory. I pretended not to notice that we were going at 15 miles an hour.

After we'd crawled along for about ten minutes, Melvin looked at the map and said sanctimoniously, 'I was an army navigator and I do believe we are on the wrong road, young lady. You are taking us, like, several miles out of our way.'

I glanced at a road sign. 'I suddenly had the idea you'd like to see the chateau at Chantilly.' Quick thinking there, Clio.

'Oh, that's nice. Thank you, dear, that is so kind. We'd just adore to,' said the lovely Kay.

'Me too,' added Joe. 'Whatever you say, Clio. You're the team leader.'

'What about the battlefields?' growled Melvin.

I assured him they could wait and he relapsed into silence, periodically staring at the map and telling me how many miles it was to Chantilly.

*   *   *

'Would you look at that!' gasped Kay. 'That is one gorgeous chateau. Give me my camera, dear. Do we have time for a picture? Can we go inside?'

There followed an argument about the itinerary, which was entirely my fault. Silently I told myself I should have stuck to the plan, should have been on time in the first place. I shouldn't have taken the wrong turn and I definitely shouldn't have tried to disguise my mistake by introducing an extra sight to see.

'Well,' said Joe diplomatically, 'I'm easy. I have time to spare, and if the tour runs over, I don't mind.'

'But, goddamn it, today was scheduled for World War One. They should have a man covering the battlefields. This is very unprofessional,' said Melvin, his beard bristling with disapproval.

Trouble is, he was right, I thought. Not about the need for a masculine guide, of course, but about the unprofessional bit. 'We can still fit in part of the Somme today, except that we had better get off there straight away. At least you've had a quick look at Chantilly,' I began.

Kay clutched him. 'Melvin, honey, I would just love to stay here and look over the chateau and the Horse Museum. We have the time. We have the money. You said you'd picked the kind of tour where we could fix in last-minute changes. You said that was the smart thing to do.'

Melvin took a deep breath and patted her arm. 'OK, Momma. OK. We'll do what you want.'

Blimey, I thought, as they wandered off hand in hand.

'There's true love for you,' said Joe with a smile, as we followed behind. He took my arm when I stumbled on the cobblestones, but let go politely at the appropriate moment. Correct behaviour, of course.

So I took them round and Kay marvelled about the ceiling heights and the gilding and the opulence of it all. And the paintings in the museum were just lovely, she thought. She adored the sweeping views of the park from the windows too. When I mentioned for Melvin's benefit that Chantilly marked the furthest advance of the German Army in this direction in 1914, she told me how clever I was to know so much about everything. The gallant Joe concurred.

'I just make notes from books and carry them around,' I confessed.

Kay squeezed my arm. 'Yes, dear, but you pick out the inter-
esting parts for us. Sometimes tourist guides can be kind of dull.
We've hired people before, so we know. And I just love your cute
English accent.'

Melvin snorted and asked me the date of that tapestry over
there, so I read the little notice in French and told him. He wasn't
impressed that I had to look it up.

They changed their mind about the Horse Museum. 'We have
horses in the US. Don't have to go to France to see them,' Melvin
said. 'I need to eat.' So I drove to the town and found them a
little restaurant, nice and simple.

I explained about the set menu being the best value and
suggested local beer or a reasonable wine. Joe loved it all and
kept saying so, but Kay was flummoxed when her prawns arrived
with their shells on. She managed to peel a few, but obviously
found the process distasteful and messy. Joe and Melvin both ate
with gusto, Melvin going for steak and chips, but Joe choosing
the local dishes I recommended. Deliberate flattery or not, I
couldn't help being pleased that he did so. He looked happy and
amused – he'd catch my eye from time to time, as if we were
sharing a private joke. Either that or I was the joke.

'Darned good steak, but Momma sure had a prawn problem.
We should try a more expensive place next time, where they
serve the food kind of properly presented,' said Melvin, now in
a better mood after a couple of beers. He divided the bill carefully, but with another irresistible smile, Joe insisted on paying
for my lunch.

Clients often pay for my meals, so I didn't read anything into
this gesture. To make things clear, on the way back to the car I
mentioned that 'my partner Philippe' liked coming to the races
at Chantilly. Kay asked me about him and I told her briefly that
we lived together and that I had a child by my first marriage. I
omitted to mention husband number two, as he's pretty irrelevant unless someone wants to know every picky detail about me.
Pacing along beside us, the amiable Joe listened to all this.

They declined a visit to the Museum of the Great War at
Péronne. 'Enough time indoors today,' said Melvin. Pity to miss
it, but I didn't mind. It would take for ever and I didn't feel like
arguing. Instead I took them on my own private scenic route

through the beautiful Somme lakes, along narrow roads over tiny bridges and past little white summer houses overlooking the tranquil water. Then as I drove up and along the plain, we began to pass cemetery after cemetery. We stopped and looked at some of them.

Even though I've been here many times, I'm still moved by the rows and rows of simple stone crosses. Those young boys, some of them only teenagers, it's heartbreaking that they fought so hard and so long for such small advances, and then were killed before they'd even begun their lives. Poor Kay was in tears, and even Melvin looked sombre.

We drove to Albert, still a bleak little town. I explained it was the site of one of the bloodiest battles in 1916, when thousands of Allied soldiers went over the top, only to be mowed down by machine-gun fire, and when the Front halted four months later, the Allies had advanced only five miles. They say farmers still plough up grenades and bombs in the fields around.

I had promised we would visit the underground Trenches Museum, but when we got there, it was closed for restoration. Melvin was not impressed. I should have known, he said, and he was right.

I gathered them back into the car and he was temporarily quiet when we visited some of the numerous war memorials dotted around the fields and woodlands. Silently we stood and looked at the thousands of names inscribed on these lonely monuments. But the mood changed when I mentioned en route that we were to spend the night in Arras. Melvin got out the map and told me how to drive and where to turn until I thought I would clock him one. I might have done if Joe hadn't suddenly said in a firm tone of voice, 'Hey, you guys, let's give Clio a break. She knows what she's doing and she's doing it fine.'

Surprisingly Melvin was quiet after that, but I heaved a huge sigh of relief when we arrived at our hotel and I could escape for a while. Then I told myself to stop whingeing. If old Melvin was the biggest hardship one had to face, life couldn't be that tough, and anyway, dear Kay compensated for his grouchiness.

'This is the cutest hotel. An ancient Jesuit monastery, you said? So romantic, just beautiful. I just adore these old stone walls right here in the lounge area,' said Kay, sipping her cocktail. She had changed out of her sporty tennis-shoe outfit into a matronly cream trouser suit and matching pumps.

Melvin looked around. 'Kind of touristy, though. We didn't come to France on what was billed as an exclusive Insider Tour to be, like, totally surrounded by people speaking English.'

'Look,' I said as patiently as I could, 'Arras is a small town and this is one of the best hotels, so naturally tourists gather here and naturally quite a few of them are British.'

'Yeah, but it spoils the atmosphere,' said Melvin. 'We kind of wanted local colour, like it said in the brochure.'

'Right,' said Joe, 'why don't we go out to eat? Shall we go hunt out a tourist-free place, or do you have a suggestion, Clio?'

I walked them to a typical local restaurant with thick white table-cloths and red carpets and platoons of waiters in black coats. Joe loved it, and even Melvin looked pleased by the formality of French dining. Unfortunately, though, steak and chips was not on the menu. I suggested the specialities, like langoustine ravioli or crab pancakes, but Melvin insisted he wanted French fries. When I tried to order them on his behalf, the waiter pointed out, reasonably politely, that this was a restaurant *gastronomique* and maybe more simple fare would be available in the brasserie down the street. I translated this even more politely, but Melvin was unhappy and spluttered we should darn well go somewhere with better service.

Dear Kay saved the day by saying she was real tired and this looked like a nice restaurant and how about we try some genuine French food, honey. Again, when faced with a direct request from her, Melvin backed down. 'OK, Momma, whatever you want.' His love for his wife was his redeeming feature as far as I was concerned.

Kay explained with an aside that Melvin's late father had also been particularly fond of French fries, but being English, he'd called them chips. Did I call them chips too?

'Oh, yes, all we Brits eat tons of them,' I said, attempting to be conciliatory.

Unfortunately I hadn't noticed that the set menu Kay chose began with pâté de foie gras. 'This liver sausage is kind of rich,' she said, pushing it away.

Actually, I'm not wild about foie gras either, mainly because of the poor geese, but it seemed a shame to see it go to waste. Another shock for the waiter, I thought.

Kay watched as Joe and I shared a plate of oysters. 'How can you swallow raw seafood?' she faltered.

I didn't like to tell her that the critters should still be alive.

I don't know if I was imagining it, but Joe seemed to be surreptitiously flirting, gazing steadily at me over the oyster shells nestling on their icy stand. While alcohol obviously loosens the inhibitions, I don't subscribe to the notion that food can be an aphrodisiac except in so far as it's auto-suggestive. If your mind feels sexy, then the rest of you will follow. If you want it to, which of course I didn't, so I avoided flirting back despite his undoubted charms.

Fortunately they enjoyed their main dish of duck breasts – not too rare, I warned the waiter – and the orange *sabayon* dessert was real pretty, according to Kay. This time Melvin and Joe divided the bill between them, both waving away my offer to pay my share. I wondered if Kay had given Melvin a talking-to.

When we reached the doorway of the hotel, Joe said he'd like to go for a walk around the town and how about I went too. I hesitated.

'You'd better come along,' he said. 'I could get lost and then you'd have to report to head office that one of the clients had gone AWOL.'

'Yes, you two young ones go have fun. My old legs have seen enough of the town. Goodnight, then, and thank you for a great day, Clio. You're a lovely woman,' said Kay sweetly. 'I hope you never lose your bounce.'

Me, bouncy? How appalling.

Walking along the street, trying not to bounce, I said, 'Nice to be considered a young one. I love Kay.'

'I love her too. She's a sweetie pie,' said Joe. 'And she's right about you. You're quite a girl. You handle old Melv well.'

'Practice makes perfect,' I said. Does Joe think I'm over-enthusiastic and hearty? Maybe it's the job.

Then, unable to stop myself, I started to point out some more of the local sights.

'Relax. You're off duty as of now.' After a pause he asked, 'So tell me about this guy Philippe.'

'Not much to tell,' I said casually. Never be rude to clients, but avoid getting too personal, that's Miss Piggy's advice.

'So have you been together long?'

'It's a while now.'

'How long is a while?'

Persistent bugger, I thought, though not in a hostile way. 'Three or four years. How about you?'

'How about me what?'

'Are you married?' I asked boldly.

'Not particularly.'

I smiled. 'What kind of answer is that? If you insist on specific answers to your questions, you've got to give specific answers in return.'

'I'm separated.'

'Ah.'

We walked on for a while. Then, against my better judgement, I asked, 'How separated?'

'Five years.'

'Long time.'

'Mm.'

I could have left it there, but curiosity got the better of me. 'So you're not actually divorced?'

'Not yet.'

If I'd probed further, I would have sounded either intrusive or interested in him, so I told myself to change the subject. 'Beautiful old town this, isn't it? Lots of restoration after it was so damaged in World War One. This square always reminds me of Brussels. Apparently there are other squares like this all over the Low Countries. All to do with the Spaniards colonizing the whole area in the seventeenth century.'

He stopped me in mid-flow. 'So are you going to stay with your Philippe, or is it a temporary arrangement?'

I stared at him. 'Aren't you interested in my fascinating exposition on the history of Arras?'

'Of course I am. You're brilliant, as Kay says.' Underneath the street light I could see he had this irritating quizzical smile on his face.

'I take it seriously,' I said, a mite sulky. I don't mind taking the mickey out of the tourist business myself, but I get annoyed when people don't recognize the hard graft that goes into it.

He put his hand on my arm. 'Don't get me wrong. I think you're a terrific guide, like I said about five times, but right now I need a break from facts and figures. My brain is suffering from information overload.'

I moved away just a little. 'Sorry. I know what you mean. I went on a one-day tour of the Loire when I first came to Paris and the leader kept talking about Louis the Sixteenth this and Louis the Fourteenth that – we had what seemed like the whole of French history stuffed down our throats. She never drew a single breath from dawn when we got on the bus until seven at night, all in French the whole damn day, and I ended up with a splitting headache. Now it seems like I'm just as bad, can't stop talking. Must be a form of showing off.'

He laughed. 'You're entitled to show off, I reckon.' Then after a few more paces he said, 'So are you going to marry the guy?'

'What an old-fashioned question. You sound just like my mother.'

'So answer us, me and your mother.'

I sighed. 'Look, I don't know. OK?'

I must have sounded annoyed because he was silent for a while.

'But it's a happy relationship?'

'Of course it is,' I said quickly.

So we walked on and suddenly I realized I was on the verge of being lost – me the famous tour guide – but luckily there's a church tower you can see from most parts of the central area, and hoping he hadn't noticed, I found our way back, with only a few wrong turns, to the Grande Place.

'Let's have a drink,' he said.

But I chickened out. I didn't want to sit there opposite this nice, kind and, let's face it, rather attractive man in a dark, little French bar in case I started to pour my heart out, the way you sometimes do to sympathetic strangers. And he did have a very sympathetic manner. Could be natural or could be part of a deliberate ploy with women.

On the way back to the hotel, I asked him if he had any children and he said two grown-up daughters, both married, and then he asked about my family, so I rabbited on about Alexander. I must have bored him to bits, but he listened politely.

We went up in the lift together and parted in the corridor to go to our separate rooms. Exactly as per Miss Piggy's rules. Not that he had invited me to break them, and not that I had expected him to. He was basically a proper kind of guy, as I'd thought all along.

Three

Vimy Ridge impressed them all. It's such a fine site and even Melvin admitted that the Canadians maintain the vast park beautifully. So many of the other battlefields have returned to nature, as indeed they should, but here you can see craters and trenches spread out over acres of ground.

Kay took about ten photos of the memorial, a tall, simple white stone tower with a weeping woman on top. It's amazing silhouetted against the blue sky like today, as she said. Melvin and Joe went to study the small museum – how men love weapons – while Kay and I walked amongst the craters. I told her all that *Birdsong* stuff about the soldier-miners who worked underground trying to blow up the German trenches. We saw gaggles of English schoolchildren and I wondered what it all meant to them, if anything.

We were silent and thoughtful as we left the area and drove back towards the south-west. Then I mentioned Monet's garden tomorrow morning and the promise seemed to cheer them. Kay began to tell us about their family, her story punctuated from time to time by polite comments from Joe. Melvin dozed off, fortunately.

They all loved Les Andelys and the tiny picturesque hotel nestling in a bend of the Seine. I warned them that its restaurant had a Michelin star and would not serve French fries. Melvin said of course he knew that.

One of about six serious-faced waiters in black served us with *amuse-bouches* in little ramekins before we had even chosen our meal. Hastily, before Melvin could complain about not having ordered them, I explained that these free extra dishes seemed to be obligatory in any restaurant that fancied its chances for a mention in one of the numerous French food guides.

Kay wanted to know about Michelin, so I told her that I couldn't afford either the calories or the cost of three- and two-star restaurants but that in France one star provides wonderful, interesting cuisine at amazingly cheap prices. Melvin said that all the same by American standards this meal was still gonna cost big bucks.

Knocking back his aperitif, he asked me to translate the menu. I muddle through in French reasonably well for a Brit, but even though I ought to know all the gastronomic vocabulary, sometimes food terminology throws me. Today I had to swallow my pride and look up one of the specialities in my food pocket dictionary, a useful book, I said, waving it about, if you want to avoid ordering tripe sausages by accident. Joe smiled kindly at my endless prattling. To my relief, the *ombre-chevalier* on the menu turned out to be a kind of salmon trout. I was afraid it might be horse meat, which would have upset the sensitive Kay.

Even Melvin admitted that the service was good. Too good. The waiters kept filling up our glasses and then another bottle of wine appeared from nowhere. It must have been Joe who ordered it, but I didn't notice. I seemed to be gulping wine rather swiftly this evening. Could be the combined effect of disliking Melvin and fancying Joe more than was comfortable. Joe was still giving me the occasional long, steady look, which made me catch my breath in a stupid girly manner. Fortunately Melvin had drunk far too much to notice, and Kay was too innocent to catch anything in the air. If there was anything to catch.

Finally, talking and laughing loudly, and full of rich and highly satisfying food, we all staggered up to bed. As I lay there alone listening to the river, I thought about Joe, not so very far away down the corridor. Advising myself to take a cold shower, I eventually fell into a restless sleep.

This time the late start wasn't my fault. Kay took an age over breakfast, and then halfway to Monet's garden in Giverny we had to turn back because she said she'd left her spare glasses in the hotel bathroom. I was dismayed, though I didn't say so, because last night I had stressed the importance of leaving early to be first in the queue. Unfortunately by the time we arrived, the line was snaking halfway round Giverny, which didn't please Melvin.

But dear Kay was just enchanted by the whole place when, after a long, long wait, we eventually reached the gardens – never mind that you couldn't move for camera-touting tourists from Tokyo, never mind that the green Japanese bridge was overloaded with gardeners from Ghent, never mind that you could only get a glimpse of the famous water lilies by brutally elbowing hausfraus from Hanover out of the way. I made Kay queue up for a souvenir book so at least she could see the archways and pergolas properly and study the wonderfully imaginative droves of one-colour planting.

'Just like the paintings,' she sighed happily.

She raved about Bayeux too. I've never had such an appreciative tourist. She almost made up for Melvin.

'I didn't realize the tapestry was so narrow and so long. Like you said, I guess it's just about the most famous piece of cloth in the whole world,' said Kay.

Joe peered at the sign. 'Says here it's seventy metres by fifty centimetres.'

'What does that mean in our measurements, dear?' asked Kay. I told her 230 feet by 1.5 feet, and so it was really more of an embroidered scroll than what we think of as a tapestry. I had to explain that it was about the Norman Conquest of Britain in 1066. She didn't even know about King Harald's death with an arrow through his eye, which was about the only piece of history I remembered from my days at school. Until I became a tour guide, that is.

I told her that basically, though the French dispute it, this tapestry was embroidered by the British therefore it should actually be in England. That made them laugh, especially Joe, who seemed to appreciate whatever pitiful attempts at humour I might be able to drag into my talk.

Handsome in a slightly crumpled cornflower-blue shirt and cream linen jacket, Joe sat down opposite me at a table for two in the Bayeux hotel restaurant. 'So what happened to the others?' he asked.

'They decided to eat in their room. Kay didn't feel too well and Melvin is looking after her.'

'This is a bonus, dinner alone with the beautiful Clio,' he said.

I love flattery, especially when it's dished out by the right man, but I managed to avoid simpering. Briskly I asked him what he wanted to eat.

As we consumed our way through another long and serious French meal and drank a delicious amount of wine, I rather forgot the brisk attitude. Without much prompting, I gabbled on all about the mess that had been my life, even about husband number two. I usually avoid mentioning the broken nose because it sounds as if I'm touting for sympathy, but tonight I confessed all, within reason. This stupid muddled autobiography would certainly put him off me, which would be no bad thing, I thought at one point.

Trouble is, he actually listened and seemed to take me seriously. He even remembered what I'd said last time we talked. Most unusual for a bloke.

To divert his probing questions, I asked him the what-do-you-do stuff and he told me that he trained as a lawyer but then went into the paper trade, sawmills, that kind of thing, but his business – he was the owner – had been bought out by a multinational. He didn't want to sell, but they made him an offer he couldn't refuse, took on all his staff and gave him a job as director.

'Impressive,' I said. His bright intelligent eyes were gazing into mine as he spoke. At the age of eighteen I'd have been bowled over, but as a sophisticated woman of the world, I gazed calmly back.

Just about.

He was saying modestly that it wasn't a big deal being a director. In that company, everyone is a vice president or whatever. He tried working for them but couldn't hack it after being his own boss for so long, so now he was in Europe checking out other business interests, seeing his daughters in London and just travelling around.

'Travelling around' could be a euphemism for unemployed, feckless and unreliable, my mother would say. 'A rolling stone gathers no moss' is another of her favourite axioms.

Joe was talking about the former family home in Ireland. He might visit it before he went back to Canada, he reckoned.

'Ireland? So how Canadian are you?'

His family had emigrated when he was eight, so he'd been brought up there for a while, but then his father, a self-made man from Belfast, went to work in Hong Kong. Joe, too, had been posted in the Far East and his daughters had been born in

Thailand. So he never felt really Canadian, or really Irish or British, or really anything. More of an international gypsy.

'Citizen of the world sounds better,' I said with a friendly smile. I was still ignoring the sexual tension that was building up. I really was.

'Citizen of the world, then.'

'And your daughters?

He told me they both worked in London. Both clever and beautiful, of course, he said.

I saw an opening. 'Like their mother?'

He smiled wryly. 'Exactly.'

'So tell me about her.'

He shook his head. 'Nothing to tell. She's history.'

'Really?'

'Yes.'

'And is there anyone else?'

He smiled. 'No.'

I was delighted. Quite mad, because I was not interested, no way. There was Philippe and this little flirtation was not going to lead anywhere. Joe and I had found ourselves together and were just being polite, passing the time. A kind of blind date. Back home, we would've told Cilla we'd hit it off fine, but wouldn't be seeing each other again. She'd have been disappointed but would wave us goodbye with 'Ta-ra, then, chucks. We wish them well, don't we, ladies and gentlemen?' I smiled involuntarily.

'What are you thinking about?' he asked.

I started to explain about that great British institution, Cilla Black, and how many years ago she used to host a tacky television programme about strangers who go on a blind-date holiday, but I could see it meant nothing to him and he probably thought I was nuts. Maybe they didn't have *Blind Date* in Canada, or maybe he's too intellectual to watch trash TV.

Or maybe he suspected I'd really been wondering about what might happen after dinner.

Nothing, of course.

I confess I was feeling pretty churned up and excitable as we walked up the stairs. It was only half lit and I had to press one of those irritating timer buttons to turn on the main lights so we could see where we were going.

So there we were outside his room.

Joe said, and his voice was husky, 'Would you like a nightcap? I think I saw some Scotch in the minibar.'

I'd been thinking hard about my answer if this question were asked, and there had been a few signs that it would be. I took a deep breath. It was touch and go but some virtuous guardian angel popped into my head and I managed to stutter, 'Look, I'd love to, but having nightcaps in clients' rooms is not something I do. Just in case there is a misunderstanding.'

'Ah,' he said. 'Still, there's always another day.'

I smiled more confidently, looking up at him. 'Sorry, not for us.' Then I added unwisely, 'Much as I'd like it.'

'So kiss me goodnight, Ms Tour Guide.'

Just as Joe bent down towards me, the main light in the corridor ran out of time. He may have intended a fraternal goodnight peck on the cheek, but in the semi-darkness our mouths met and it became a tender, exploratory kiss. I couldn't help kissing him back.

Suddenly a door opened and the lights flashed on again. There, to my horror, was Melvin standing in blue pyjamas just a few feet away.

Scarlet-faced, I stepped back. We were both rooted to the spot gaping at Melvin, waiting for him to leave, but he said, 'Been trying to call your room, Clio.'

Nervously I smoothed down my hair. 'Right.'

He spoke rapidly. 'Kay needs to get back to Paris. She has some kind of health problem. I'd like to have a doctor check her out, so I called our friends at the US Consulate and they're going to make her an appointment at the American Hospital.'

'Right,' I repeated. 'Poor Kay. What's the matter? Is she in pain? I have some aspirin.'

'That's OK. I gave her some. But we need to get you to drive us back to Paris tomorrow.'

'OK, right. Is it serious? An emergency? Should we call an ambulance? The hotel will know a doctor.'

'No, no, nothing serious, not an emergency. She just needs to take it easy,' he said impatiently.

I smiled in relief. 'That's good. This is just a vague suggestion, but you don't think she might be well enough to go with you by train tomorrow? Only the trains are excellent here, quicker than the car, and I should really finish the tour. Just an idea, in case she—'

Melvin was incensed. 'My wife is not going on some French train. Goddamn it, don't you know how to take care of your clients?'

'Like I said, I only meant to suggest it as a possible course of action, because—'

'Don't worry about me. I'll take care of myself,' said Joe. 'I'll hire a car and do the D-Day beaches on my own.'

Melvin gazed furiously at us both. 'I want to leave at nine thirty tomorrow morning, Clio.' He retreated to his room, slamming the door behind him.

I became all brisk again and apologized to Joe, told him he'd get a refund from Insider Tours for the curtailment of his trip and offered to arrange a hire car for him. He said he could do it himself and not to worry.

'Maybe you should write me a letter about the refund, though. There's some hotel writing paper in my room,' he said with a twinkle in his eye.

I grinned. 'I'll give you a note tomorrow. Goodnight, Joe. See you at breakfast.'

Sadly, so it was. We said goodbye over the croissant crumbs. Well, in the car park, actually.

He helped me load all the cases into the car. All he said was, 'I've got the office address and your cell-phone number. Guess I'll take another Insider Tour one day, next time I'm in France.'

'Do that,' I said, giving him a casual little wave. Then I bundled a pale Kay and a worried Melvin into the car and set off for Paris.

Philippe appeared pleased to see me back early and I was relieved to be home. After another long drive with Melvin breathing down my neck and rustling his map and telling me how to drive, my nerves were worn to a frazzle. As I dropped them off at their friends' apartment, I could hardly bring myself to say goodbye to him. Only the presence of poor Kay stopped me from being seriously rude. I didn't want to upset her. Not that she appeared to be all that ill. Maybe it was just stress and exhaustion from having to live with pernickety Melvin.

I was rather hoping for an early night that evening, but Philippe followed me up the stairs straight away. As I undressed, he began to help, licking the back of my neck and then pulling off my bra to kiss my nipples.

He thinks this turns me on more than it does. I never have the nerve to say what I like or don't like in bed. I tried it once with husband number two, but he got stroppy and didn't speak to me for days afterwards.

Philippe is a skilled and reasonably patient lover, always keen to try new ways, some more comfortable than others. He isn't boring in bed. It's just that sometimes when we go through the whole routine, I feel my heart isn't in it, even if my body is enjoying itself, the way bodies do.

Tonight I closed my eyes, focusing on my own sensations, and gradually I began to feel as enthusiastic as I pretended. I was fantasizing that I was with Joe, that it was he who was caressing me so intimately, running his fingers down my stomach, pausing, teasing until I was desperate. Eventually the fantasy worked.

'You're a great lay,' Philippe repeated happily. He often says something like that afterwards. He likes American slang and it doesn't sound vulgar in his admittedly charming French voice.

I smiled, but tonight I felt strangely remote.

Four

Miss Piggy's eyelashes were not fluttering today. She was staring at me in an uncomfortably malevolent manner. 'So you had one or two problems, Clio, huh?' It was clear she was not in the best of moods.

'You bet I had problems,' I said. 'Elaine, you have no idea what that Melvin guy was like. He was just about the most tiresome client I ever had, most unlike an American. You know how they are very friendly and appreciative normally, but he was so damn bossy and demanding. Well, I suppose he was born a Brit, but even so . . .'

'You received a whole lot of training on how to deal with problems,' began Miss Piggy impatiently.

Training! I think she once dished out one of those self-help manuals, probably something like *The Seven Habits of Successful Tour Guides*, or *Twelve Steps to Avoid Killing Clients*.

I tried to keep my temper. 'Look, Elaine, I did the best I could and now I'm pretty exhausted, so can I take my money and go?'

'You certainly can. Here is a cheque for your fees for the last month, including the trip you just did. If you've brought along your receipts for expenses on your last trip, I'll pay them. If you have, like, lost or forgotten any, then you won't get reimbursed. The new chairman says we need to tighten up on our accounting. The company rule is expenses have to be submitted immediately and in full. No receipts, no dice.'

'Oh, come on!' I moaned. 'You can't do that. Sometimes I don't have time to write up all the accounts straight away. It isn't fair. Look, Elaine, if you're going to mess me around like this, I'm going to quit.'

'Yes, you're right about that. You do quit. Insider Tours doesn't have room for guides who, like, break every rule in our code of conduct.'

'Code of conduct – never heard of it!' I said unwisely, not really believing that she was firing me.

'Exactly. I have a problem with your attitude, Clio, and so, incidentally, did Melvin Hooper.'

'*What?*'

'He said you were unpunctual, incompetent and not that polite. He had a problem with the restaurants you chose and thought you didn't give enough advice about the differences between US food and French.'

'Elaine,' I said heavily, 'Melvin Hooper is a major fusspot. Out of hundreds of clients this is the first complaint you've had about me, isn't it? Call Joe Dryden, or ask Kay Hooper. They both thought I was fine, honestly.'

'Mr Hooper said you were flirting with Mr Dryden.'

'Nonsense,' I snapped, not entirely accurately.

'Kissing sounds like flirting to me, so Mr Dryden is not likely to give us an unbiased opinion, is he?'

'Oh, that – it was nothing. Just a friendly goodnight kiss. You know how everyone kisses everyone in France,' I said airily.

'Yes, but North Americans do *not*. I am told that Mr Dryden is a married man.'

'But he's separated, or so he said.'

'Whatever. You should be more careful. Our company has its reputation to consider. While we're on the subject, Mr Hooper also reported that your skirt was too short.'

'So that's why he was staring at my knees the whole damn time. It was the usual Paris length, for God's sake. Anyway, who the hell cares what he thinks?'

Elaine compressed her thin lips. 'As it happens, *I* care. I can now reveal to you that Mr Hooper is the new chairman of Insider Tours. He has just started his travels around the world to test out the local organizations. He says he does this by acting a little grouchy and difficult as a client, and you failed his test, which kind of reflected badly on me too. I promised I'd send a really great guide, and he said if that was the best I could do, he wasn't impressed.' She stood up and pushed the pay-cheque envelope across the desk towards me.

I sat down with a bump. 'He was the new chairman and you didn't even think to warn me!'

'Didn't even know myself. He said it was company policy. It wouldn't be a proper test if we knew who he was.'

'But Kay, his wife, didn't she know? I mean, she behaved completely and utterly like a genuine tourist.'

'Mr Hooper said he had not informed his wife he's the new proprietor of Insider Tours. He wanted her to act natural.'

I swore under my breath. Aloud I said evenly, 'So just what are you going to do about a replacement for me, Elaine? I have a whole load of tours scheduled, if you remember.'

'You can forget about your schedule. I have already given it to a British Embassy wife. I engaged her yesterday, through Mary. Seems like they are the kind of classy people who know how to be polite, and this lady is a graduate from Cambridge. Pretty good, huh? Now, before you go, will you please give me your company mobile?'

Sullenly I fished the mobile out of my handbag and plonked it on the desk. 'Elaine, this really isn't fair. For all you know, sacking me like this with zero notice could be against French employment laws. I could . . . I could go to a tribunal or something.'

'No chance. You're part-time.'

'Every chance. Everyone has rights in France – the great European Union cares about us little workers.'

Her fat cheeks quivered in anger. 'Clio, you might, if you ever learn to behave in a more graceful manner, you just might get some temporary work with us now and then. And maybe, if that goes OK and we get no more complaints, it might lead to a bit more work. But if you get this company involved in a goddamn tribunal, you are *toast*.'

'We'll see about that,' I said, standing up and taking the cheque. Of course, there was no way I was going to throw myself on the mercy of French bureaucracy, because I wasn't at all sure that once you got yourself into the quagmire, you'd ever dig your way out again, but I hoped that Miss Piggy would stew there in her sty worrying her socks off.

'Anyway,' she said as I was sweeping out, 'Joe Dryden complained about you too.'

I flinched. Unable to speak for a moment, I spun round. 'So –' I cleared my throat, – 'so what did he say?' I stared at the wall above her head, hoping she wouldn't notice how much I minded.

'He said he was disappointed.'

'In what way?' I stuttered.

'He didn't specify. Probably the same way Mr Hooper was. And I have to say I am kind of disappointed too. Seems like you do need to take a career break, Clio.' Her expression was pure malice.

Too upset to think of a retort, I backed out, slamming the door behind me.

Philippe was not impressed that I'd lost my main job. He was always an expert at rubbing salt into a wound. 'You can be too outspoken and blunt, Clio, as I have told you before.'

'Me? Outspoken? By French standards I'm the soul of tact,' I said coldly.

'You will have to pay more attention to your journalism now,' he said. 'After all, you need the income.'

'Look, I get a set fee from the mag, regardless of how much attention I pay to it, and I always meet the deadline. Well, mostly.'

He shook his handsome head patiently. 'Exactly, mostly. You should try to sell your articles to a few more magazines – the *Herald Tribune*, or the airline journals, something that pays a little better.'

'I know, I know,' I said.

But I felt it would be a mammoth hassle, which I didn't really want to get into. Doing major research, sending off endless query letters and getting endless rejections, not being paid for months even if you do get a commission – I couldn't face it. That's why I like good old Batsford Berryman and his amateur little travel monthly, *French Fantasia*. He pays me a small but steady sum every month, come rain or shine, and in return I do the best I can for him.

Berryman, or BB as he's generally known, is aged at least seventy and is the worst editor in the world in that he embell-ishes every sentence you write with borrowed poetic phrases by the bunchful. He desktop-publishes the mag all by himself and distributes to about two thousand personal subscribers. I bet some people subscribed to it originally because they thought it was a porn or a fantasy mag and then couldn't be bothered to cancel when they found themselves reading about Monet's garden and beaches in Brittany. ('Monet's bee-loud glade or Brittany's sandy shores oft-bestrewn with aged rose-pink rocks half as old as time,' as BB would say.)

I would dash off my articles for him in the slack periods between trips, and of course I could sometimes do research for BB on an Insider Tour. I don't take long over *French Fantasia* pieces because if I muse about and search for a good adjective or descriptive noun, sure as fate BB will rewrite and redecorate the whole thing in his flowery version of English. He pays my expenses, of course, but I'm careful not to charge both Miss Piggy and BB for the same hotel. Though poor, I am ethical. I have to confess that Miss Piggy didn't actually know about my other job and nor did BB. It's immaterial now, anyway.

I fumed for a while about being sacked by Elaine, but what hurt me most was Joe's treachery and, to a lesser extent, the fact that Kay didn't stick up for me. Maybe Melvin has told her nothing about it. I should go and see Kay. She'd be much more effective than a French tribunal. Melvin would listen to her and then tell Piggy to reinstate me. I loved my tour job and wanted it back. I suppose I could try one of the big companies, but that would mean ferrying around coachloads of tourists and there would be French exams to take, and strict hours and general hell on earth.

So, yes, I'd try lobbying Kay.

I dressed to kill in a fiendishly smart black suit and off I set. I could remember the address where I had deposited the Hoopers, but when I got there, and it wasn't far, I began to doubt the wisdom of my actions. What if Kay wasn't there? I could find myself having another pointless battle with Melvin. So I changed my mind and went home to compose a letter.

Two hours later I was back outside the grand block of flats. I rang the bell and, avoiding a tough-looking concierge hoovering the stairs, I went up in the lift to the third floor where I was faced with the usual tall, imposing double door. Quite sensible from the furniture-moving point of view, the wide Parisian entrance, but daunting until you get used to it.

A tiny young Asian maid in a pale green uniform peered round the door.

'*Bonjour*,' I began.

Screwing up her pretty face, she giggled sweetly, 'No spik Flenj.'

'English?'

'Little bit.'

'OK, please may I talk to Mrs Hooper?'

'You like spik madame, madame?'

'I would like to speak with Madame Hooper.' I relapsed into pidgin. 'She stay here two days ago.'

The maid stared at me, perplexed. 'Madame no home. She and sir go out.'

'I like speak Mrs Kay Hooper,' I repeated, still not sure who we were talking about.

'Mrs Hooper? Ol' American lady?'

A breakthrough.

'Yes, yes, thank you.'

'She no here, madame.'

'Do you know where she went?'

The girl looked confused.

I tried again. 'Is Mrs Hooper coming back later, or has she moved to a hotel?'

'She gone.'

I gave up and said would she mind asking someone to send my letter on to Mrs Hooper. I wasn't terribly confident that anything would be done about it, but she took the letter and, with another shy smile, gently closed the door after me.

I met my former colleague Mary for lunch at one of those close-packed pavement cafés where you sit on a basketwork chair at a tiny round marble table and the waiters are thin, cross and efficient.

Immaculate in a conventional blue dress with silk scarf, Mary was distraught. Shaking her head, she said, 'I had absolutely no idea Elaine was going to sack you. She asked me if I knew of anyone else who wanted a job. I thought she needed extra staff, so I recommended my friend Sarah. This is appalling. If I'd known, I wouldn't have mentioned her.'

In between ordering the *salade du jour*, I told her it wasn't her fault. Then I raved on about how fed up I was, and how upset about Kay and, particularly, Joe, how he'd seemed like such a kindred spirit.

'Your Canadian client? Oh, he phoned when I was sitting there in the office waiting for Elaine to dish out assignments. She was all smarmy when she talked to him.'

'So did she tell him I'd been sacked?' I asked carefully.

'She just announced you were no longer with Insider Tours. Then he asked for your phone number or your email – or at least he must have, because Elaine put on this incredibly snooty voice and said she never gave out the staff's private details.'

'Huh. If he'd wanted to, he could have phoned my mobile before I gave it back to Piggy.'

'But how was he to know?'

'Good point.' I picked up a hunk of baguette and ate it before I remembered I was meant to be slimming. 'Anyway, I don't want to speak to him, not after he did the dirty on me.'

Mary looked thoughtful. 'From where I was sitting trying to eavesdrop, I think he was asking her to pass on a message to you, but she wouldn't. Then he seemed to get a bit stroppy because Elaine said something like she hoped he would be using Insider Tours again on his next trip to France. It was obvious he hung up on her.'

'Yeah, he's a two-faced bastard. Smarmy flirty one minute, then knifing you in the back the next.'

'You don't know what he said to Elaine. If anyone's two-faced, it's her.' Mary rarely says anything unkind, but Miss Piggy doesn't bring out the best in people.

Before Mary left to go off and do her diplomatic good works, she fished a piece of paper out of her pocket. 'If you want to get in touch with this Joe chap, I got his email address off the office computer when Elaine was out of the room.'

'Thanks but no thanks. Very kind, but . . .'

'Just in case you change your mind.' With an innocent smile she put the note on the table.

So as not to be rude I picked it up and stuffed it into my handbag, intending to throw it away as soon as she'd gone.

Five

Mary had failed to cheer me up and I couldn't face the thought of going home to write this month's chunk of articles for *French Fantasia*. I just wasn't in the mood. Anyway, there were days and days until the deadline.

Shopping was one possibility, but I didn't have any money and clothes shopping in Paris isn't always good therapy for me. I'm only a size 14 – mostly – but all the assistants stare as if I'm a freakish giantess because I don't have a 22-inch waist. They just shrug their shoulders and say they don't have it in my size and how about I go up to the department called Classiques. For classic, read matronly.

Sometimes I don't even fit into Classiques and then the skinny, hard-faced assistant suggests other designer gear for large-breasted, generously built Continental ladies. I don't look good in these supa-garments either, not having the boobs and not particularly wanting to spend a month's wages on drapery, however well cut and elegant such drapery may be.

I could go and buy something especially delicious to cook for dinner, but in my current mood I'd probably ignore the fish-monger and go straight to the boulangerie to buy *pains au chocolat* or *tartes au fraises* and slices of four-cheese pizza. Then Philippe would sigh and ask how I was ever going to keep what passes for my figure if I ate all that saturated fat.

To avoid both work and shopping, I decided to go and see Philippe's elderly aunt Isabelle. Isabelle never married but had a sugar daddy, who died and left her pots of money. She's disapproved of in the family because of that and because, though childless, she has never given any of her money to Philippe and his sisters. These sisters, thin and nervy, are both happily married to fat, square men who are rich enough to keep them in some style, but nevertheless Aunt Isabelle is, in their view, selfish and stingy.

She lives in the ultra-fashionable seventh arrondissement in a chic little terraced house wildly over-decorated with ornate furniture covered in porcelain figurines and strange knick-knacks, half valuable and half rubbish, according to Philippe, who knows about these things. The walls are crammed with paintings, both traditional and modern, hanging alongside gaudy decorative china plates dotted about at random. It's like a junk-shop-cum-gallery, except more cosy as it does have large luxurious Persian rugs scattered about and, by French standards, relatively comfortable chairs. The house, her dim-witted standard poodle and Aunt Isabelle herself are all tended by a highly strung Greek butler, who also acts as chauffeur, and a doddery Filipina maid of all works.

Plump and well preserved with hair dyed jet black and a skil-fully lifted face, Isabelle is always kind to me because her main aim in life is to annoy her younger sister, Camille, who is not my number-one fan. Camille hates me because I am upstart English rather than well-bred French, and because I am supposed to have broken up the marriage of her favourite child, Philippe. In fact, the villainess was some other earlier mistress of his, but Camille conveniently forgets this. I didn't even meet Philippe until he had been separated for about two years.

No, he isn't yet divorced, and he still goes to see his wife from time to time, which doesn't thrill me through and through, but I am a tolerant person and possession is supposed to be nine-tenths of the law. Philippe and Françoise don't have any children, so they could easily take the final step to split, except that in the eyes of Philippe's mother, who is devoutly religious, they are still and will always be married. Philippe, like his aunt Isabelle, takes a secular view of life and claims that his visits to his ex are to talk about legalities to do with the divorce.

Heard it all before? Yes, say all my wise friends.

Today, as usual, Isabelle greeted me like her favourite long-lost daughter and then summoned Nicos, the nervous butler, to bring me tea and cakes. I ate three madeleines to comfort myself while I told her all about losing my job. Gigi the poodle fixed her eye on the cakes, wanting a piece of the action, but I ignored her. She's quite podgy enough already.

I told Isabelle blow by blow about Melvin and Kay. Obviously not finding the subject that fascinating, she then asked me about my dear little Alex, as she calls him. I was in the middle of telling her about his forthcoming sports day and what a marathon trip it would be for me when the butler came flapping in, almost incoherent with distress. Rosa, the maid, had fainted and, the shock of it, she had actually been so inconsiderate as to collapse in the corridor so no one could get past.

We all rushed to examine her, the dog leaping about in a hysterical manner and getting in the way. There was talk of summoning the fire brigade, who are called in any kind of French emergency – it doesn't have to involve flames. The *sapeurs-pompiers* are usually young and handsome, so I perked up. Then an ambulance was suggested. Isabelle, who has her economical moments, as we all do, said that ambulances were expensive and asked whether Rosa was that ill. Rosa opened her eyes at that point and half sat up. She looked a funny colour, so I offered to take her to the doctor, but then, as she complained of a sore wrist, Isabelle decreed I should take her directly to casualty.

It was efficient, the old-fashioned hospital, and the queues were short compared to the National Health back home. But endless forms had to be filled in and there is no way Rosa could have managed it on her own. Her written French is non-existent and she doesn't speak it well either, particularly when she's frightened, as she was today.

The doctors couldn't find much wrong with her, but just to be on the safe side they kept her in overnight. They were worried about her wrist and a full body scan was required. A full body scan, all on the French National Health, for a swollen wrist. Just like that.

I returned to the hospital next day to be there for the scan. Rosa wasn't pushed into one of those tunnels – she just had to lie on a trolley with various spooky machines hanging over her. All the same, she was terrified and I held her hand until the scanner began its weird journey skimming over her just inches away. Her normally placid old face went a peculiar shade of grey coffee and she trembled so much that I thought she'd fall off the bench. But no, after another few zillion tests, they decided there was nothing wrong and I was allowed to take her home.

'Aunt Isabelle tells me you are a heroine, almost saintly in your compassion to her maid,' said Philippe, putting down the telephone.

I shrugged modestly and said it was nothing.

'No, no, it sounds quite something,' said Philippe, opening a bottle of Entre-Deux-Mers and pouring me a large glass. Unusual that. He normally tries to restrict my intake so as to help me with my weak-willed struggle against excessive calories and the pleasures of eating and drinking. 'It's good you get on so well with Isabelle. You are the only one of the family who does.'

'Of the family', he'd said. Wow! No one, least of all Philippe, has *ever* suggested I am part of the family. This was a big step forward.

'She's not hard to get on with,' I said, smiling happily.

'Compared with my mother, you mean.'

I avoided that dangerous ground and went on to tell him about the great drama.

'You can be quite amusing. Keep up the good work with my dear aunt,' he said finally, and then returned to his piano. This Steinway baby grand, one of Isabelle's rare gifts, adds considerably to the elegance of the flat, but it's not purely ornamental. Philippe practises frequently and, as far as I can tell, plays well. It is one of his numerous talents. I am not musical, but fortunately this is another of my imperfections that he is prepared to forgive.

We made love that night. As usual, he seemed well satisfied with me and with himself. Somehow I felt absent from the whole proceedings and ended up faking it. Easier than a cross-examination about why I didn't come. Which, if it happens or rather doesn't happen, is all my fault for lapsing back into the behaviour of an uptight English prude.

Six

At Alex's sports day Samantha was dressed to kill and so was I. As she wore floaty floral and I had selected a plain cream shirt-dress, it might have been a draw, but I decided she'd won on points because, though not that great looking, she's a lot younger and peachier, and her pink sandals were delicious. She also has a nicer nature than I do. Samantha is my first husband's third wife and, surprisingly, I like her, though I'm not entirely sure she likes me.

The day had begun badly because I left in a rush at dawn to drive to Le Shuttle at Calais and was halfway out of Paris before I realized I'd left the picnic behind, but it was too late to go back. So, having negotiated the Channel Tunnel, Kent and the traffic-sodden M25 before I reached the school in Berkshire, I had to dive into a petrol station to buy some plastic sandwiches. The whole journey had lasted over five hours, so even before the marathon that is sports day began, I was feeling, and no doubt looking, somewhat jaded.

Alex's school is in a beautiful Queen Anne house with extensive grounds and cricket pitches galore. On sports day the routine is that parents inspect the inevitable classroom displays guided proudly by their offspring, eat their joint picnic lunch by the lake and then sit watching the boys rushing around doing hearty gymnastics, relay, long jump and other athletic stuff. Then there's tea, followed by speeches and prize-giving. It all takes for ever, but at least you get to take your darlings back for half-term after. Except that this year Alex was going to his father's.

Pushing this unwelcome thought aside, I concentrated on parking. One of the problems about this upmarket scene is that my old car doesn't look good among the other parents' posh vehicles, the Mercs, the BMWs, Volvos and the various faux off-roaders. I have to try and hide it in a corner underneath a bush so as not to shame Alex.

Of course we were thrilled to see each other. We hugged tight

– or as tightly as his schoolboy self-consciousness would allow – and I couldn't stop myself from saying he'd grown even taller. On the verge of early manhood but still basically a charming enthusiastic child, he already shows signs of inheriting his father's heartbreaker looks, though his hair is mouse rather than Greek-god blond like dear Harry's.

We zoomed around inspecting Alex's neatly written French project and his paintings in the art room – showed talent, I thought proudly. Then, while we were on our way to see the school pets, he told me that his father and Samantha were coming to sports day too.

'But I thought I was supposed to drop you off at your dad's tonight on my way to Granny's,' I said, trying not to look dismayed. Having driven all this distance, I selfishly didn't want to share Alex today.

He said, no, he'd had a message from Dad saying he'd be here for a late lunch. 'And they've got a new puppy!' he added excitedly.

'How lovely!' I said, even more jealous. It's Alex's dearest wish to have a pet, but unusually for a Frenchman, Philippe disapproves of dogs and I have to agree there are far too many of them crammed into Paris flats or performing on Paris pavements. Unfortunately he won't hear of a cat or a gerbil or another form of animal life either. Alex and I managed to smuggle in a gold-fish at one point and Philippe just about tolerates this dreary creature, despite the fact that it is the height of naff bad taste in his view. It has to be hidden away in Alex's room of course.

So Harry and Samantha had definitely stolen an advantage by acquiring a puppy.

Harry was handsomer than ever and still fit-looking, despite his age and murky past. Usually I sense a small frisson of attraction every time I see him, but today I stared into his fallen-angel blue eyes without a tremor. I must be growing up at last, and not before time, I thought.

He was dressed for the occasion in appropriate country gentleman's summer gear complete with the adorable black Labrador puppy on a lead. The lead was crucial as the puppy was wriggling with plump enthusiasm for everyone and everything. It was clearly love at first sight as far as Alex was concerned.

I wondered what Samantha's baby made of it all. She's a beautiful but fractious two-year-old, with Harry's blond, wavy hair and Samantha's serious gaze. Her name is Flora and today she was traditionally but possibly impractically dressed in a smocked blue Liberty lawn dress.

Restraining Flora from pulling the dog's tail, Samantha invited me to join their picnic. Full marks to her, I thought, as she actually managed to look as if she meant it. Accepting, I opened my mouth to say that I would go and fetch my garage-bought contributions when I remembered Harry had once said something about Samantha's amazingly efficient domesticity.

Too right. She had handed the baby over to Harry – funny how he was such a good father these days – and was extracting from the back of the BMW a smart folding table, a pink starched linen cloth, six chairs and a wicker basket full of carefully wrapped goodies. She then produced a jug of Pimm's which she poured into three real cut-glass tumblers, complete with cucumber and sprigs of mint, of course. Flora and Alex were offered fresh orange juice in practical but stylish plastic glasses decorated with a strawberry motif. To accompany this were home-made crisps and sausage rolls for the children, plus unbearably lovely cheesy things for the adults. While we were consuming these wonderful offerings with much over-polite jollity, Samantha laid the table with proper silver knives and forks and, the final touch, a silver vase of roses.

I was so impressed I couldn't speak. I had always wondered why Harry married her, seeing as he normally prefers the model-girl type, but now I knew. Samantha is the perfect Stepford wife and a true domestic goddess.

Only Flora spoilt the perfection of the occasion by pouring her orange juice over herself and the dog. Samantha was ready for everything, however, and quick as a flash she led the weeping Flora away, whipped off the Liberty frock and replaced it with another one, pink this time but equally sweet and pretty.

Meanwhile an astonishingly docile Harry had taken over laying out the lunch. Spinach and ricotta quiche, fresh salmon, an elegant aubergine salad, anchovy and something or other stuffed peppers, accompanied by sun-dried tomato and Parmesan bread. I was thinking, cattily, that the children wouldn't want this sophisticated stuff, but then good old Samantha produced some barbecued chicken legs and cute little mini hotdogs. We then had strawberries, meringues and crème fraiche, while the children were offered home-made fairy cakes. I sampled one and they were ultra light and delicious.

It was all too much. Shamefully, I had been hoping that even if we adults were having a lovely time, Flora would throw another tantrum. But for the time being she was behaving like an angel and the perfection of Samantha and all her works made me sick. I was very much afraid that she was a better mother than I was.

After lunch I made an effort to push away these unworthy thoughts as we all got ready to watch the little boys running races and generally being athletic and cute. Alex and I walked back towards the school alone.

'Gorgeous puppy,' I said.

'Mm,' he agreed enthusiastically. Then he patted my arm, 'Don't worry, Mum, I do understand we can't have a dog in Paris.' Then he ran off to change into his sports gear.

It was an exquisitely English country scene with the daddies – stockbrokers and accountants – in summery beige jackets and the lovely young mummies in cool designer white, or the less hip, less gorgeous girls in sprigged flowery numbers like Sam. Where do they find those fancy frumpy dresses? They're unobtainable in France: I thought they'd gone to fashion heaven years ago.

Alex was very kind to little Flora and helped her run in the baby sisters' race. Despite his careful coaching, when the race began and the other little girls ran towards the finishing tape, Flora stood perplexed on the start line and then toddled off in the wrong direction. Alex grabbed her by the hand and, roaring with laughter, brought her back to us. They made a sweet pair, my son and his sister.

Alex himself didn't star this year in the athletic events. As he explained to me gravely, he is more into tennis and cricket and stuff. He's in the second eleven cricket team, but on the rare occasions I manage to come and watch him, he's always out first ball. Today I could tell that because I was here, he was especially keen to shine at something sporty, but it was not to be. I sometimes worry about how seriously Alex takes life at the moment, but no doubt all will change when he becomes a teenager.

After the athletics, tea was served in the marquee, where both the French and the History masters approached me and said what a smashing and clever chap he was. This delighted me, of course, but then I saw in the distance another elderly teacher talking earnestly to Samantha. She's not his mother, I wanted to scream. Don't you dare discuss my son with her.

Ashamed, I told myself I should be glad she's taking an interest. It wasn't as if Harry was available for parent–teacher discussions. He'd disappeared; too busy chatting up all the prettiest mummies probably. No change there, then.

It's only recently that Harry has started to pay much attention to Alex, and I've concluded Samantha is responsible. She is a woman with a conscience, and I'm happy to have her as Alex's stepmother, really I am. Bearing in mind Harry's previous bimbettes, she could be a lot worse.

Though Harry always coughed up child support without question, there were years and years when we hardly heard from him and I don't think Alex minded that much because that was what he was used to. But nowadays, since Alex has grown up to be a reasonably successful and pleasant young chap, Harry has obviously decided his son is interesting after all. Maybe he is reliving his schooldays through Alex. Yes, this is the prep school my dear ex-husband attended.

'Hello again, darling,' drawled a voice in my ear.

'Oh, hi, Harry.'

'Did I say you were looking stunning?' He seemed to have had a glass or five of Pimm's. Not that he needs alcohol to switch into flirt mode. It's his default status. 'Did I say I loved your outfit? Very chic and Parisian.'

I raised my eyebrows. 'You did, thanks, m'dear.'

'Still fancy you, you know.'

'I know, Harry, just like you fancy us all.'

He grinned. 'Not true. I'm very particular.'

'Come on,' I said briskly, 'we should have a quick word with the headmaster now I've got hold of you.'

His eyes twinkled. 'You can get hold of me anytime.'

'Save it, Harry. Heard it all before,' I groaned theatrically.

He took my arm as we walked along between the tidy rose beds. 'How's old Philippe?'

'Fine.'

'Paris OK?'

'Yep.' I didn't elaborate because Harry isn't much interested in anything outside the circle that revolves round himself. In fact, we didn't even get as far as the headmaster because Harry suddenly saw someone in the distance he just had to talk to. A business colleague. Needless to say, the colleague was a leggy young blonde in sleek olive green. With some amusement I watched him saunter over towards her. Good old Harry.

I told myself that in some ways I should be glad he's more interested in chasing women than in discussing Alex's future. If he were obsessive about his son, my life would be considerably more difficult. The trouble is that despite Harry's relaxed attitude, and despite the fact that he and I have such a civilized, friendly form of joint custody, I always have an irrational fear that he and Samantha are somehow going to steal Alex away.

And when, at the end of the long day, I found myself driving back alone to spend the night at my mother's while they'd whisked my son off in their jolly little family unit, complete with jolly little dog, I was thoroughly miserable.

Alex had hugged me tight before he left. I knew he was concerned about my feelings, so I'd put on a cheerful face as I waved them goodbye. A boy of his age shouldn't have to worry about his mother, but maybe that's one of the snags about being an only child.

My visit to Ma was mercifully brief and soon I was back in Paris, where I felt a little better, but not much. If I had been well organized, I would have brought Alex with me, reckoned my mother. Apparently my sister's children visit her regularly, but then Rosalind has brought them up very nicely.

Seven

'You are so good for Philippe,' said Aunt Isabelle. She was sitting in a high-backed chair, her puffy ankles supported by a stool upholstered in crimson damask. Her grey suit could have been worn by an English country lady up to London for the day, except that it was much better cut. The gold YSL buttons proclaimed its provenance.

Gigi the poodle had calmed down a little and was lying on the floor, her face alert, eyes fixed on my face, beseeching me to take her for a walk.

I smiled at them both with their black curly hair and beady brown eyes. Well, maybe I was stretching the comparison. Isabelle's IQ is a hell of a lot higher than Gigi's, and Gigi's hair colour is natural.

'Yes, so good for him,' repeated Aunt Isabelle. 'Françoise was such a tense and serious woman. Everything had always to be perfect, and a perfectionist is impossible for any man to live with.'

'Um. Well, that's something in my favour. No one has ever accused me of being too perfect. On the other hand Philippe himself, well, he has high standards, so he and Françoise together . . .'

'Were a pain in the neck,' finished Isabelle. 'But you are teaching him to laugh and to relax.'

I smiled. 'The way he sees it, he's teaching me to become a Parisienne, *une femme sérieuse*.'

'Oh, that would be a mistake. Please don't change. You are so charming and refreshing as you are.' She waved her wrinkly hand. 'Now, will you do me a small service, my dear?'

I put down my teacup. 'Of course. I was just thinking Gigi needed a walk.'

Gigi leapt to her feet and began to bounce, wagging her funny pom-pom tail. She's not that stupid.

'*Doucement*, sit down, sit down, dog,' said Isabelle. To my astonishment, Gigi obeyed. 'No, I should like you to fetch something from the top drawer of my desk, a small purple box.'

'Of course. Which desk?'

She has three elegant spindle-legged desks dotted around the house, each one ornate, inlaid and gold-trimmed, and each one crammed with disorderly papers and letters. Occasionally she likes me to bring her a drawer, which she attempts, half-heartedly, to tidy.

'That one, the Louis the Tenth, of course. That's where I keep everything of the greatest importance.'

I had to smile again because Aunt Isabelle tells me each week that she is in the throes of sorting out her papers and each week she instructs me that a different drawer is full of vital stuff.

Rather to my surprise, the purple box was where she specified. It was a small velvet trinket box and I imagined she wanted me to take some jewellery to be repaired. It's the sort of thing she prefers not to ask the butler to do. 'A woman knows best,' she normally says.

She rifled through it. 'Here, my dear, this is a little present for you, for your patience. Hold out your hand.'

I gasped as she placed a ring on the middle of my palm. 'It's lovely. Thank you. Thank you very much.' A gold ring set with a large pink stone with what must be fake diamonds on either side, it was most attractive, old-fashioned and solid. The stone was too large to be anything but costume jewellery. A nineteenth-century dress ring, I thought, but I was mistaken.

'It is a pink sapphire. Monsieur gave it to me,' she said with a wink. Her late boyfriend is always referred to as 'Monsieur'. 'You must get Philippe to insure it as it is valuable.'

'Valuable? But I thought . . . But I can't accept such a present if it's . . . What about your family?'

'I insist. And this ring is a personal thing, nothing to do with the family. I shall not speak to you again unless you accept my gift as graciously as I am presenting it to you.'

'Excellent,' mused Philippe, holding the ring up to the light. 'An excellent stone. You have done well, *chérie*.'

I felt uncomfortable. 'Yes, she's very kind, your aunt.'

'Extraordinarily kind,' he said. 'One must have this valued.' Then taking his eyes off the ring for a moment, he said sharply, 'Did she put any conditions on this gift?'

'Conditions?'

'About it staying in our family or something of that nature.'

'No,' I said quietly. 'No, I hadn't thought, but I got the impression that it was just a present to me. I can check with her.'

'No, no, don't check. I shall do so, but I am delighted she should give you a personal present of this value. Delighted. You should wear it to lunch this Sunday, at my mother's. Better wear it on the right hand for now.'

'Sure,' I said. I admit I was rather looking forward to Camille's face when she saw the ring. It would drive her nuts. Then it dawned on me what Philippe had said. Wear it on the right hand *for now.*

He was gazing quizzically at me.

'What do you mean?' I asked, flushing.

'Eventually,' he said, 'it could fit the third finger of your left hand.'

I stared at him. If this was a proposal, I wasn't ready for it.

Nor was he, it seemed, because suddenly he twirled me round. 'It is safer on the right for now, *ma petite,*' he said, and suddenly left the flat.

I stood rooted to the spot. I ought to be over the moon, but my feet were firmly here on the ground.

Camille, Philippe's mother, sat squarely at the head of the table in her dark and formal Saint-Cloud dining room. As usual, she was watching us all with sharp, hooded eyes. Sometimes she reminds me of a crocodile.

When we lunch there on Sundays, as we often do, I always feel she's waiting for me to make a mistake of some kind, social or grammatical. She doesn't have to wait long because I take great liberties with the French language in order to get the words out. If I hesitated until I'd formulated a perfectly constructed, perfectly pronounced sentence, then I would never speak at all. I'm always at my worst *chez* Camille. Usually French people are kind and don't mind the mangled way I rave on in their language as long as they can understand the gist of what I'm trying to say, but Camille corrects the pronunciation of every other word, so that whatever I am trying to say sounds sillier and sillier, until it is clear it wasn't worth saying in the first place.

Today I remained quiet, eating the admittedly delicious lunch and occasionally glancing at the pink sapphire that I was wearing on the third finger of my right hand. No further discussion about moving it to the left had taken place, but Philippe was being surprisingly nice to me at the moment.

It was Marie-Clementine, the younger of his married sisters, who noticed. 'How charming your new ring is, Clio,' she said. 'It reminds me of one Tante Isabelle had.'

I swear they've made an inventory of everything in Isabelle's house, those girls.

'Yes, actually she gave it to me last week. A present,' I added firmly. 'Wasn't that kind? She is always so *sympa*.'

There was a deadly silence. Then Anne-Sophie, the elder sister, spoke as if in deep shock. 'To you? She gave that ring to you?' She glanced quickly at her hands as if she was afraid I had snitched her precious diamonds too.

A whisper of stunned French disapproval rippled through the room. '*Pour elle, la bague? Pourquoi à elle, l'Anglaise?*'

Why give the ring to the perfidious Englishwoman? Why indeed? I didn't know, except that if it was one of Isabelle's attempts to irritate Camille, then she had succeeded in spades. The girls were put out, but Camille's face darkened with anger.

After lunch she asked to inspect it. I held out my hand. I certainly wasn't going to take it off in case she confiscated it. Whether she noticed my badly filed nails or not I don't know, but she stared hard at the ring and then turned away without another word.

Sometimes I think she is one of the rudest women I've ever met. The trouble is, she can be perfectly charming at other times, and you forget and begin to relax in her presence, half assuming that she quite likes you after all; then suddenly she'll bite your head off and you feel all the more upset because you weren't prepared. Maybe I should answer her back more than I do, but I always feel quarrelling with her would be counterproductive. She would win.

One thing in her favour is that she is always sweet to my son, my Alexander. She cooks him special food, admires his clothes and helps him with his French. She often says rather pointedly how good his pronunciation is. Amazingly he and *les cousins*, fat sons of the thin sisters, get on well and play football together in the park near Camille's house. All four of them are younger than Alexander and they appear to admire him, so at least one of us is held in some regard in Saint-Cloud.

Perhaps I am being unfair to Marie-Clementine and Anne-Sophie, as they can be quite chummy when we meet away from their mother's territory. It's only in Saint-Cloud, when their mother is watching them, that I get the cold shoulder. Both girls keep a firm eye on me if I am talking to one of their timid husbands. It's as if they think I am a seductress about to drag an innocent off to my lair, though frankly both husbands have about as much sex appeal as yesterday's scones.

Philippe's quiet and charming father, Edouard, stays out of all family controversy. He's the tall, thin, stooping professor type and spends most of the time in his library or away down in the Loire in their dilapidated country house, attending to the business of their small unprofitable vineyard. He used to be a civil servant and has retired on a good meaty French pension, according to Isabelle.

Occasionally he will lean forward at lunch and ask my opinion about a political matter or try to discuss with me some arcane point about Britain's international affairs. I have few opinions in English about politics, let alone in French, so usually I sit there opening and shutting my mouth like Alex's goldfish, showing about the same amount of brainpower.

Eventually I developed one way of dealing with him. I would study some peculiar, faintly quirky and unusual fact about, say, Polish woodcutters being eaten by reintroduced wolves or Swiss glaciers being air-freighted to Saudi Arabia, then I'd learn a few fancy phrases in French on the subject and spout this out, regardless of what he asked me. He'd want to know my views on Britain's position vis-à-vis the European Union and I'd say something like, 'Funny you should mention that because only yesterday I was reading about Austrian manufacturers protesting about the new EU regulations on cuckoo clocks . . .'

Today, however, even Edouard didn't dare to speak to me, so I sat quietly watching my new sapphire winking in the pale sun shining through Camille's windows.

★   ★   ★

Back at the apartment, we drank a glass of Armagnac and then made love in the afternoon, as we often do on a Sunday. One needs to relax after lunch *chez* Camille.

When we were done, instead of turning away, Philippe took my hand gently. 'We should get married one day,' he said.

I held my breath. My heart was thumping uncomfortably. 'I'm not so good at marriage.'

'Yes, but, darling, you have been very unlucky.'

This tenderness unnerved me. I held him close without speaking. Then I said, in a light, casual whisper, 'But you are still married to Françoise.'

'Of course, but I will speak to her about the divorce again soon.'

I was silent. If he was stalling, so was I. Part of me wanted him, his extended family, his settled French life. If I were a daughter-in-law, Camille would have to accept me. Her well-developed sense of family would force her to conquer her dislike. At the moment she was still fighting to dislodge me, but if I won then she would have to be gracious in defeat, I reckoned.

And Philippe and I were happy together. Happier than many couples I knew, anyway. As happy as one could reasonably expect to be. Not madly, deeply, deliriously in love, but that was a dangerous state and never lasted, as I knew only too well.

If I married Philippe, Alex would have a settled home in France and a family background that would be strong against Harry and Samantha and all their works.

'Yes,' repeated Philippe. 'I shall speak to Françoise very soon.'

I was still silent.

As if sensing my unspoken thought, he said, 'I expect you imagine one would be better to speak to a lawyer than to her, but a divorce is always cheaper and better if it is amicable.'

'Of course,' I said.

'So I will settle things with her finally. Then together we shall go to the lawyers. But it will take time.'

'Right,' I said. 'Whatever's best.'

He smiled down at me. 'You are a very understanding person, my Clio, and I adore you.'

Hm, I thought.

'I'm always happy when you are near me,' he murmured, still in this surprisingly romantic mood.

I didn't reply, just snuggled closer to him as we drifted off to sleep.

Something jolted me awake: the illogical thought of Joe. He often swam in and out of my mind without permission. The distant, unattainable stranger factor.

Doesn't mean anything, of course. Just a fantasy.

Eight

I had to tell someone, someone discreet and someone who knew none of Philippe's friends. 'He proposed. Well, more or less,' I confided to Mary.

As both Philippe and her husband were away, we were having a girly, giggly supper together at her posh diplomatic apartment, while her two young children slept peacefully at the other end of the long corridor. We'd eaten a huge, fattening, wonderfully cheesy lasagne and drunk rather too many glasses of red wine. We'd finished pulling Elaine to pieces for now and I'd heard all about her latest dim-witted Insider Tours clients. As there was a pause in the conversation, I decided to make my thrilling announcement.

'Who proposed?' she asked with a grin.

'Philippe, of course.'

'Oh, er, good. Congratulations.' She gave me a hug, but I noticed she didn't sound miles over the moon for me.

I gushed on, 'It's a secret, completely hush-hush at the moment. We haven't told his family.'

'Why not?'

'Good question. But of course he's not divorced yet, and then there's his mother. She hates me. Not that that matters, but it's a bit more of a problem in France what with families being so close, you see.'

'I do see.' She looked puzzled, and then she asked in a kind of airy voice, 'So you accepted, did you?'

'Oh, yes, or at least I think I did. Well, I didn't say no or yes.' I took another sip of wine. 'I'm prevaricating, aren't I?'

She smiled without replying. Then she began, obviously picking her words even more tactfully, 'But if he isn't divorced, you've got plenty of time to decide.'

'I made my mind up ages ago that if he asked, I'd say yes.'

'Still, one shouldn't rush things – there's plenty of time to decide if he really is what you want.'

I stared at her. She was being astonishingly outspoken for Mary. *In vino veritas?* Her eyes were bright and her cheeks were flushed, but she wasn't that pissed, was she? People like Mary, respectable representatives of Britain, just don't lose control.

I took a deep breath and blurted out, 'You don't like Philippe, do you?'

'Course I do. Course I do,' she said quickly. 'He's always charming when one meets him, absolutely charming. Good-looking too. Definitely.'

'I can feel there's a "but" coming. But what?'

She looked embarrassed. After a moment's hesitation she said, 'Well, from the sound of it, he isn't always that nice to you.'

I must have been moaning more than I realized.

'Look,' I said. 'You know what men are – up and down, a bit moody according to what's been going on in the office, that sort of thing. He's really sweet to me sometimes.'

'Mm.'

'Yes,' I said defiantly. 'When he's nice, it's like, er, spring and summer combined. I mean, if he was sunshine and light all day and every day, one wouldn't appreciate the bright periods half so much.'

She didn't look convinced.

I raved on. 'No, well, I mean, no one's perfect. I'm certainly not. Even my own mother says I'm not much of a catch. And I'm hardly love's young dream.'

She clutched my arm. 'You are a total gem, Clio, and don't let Philippe forget that.'

'And you're a total mate,' I burbled, embarrassed. 'And an utter gem too . . . Um, have we had too much to drink?'

'Probably. But the point is, what about Joe?'

I flushed. 'Joe?'

'Joe Dryden as you perfectly well know.'

'He was just a ship that passed in the night. No, not the night. We didn't have a night. It was perfectly innocent. Well, not perfectly but just a kiss, you know. Nothing else.'

She grinned. 'I'll believe you. Thousands wouldn't.'

''Sperfectly true,' I slurred. 'Goodness, what's the time? Mustn't miss the last metro.'

'Get the bus, safer,' she said. 'Anyway, there's loads of time. But have you heard from Joe?'

I was hoping to have distracted her. 'No way. Forgotten all about him,' I lied.

'So you didn't contact him? He hasn't forgotten about *you*. He keeps emailing the office, as I discovered today when I held the fort for Elaine – she had some great dental crisis.'

'Poor Elaine, what was wrong?'

But Mary was not to be diverted. 'He's been sending message after message, so I replied, giving him your email address. Thought it might be indiscreet to give him anything else.'

'You did what?' I was so startled I was almost shouting.

'Calm down,' she said. 'How was I to know you and Philippe had come to some sort of understanding? I thought you liked Joe, so I was just letting what I thought might be a little new romantic light into your life. Sorry, should have asked you if you minded.' She looked a bit sheepish.

'Too right you should. It doesn't matter, though. I just won't answer the emails. No harm done.' But my heart was thumping hard in my chest. 'Did you tell him I'd been sacked?'

'I did. I told him about Melvin complaining about you and how Elaine alleged he'd complained too.'

'Mary, you're nuts to put all that on the office computer. You'll get sacked yourself.'

'Don't worry. All double-deleted in an instant. The point is, have you heard from him?'

No, I hadn't and did I care? Of course not.

Just then who should appear but Mary's nightmare nanny, back from a romantic dinner with her married lover, so the conversation about Joe was interrupted, to my relief.

Virginia, the most unlikely nanny imaginable, is the original vamp: dark, sultry and a pain in the butt. She tries to be Liz Hurley and a younger Liz Taylor all rolled into one great sex bomb. Sometimes this works, sometimes her male victims run a mile. To be fair, her skin is pretty good for someone approaching forty, she has an excellent figure with an impressive bosom, and she doesn't dress like Liz Hurley these days. Paris has had a good effect on her fashion sense, as with all of us. It's just her manner that is so irritating. She can be perfectly normal, charming and matey with women and children, but as soon as a man comes into the room, any man, she becomes a sexual being, all smouldering eyes, throaty voice and swinging hips, along with arm-clutching and face-stroking if she can get near enough to the bloke in question, and she usually does.

Tonight she stood momentarily in the doorway of the salon, looking pale, dishevelled and not at her best, I thought.

'Hello, Virginia. You're back early,' said Mary.

'Yes. Oh, hi, Clio. Won't interrupt,' she said shortly, and stomped off to her room.

Normally Virginia enjoys a good chinwag. Mary and I raised our eyebrows. It looked as if the path of untrue love was not going smoothly.

According to Mary, the story of how she came to engage her as a nanny goes something like this.

Mary was innocently doing the ironing in her neat Victorian semi in Richmond, feeling that all was very well with the world. Her husband, Tim, had recently been told by the Foreign Office that he was to be posted to Paris. Naturally they were both delighted, particularly in view of the fact that less salubrious possibilities like Lagos, Kinshasa or Bogotá had been floated about by the HR department during the last few months.

She had just finished the last of Tim's striped shirts when the telephone rang.

'Mary, sweetie, is that you?' said a deep, breathy female voice.

She recognized it immediately: Virginia, her husband's first cousin. OK in small doses but a little went a long way.

'Hello?' she said cautiously, rather hoping she was wrong about the identity of the voice.

'It's me, my love. Virginia risen from the ashes. So sorry not to have touched base for such yonks, but life has been a teeny bit fraught of late.'

'Lovely to hear from you. How are you?'

'Oh, you know, one or two probs, but basically fine and dandy and raring to go.'

There was a pause.

Mary's diplomatic training meant she automatically filled in pauses, so against her better judgement, she asked, 'When are we going to see you?'

'Well, my love, I thought I might pop round more or less straight away, if you're free. Dear old Timbo says you aren't too busy this week.'

If Mary had not been in such a generally good mood, she might have been pretty annoyed not to have been warned by dear old Timbo. As it was, she said, 'Of course. I mean, when?'

'Well, sweetie, since you've both always been so kind to me, what I thought was that I could come tonight or soon, or whenever you say, and cook you dinner. I'd bring every last morsel of food with me – well, not flour and oil and stuff, but absolutely everything else. Then we can all celebrate your new posting together and you'd have an evening off and wouldn't even have to get a babysitter. How does that sound?'

Mary was taken aback, but she said, 'Sounds wonderful, I must admit, but how did you know about Paris?'

'Heard it on the old grapevine and so I phoned Timbo and said how I'd love to get together before you go. He said something feeble about babysitting problems and so I had this totally brilliant idea. I owe you so much hospitality – you've always been such angels – and this just seems the only way to pay you back. So how about it? When can I come and cook you a dream dinner?'

Mary had been gearing herself up to go to Waitrose and suddenly the idea of not having to produce yet another meal was rather attractive, so rashly she said, 'Anytime.'

'Tonight, then? Let's strike when the iron is hot. See you at seven, then, OK?'

Mary gulped. 'Yes, yes, but, Virginia, don't go to too much trouble. I'll lay the table and all that, but how many for? Sorry not to know, but like you said, we haven't heard from you for a while. Are you, er, *with* anyone at the moment?'

'Not in England, my love,' said Virginia. '*A bientôt.*'

As soon as Mary had put the phone down, she began to worry. There must be some kind of ulterior motive, but what? The first thought that sprang to mind was that Virginia hoped for an invitation to visit Paris. Fair enough. Now that their new posting had been announced, quite a few people suddenly remembered what good friends they were.

'Not in England.' Did this mean a man abroad, and could this man just possibly be in Paris? Frequent visits from Virginia might well be a nuisance, but there would be ways of dealing with her, like saying they were fully booked with family or official visitors.

Virginia arrived in a flurry of kisses and lovely-to-see-yous and Sainsbury's bags. The children should have been in bed, but instead they were jumping around in their pyjamas, excited to see her. At least, six-year-old Toby was. Four-year-old Kate claimed she was 'cited too, though it was unlikely she could remember Virginia.

Dressed to kill in youthful sequinned-denim rock-chick gear, Virginia made an immediate hit with both children by producing two Dr Seuss books as presents and then offering to read a story. Usually shy with strangers, a giggly little Kate took her by the hand and led her upstairs.

Mary settled on the sofa with a large glass of red wine and marvelled at the peace. She'd toyed with the idea of unpacking the shopping but was reluctant to interfere. After all, Virginia used to be a professional cook at one stage during her long and chequered career.

May as well lie back and enjoy it. Mary undid the waist button of her too-tight jeans and kicked off her Russell & Bromley flatties. She was suddenly conscious of the comparison with Virginia's sexy sandals. Never mind, even in her twenties she had never been able to compete with lithe and unconventionally fashionable women like Virginia, so why worry now? After all, she was the one with the husband and family. Mary gave a self-satisfied sigh, but there was a little cloud at the back of her mind.

A while later Virginia came down and, refusing help, began to rattle around in the kitchen, occasionally shrieking, 'Where's the colander, my lovely? Haven't you got any fresh basil at all? Oh dear, sweetie, is this the only square entrée dish you have?' Delicious garlicky smells wafted around the house.

'I say, Gins, jolly good fish,' said Tim later, wolfing it down. The evening sunlight was shining through his thinning hair like a halo. Sometimes he reminded Mary of a plump little Friar Tuck.

'Delicious sauce,' Mary said. It really was. She wondered about the calories, both for herself and for Tim, who was reluctant to admit the need to watch them.

'Tuna is so healthy, omega-3 and all that,' purred Virginia. 'I'm frightfully careful where I shop these days. Of course, it will be fantastic in Paris. Such marvellous ingredients in the markets.'

'Mm,' said Mary warily.

The tiramisu was even more delicious.

'Timbo's always had a weakness for puds like this, haven't you, sweetie? Just like your father.'

Cue for childhood reminiscences, thought Mary resigned.

But instead Virginia asked casually, 'What will you have in the way of staff in Paris?'

Mary said she'd look for a Filipina for cleaning and a bit of nannying, but unfortunately their predecessor's treasure was leaving the country. It was always difficult settling the children in at first, and there were bound to be endless official functions, so from the start they'd have to face the problem of strange babysitters in a strange country.

'But if you had a live-in dinner-party-cook-cum-nanny, it'd be better for the children. Then you could just get a cleaner once a week or something.'

'Of course, that would be ideal if one could afford it, but . . .'

Virginia stared at them both under her annoyingly long eyelashes. 'So how about little old *moi*?'

Mary tried and tried in the most tactful manner to put her off the idea, but Tim was no help at all. 'Brilliant, brilliant, great help, but better stick to three months, Gins. We might get sick of each other after that.'

Later, after Virginia had gone – and she'd even done all the washing-up – Mary explained her misgivings more forcefully.

Tim patted his stomach in that irritating way he had. 'I can deal with old Gins if she gets out of line, but think how difficult it's going to be to do the job properly if we arrive without some kind of nanny in tow. In the first few weeks there'll be endless diplomatic parties every night and you know how tricky Kate can be with babysitters.'

Mary shook her head. 'I didn't really want someone living in. We've had all those problem girls in the past. Remember the anorexic who didn't speak and that unhappy Irish one who cried all the time? More trouble than the children, most of them.'

'But Virginia is family. Won't be like some alien spotty teenager who's never been abroad before and who hates us all and Paris. No, old Gins will fit in fine.'

And that was the end of it as far as he was concerned. They always had to be nice as pie to cousin Virginia because her father, Reggie, had supported Tim when he was a boy. Tim's father had died young and Uncle Reggie had been a prop and stay and could never be denied anything for ever more. This debt of gratitude extended to Virginia, who was always to be granted any reasonable request she made. It just depended how one defined reasonable.

'Why does she want to come to Paris, anyway? I wouldn't have thought that cook-nanny was her thing at all. She's more of an It-girl.'

'*Cherchez l'homme,*' he said.

'You mean she has a boyfriend?' All had suddenly become clear to Mary.

And so it came about that, in order to help Virginia chase someone else's husband, Mary has been lumbered with her for almost a year. The three-month limit has gone by the board and it looks as if she'll be stuck with her for the duration. Virginia cooks like a dream when it suits her, Mary admits, and she does babysit, but only when it doesn't conflict with one of her assignations with her Italian lover, an international financier. The wife of Virginia's lover works in Brussels, appearing in Paris only for the odd weekend, so Virginia and Paolo have the field to themselves mostly.

She isn't content with just Paolo, though. Maybe it's to keep him on his toes, but she flirts with every man in sight. Not just the sexy Don Juan types either. She'll toy with dry civil servants or dusty professors unused to being chased by any women, let alone a nubile sex bomb like Virginia, and they either run a mile or stand there with their mouths hanging open in mesmerized embarrassment. I'm not saying she sleeps around. She just gives that impression.

Tim, normally a mega stuffed shirt, is peculiarly indulgent about Virginia's behaviour. She isn't like the rest of us, he would say. She's had difficulties with men. One has to make allowances.

'You've had difficulties with men, Clio,' whispered Mary this evening, as Virginia's heels tapped away down the corridor, 'but you don't behave like a tart.' She'd now reached the stage of speaking pretty frankly to me on the subject.

'Mm,' I said, wondering nevertheless if my secret fantasies about Joe could be classified as virtual infidelity, if not tartiness. I could hardly share these thoughts with Mary since I had spent all evening talking about my virtual engagement.

A bedroom door slammed.

'It's not going so well with Paolo. Virginia's worried about her biological clock. I reckon they've had a fight.'

'Have they?' I asked vaguely. I had rather lost interest in the Virginia saga. What I wanted to do was get back and see if I'd had any emails from Joe.

I arrived at the bus-stop and jumped up and down impatiently, checking the timetable. Probably just missed one, I reckoned, so I didn't bother waiting and hurried off along the quiet boulevards, striding out like an Olympic speed-walker. Needless to say, the damn bus passed me when I was between stops. And needless to say, a strange car with two strange men drew up alongside me. Maybe they didn't think me sexy enough because they accelerated away sharpish when I ignored them.

Actually, you're pretty safe in Paris in a district like this. There are plenty of prostitutes around, but the punters usually know who is what. One way to tell a pro is that she (or possibly he) wears white shoes, they say. Another piece of spice: apparently, in Avenue Foch the female tarts operate nearest to the Arc de Triomphe, the swingers in the middle, and the lady boys nearest the park. This is what Philippe tells me, anyway. Not sure how he knows. They, the prostitutes, don't bother people much, as long as one keeps out of their way. It's always a surprise to me, however, that they are so obvious, standing around next to respectable embassies and other grand houses. And then there are the ladies who operate in white vans parked on the edge of the park next to the Périphérique. It must be much too hot in the summer, I always think.

None of these lowlife considerations were on my mind this evening, though.

The moment I got home, I dived to the computer and called up Outlook Express.

'No new messages,' said the disheartening little blurb on the bottom corner of the screen.

Nine

I must have checked my emails a hundred times before I heard from Joe three days later. It seemed like the longest three days in my life, which was stupid because I wasn't that interested in a nomadic Irish-Canadian I hardly knew, a man who lives on the other side of the world. How could I be when I was happily semi-engaged to a respectable and respected French economist?

What does Philippe do economics-wise? I don't exactly know. He writes learned stuff about globalization, world trade, and, this is the good part, he draws up schemes and thinks up ideas whereby the richer countries can help the poorer ones. His work is theoretical and analytical, rather than hands-on stuff at the sharp end. He doesn't actually visit Africa and dish out sacks of grain, or go anywhere else in the untidy Third World, but presumably what he does is worth while as he's well paid and very well thought of by his colleagues, so he tells me.

So there I was sitting at my desk in Philippe's flat supposedly typing my *French Fantasia* contribution – an article about Chartres – but constantly interrupting my flow of thought by logging on to email every ten minutes, or every two minutes, to be more accurate.

At last the computer gave a little ping. A new message. A new message from Joe Dryden. My heart flipped as I read it.

Hi, Clio,
   Am coming to France on 20 July for a couple of weeks. Can I book a tour with you? Anyplace you choose, anytime, but maybe the Loire.
   I'm aiming to avoid Insider Tours again unless you are part of them. Your friend Mary said there had been a problem, but I did *not* complain about the Normandy tour. On the contrary, I told the boss lady you were great.
   Sincerely,
   Joe

Nice, polite but hardly a love letter, was my first thought. My second thought was that 20 July equals school holidays, and that Alexander and I would be at the seaside, far away from Paris. I was longing to see Alex, but I couldn't help the surge of disappointment that washed over me at the bad timing of Joe's visit.

Pull yourself together, Clio. Fate has decreed that you won't see him again. Which is just as well.

I'd reply to him in due course. Much later. An instant reply would be uncool. Meanwhile better get back to Chartres Cathedral and forget about him, since he is totally irrelevant. 'The current cathedral dates from the twelfth and thirteenth centuries,' I began, 'after the previous church was burnt down in 1194.'

Unless he could come at a different time.

Maybe he could.

But you don't want him to, because he might mess up your life.

Exactly.

'Take binoculars so that you can appreciate the intricacies of the richly coloured stained-glass windows.'

If you send your reply now, then you can stop thinking about it and finish that goddamn article.

Switching to the email screen again, I began:

> Dear Joe,
>   Great to hear from you. Sorry, but in July I'll be away on holiday with my son. We'll be right down in Hendaye on the Spanish border. Too far away to connect. Sorry to miss you.
>   Love,
>   Clio

Then I deleted 'love' and just put 'Clio'. Then I changed it to 'Regards, Clio', then to 'Best wishes, Clio', because that sounded less stiff.

I read it through. Nice and casually friendly. I sent it off there and then, just to get it and Joe out of my hair.

Now, I thought, I can concentrate on Chartres. I certainly wasn't doing it justice at the moment. 'Browse around the old part of town, which surrounds the cathedral . . .'

But of course I kept checking my email constantly. Eventually there was the briefest acknowledgement.

> I'm sorry too.
> What's your new cell-phone number?
> Love,
> Joe

And that was it. I couldn't believe it. If he had really wanted to, surely he could have rearranged his trip. Crossly, I deleted every dull, mundane sentence I had written about Chartres and went for a walk.

'Love, Joe' meant nothing. I was damned if I was going to send him my phone number.

I managed to relegate him to the back of my mind in the excitement of Alexander's arrival and our departure on holiday. There was the usual disorganization and drama. How I hate holiday packing. My beach clothes were all wrong, shrunk and tired, and Alex's were all lost, too small or, he alleged, unwearable owing to lack of cool. Often during these last-minute panics I feel I'd give anything not to go.

The long, hot drive to Hendaye on the Spanish border was bogged down by traffic jams, but finally we arrived at the Atlantic and installed ourselves in Philippe's holiday flat. He was due to join us towards the end of the month.

This flat is part of an old-fashioned seaside villa, faintly Spanish in style, just across the road from a long, sandy surfing beach. It's a large family house divided into six flats owned by various relations of Philippe, all thanks to some far-sighted great-grandfather or other who bought the land an age ago when there was just an undeveloped beach and a few shacks.

Philippe time-shares his own flat with his sisters and spends hours on the phone negotiating as to who has what week. It's all very complicated and French. The drawback is that the other flats are full of members of his extended family, *les cousins* or their friends. On the plus side Alex usually finds someone to play with and has a wonderful time, and that's the most important thing, as far as I'm concerned.

Hendaye, a jolly family resort, is pleasantly low on chic Parisians and international jet-setters, exactly why I like it. There's not a huge amount to do apart from the usual seaside pastimes: sailing in the lagoon, swimming and modest surfing in the Atlantic rollers and, of course, eating. The food is incredibly cheap, almost every dish in the simpler restaurants being served with *sauce basquaise*, basically tomatoes and peppers. The local vegetables are plentiful and delicious, and you can buy a ton of tuna for about fifty pence. Well, maybe I'm exaggerating, but you get the picture.

The weather can be dodgy when the sea winds from the west hit the foothills of the Pyrenees and condense into torrents of rain. If you don't fancy gambling at the casino or, more bracing but equally expensive, a thalassotherapy treatment, then the wet days pass pretty slowly. You can go up into the hills and visit a Basque village complete with pelota court and elaborately decorated cemetery, but after a while the fascinations of the Basque country in the rain begin to pall. Of course you can drive to beautiful Biarritz, a kind of Paris-on-Sea with designer shops, or scenic old Bayonne, shops ditto, but it's a long journey in both cases. We did once go and see the live seals at the Sea Museum in Biarritz, which animal-mad Alex adored. Hope we won't have to go again, as sightseeing is a bit of a buswoman's holiday for me.

This week luckily the weather was good and equally luckily I'd managed to book Alex into the sailing school every morning, which he adored. This left me free to sunbathe. I know one should avoid the sun, but Philippe thinks a tan disguises a multitude of fleshy sins and I have to agree with him. I'd already managed a pale biscuit shade by lying on the roof in Paris, but I wanted to be a slimming nut brown by the time he arrived. I'd bravely brought my old bikini with me, though really I'm too fat these days. Next year it will have to be a one-piece.

One morning as usual I went down to the beach, not too crowded yet, found a nice pitch and dug my wobbly pink-striped parasol into the sand. Then shaking out my beach mats and bathing towels, I arranged my camp. Philippe always laughs at my futile efforts to avoid sand on the beach. Studying the position and angle of the sun, I set up my beach chair, which is old and rusty and involves a major wrestling match in the style of Mr Bean.

You pull out one set of legs, but then the back won't go up, and vice versa. Sometimes it takes about ten minutes to erect, but I am too mean to buy a new one.

Peace at last, I thought, anointing myself with Ambre Solaire and wiping the sand off my feet yet again. Peering between the brim of my sun hat and an old paperback Joanna Trollope, I checked out the nearby French families – there were some depressingly slim and gorgeous young women, but the leathery grannies displaying their droopy boobs were a less pretty sight.

Relaxing back, I was deep into my book when a shadow fell across me. I looked up.

'Hey, Ms Tour Guide.'

Joe! Of all people.

Startled and blushing like a schoolgirl, I dropped *The Spanish Lover* into the sand.

'Oh, hi, what a surprise!' I said, with a wide, gormless smile.

What the hell was he doing here?

He knelt down to pick up the book and, holding it by the corner, shook it clean. 'You lost your place. Sorry.' Glancing at the title, he raised his eyebrows.

He looked fantastic. Solid brown legs and solid brown chest, not too hairy. He wasn't slim, or fat, not some muscle-bound wonderboy either. Just a very nice hunk of grown-up man. But, horrors, he was staring at me and my podgy stomach. At least I hadn't been tempted to go topless like some of the locals, though my bra had slipped down almost to the point of no return. Hitching it up, I stared at him through my sunglasses, hoping he'd put my red face down to the heat.

'Mind if I join you?' he asked eventually, and sat down on the edge of the beach mat.

'Wh-why are you here?' I stuttered.

'Came to see what you looked like in a bikini.'

'And?'

'Pretty good. Like I expected.'

I grinned delightedly. Then I managed to pull myself together. 'Didn't mean that, I meant, what are you really doing, and how did you find me?'

'Just walked up and down the beach a while, kind of looking around, and then a woman under a pink sunshade caught my eye.

So I said, Go for it, Joe. That's the one. Good body, nice face, and she can read too. Must be an intellectual.'

I grinned. 'Patronizing male bastard . . . But it's very good to see you, all the same.' The pleasant shivers running up and down my spine were still making sophisticated cool difficult to achieve.

'You too. Missed you.'

I let that one pass, and we chatted about Hendaye for a while.

'Will you have lunch with me later on?' he asked in that pleasant deep, growly voice he has.

I sifted the hot sand through my fingers. 'Alex, my son, he'll be back at twelve.'

'Dinner, then?'

My mind raced along. I could ask one of the cousins to babysit, but they might gossip. Never mind, let them. 'Which day?'

He gazed down at me. 'Tonight, of course. If you're free.'

I was.

So it was settled that I should pick him up in the car and we'd drive to Saint-Jean-de-Luz, which had plenty of good restaurants.

'Let's swim now,' he said.

I walked beside him across the sand towards the sea. He didn't hold my hand until we reached the edge of the water; then he pulled me along towards the waves, only small ones today fortunately. The larger rollers have a tendency to dislodge bikinis.

'Long way to come for a swim,' I called as we waded through the shallows.

'Worth it, though.'

My stomach fluttered again.

Finally when we were waist deep, he let go of my hand and dived into the crest of the wave. We swam out for a while, then without speaking turned towards each other.

I thought for a moment he was going to grab me and kiss me. Something – probably a guilty conscience – made me turn away and splash off hastily for the shore. He didn't follow, but stayed diving into the waves and body-surfing.

I pretended not to but I watched him, of course. Eventually he appeared again beside me.

Gazing at the wet tendrils of hair curling on his chest, I forced myself to speak. 'I ought to tell you about Philippe,' I began in a clumsy rush.

'Is he here?'

'No. Still in Paris for the moment, but . . .'

He grinned. 'Then let's forget him.'

'But . . .'

He wrapped his towel round his waist. 'See you at dinner, lovely Clio. You book the table. You're the expert.' Then he strode away down the beach. I stared after him until he climbed up the stone steps on to the esplanade and out of sight.

Our neighbour Carole, who was renting the flat next to ours, promised to keep an eye on and be on call for Alex, who had been deeply offended when I'd suggested a babysitter.

'Mu-um, chill out, would ya. I'm nearly grown-up now, remember? I'm perfectly sensible and I don't need some stupid girl, like, two years older than me, sitting around earning money for doing nothing. Anyway, I babysat myself for Dad and Samantha. I looked after Flora at half-term when they went out for drinks.'

'Did you now?' I was taken aback by the idea of Alex as a childminder, but Samantha and Harry live in a quiet village, so I suppose it's safe enough.

'Yep, loads of times.'

'But I thought they had a nanny.' My dear ex is very generous towards his latest wife.

'No, no, not now that Flora goes to nursery school. The cleaning lady babysits, and I do too when I'm there. I'm cheaper.'

I raised my eyebrows. 'They *pay* you to look after your sister?'

'Sure,' he said smugly. 'So, er, tonight maybe you could, like, pay me for looking after myself?'

I grinned. 'Nice try, but no way.'

Somewhat reluctantly he accepted the suggestion that Carole could be a back-up in case of emergency. Young and pretty, she is a distant cousin of Philippe's. I hoped that, with her four young children to preoccupy her, she wasn't the inquisitive type, but she did ask me, with delicately raised eyebrows, who I was going out with. Oh, I said casually, just 'some friends' I bumped into. If she was suspicious that I wasn't taking Alex with me, she didn't say so.

As for Alex himself, I told him I'd met one of my clients on the beach and been invited out. They probably wanted to talk business, I lied, and that's why they hadn't asked children. I was waffling, I knew.

He thought about this and then said, in the most grown-up manner, 'OK, I understand.'

I felt terrible, both about lying and about leaving him Home Alone, but luckily I'd bought a *Lord of the Rings* DVD last time I was in England. I produced this surprise present just before I left. Bribery? You bet. I don't usually abandon him when we're on holiday. It's normal in France to take your children out to restaurants. That's how they learn to behave and try new food and generally adapt to adult society and appreciate grown-up things. I know I've bellyached in the past about the French being too strict with their children, but living here, one can see the benefits.

So, full of maternal guilt, I left Alex watching the mystic battles and went to shower and change into my new slinky black sundress, plus some dusky-pink earrings and vaguely matching wooden beads. Then I tried a different dress, pale blue and feminine, and different jewellery, modern funky silver, then changed back again to the outfit I'd first thought of. I'd already washed my hair, which was frizzing for England in the damp sea air, so I bunched it up into a kind of bun with bits hanging down. It looked nicer than it sounds. I hope.

My strappy black sandals were almost sensible, rather than the teetering stiletto type, but there might be a bit of a walk involved. I fancied the idea of a stroll out along the slippery harbour wall, where we'd gaze at the sun setting over the Atlantic, and I wanted to be prepared for all eventualities. Not quite all eventualities, actually, since this was, in effect, our first date. No, I keep forgetting, it's not really a date. Just a dinner.

My hands were shaking as I started the car to drive along the crowded beach road to Joe's hotel. I drove along about 15 miles an hour, afraid I would somehow lose concentration and hit someone or something on this perfectly straight road. There were a great many tourists around, all trying to kill themselves in front of my car as they wandered back home after a late swim.

He was standing there on the steps of Hendaye's best hotel when I arrived, rather too punctually, a little after eight o'clock. My heart skipped a beat as he kissed me on the cheek.

'You smell nice,' he said, 'and you look pretty good too.'

I grinned. 'So do you.' He did, though his blue shirt was rather crumpled and Philippe would not have approved of wearing denim in the evening.

After this rather feeble conversational start, I managed to keep up some kind of inane chatter. He'd flown to Biarritz, then taken a taxi to Hendaye. Impatient, I thought. And very extravagant. I told him he should have come on the train and solemnly he said, 'Next time I will, Ms Tour Guide.'

When we arrived at the little port of Socoa, Joe made suitably admiring remarks about the scenery, the yacht harbour and my choice of restaurant. I'd booked us a table outdoors under the blue awning, with a view of the water and the neat rows of beached sailing dinghies.

After I'd downed a large glass of wine, I began to feel more relaxed, but my guilty conscience was giving me a hard time. As soon as the waiter had wafted away, I took a deep breath. 'About Philippe,' I began, 'we're sort of semi-engaged.'

A calm smile. 'Sort of?'

'That's the only way I can describe it.'

'How official is it, this semi-engagement?' he asked.

'Oh, we haven't announced it. No one knows. But there's a ring, kind of. Though he didn't buy it.' All this sounded pretty tenuous, I admit, but I was doing my best.

'So who did?'

I twiddled my beads. 'His aunt. She gave me this family ring, and, well, Philippe said it could be an engagement ring eventually.'

'So let's have a look at this famous jewel.'

'Left it in Paris. Too valuable to bring on holiday.'

There was a pause. 'What about *our* relationship?' he asked with a mischievous smile.

'We aren't even having a relationship.'

'Oh, yes we are.' His eyes twinkled as if basically he found me a bit of a joke, albeit an attractive one.

At that point an elderly waitress plonked down our first course with a cursory '*Bon appétit.*'

Joe began to tackle the oysters, but my appetite had deserted me. I would have liked another glass of wine or three, but then remembered I was driving.

I glanced around. The tables were rather too near together for discretion, except that as we were eating relatively early by French standards, the places around us hadn't yet been filled, which was fortunate. I'm ashamed to admit that I love listening to other people's conversation, but tonight I didn't want to be eavesdropped upon.

As if to put me at my ease, Joe began to talk. Lovely funny, flirty talk, the kind of conversation that could go on and on for ever. I'd already done my autobiography bit when we had dinner in Normandy, but he wanted to hear it all over again. As before, he listened with great attention as I told him about my job and how I was doing a bit more journalism now and managing to sell the odd article, but I still missed the tour-guiding. He said something about having ideas about that, which I didn't follow up. I wasn't really in the mood to talk about work. Instead I asked to hear his life story again and he filled in more of the back-ground and coloured in the details.

One detail that surprised me was that his divorce papers were coming through any day now, he said.

I digested this. 'But I thought you hadn't taken the final step.'

He'd managed to hurry things along last time he'd been home. After all, he'd been separated for years, so it was sensible to make it legal.

'Right,' I said cautiously, thinking of Philippe's long, drawn-out saga. 'So how do you feel about it, the divorce?'

'Just fine. Much better. Should have got it out of my hair before.'

I pushed my fish around the plate. 'Would you like to talk about it? Your wife and things, I mean.'

He spoke slowly. 'Maybe, one day. But it's hard to describe a long marriage, and maybe I don't want to get into negative stuff this evening.'

There was a pause.

'Was it all negative?' I asked.

'No, no, there were good times too. That's what I mean: it'd take for ever to explain it all in a balanced manner, even if I could. I'd rather kind of draw a line under it.' He smiled. 'Well, maybe I'll bore you with the whole caboodle eventually, but right now, at this early stage, I don't want to dig too deep. I need to give you the impression I'm a really great guy.'

Hm. I wonder if he was unfaithful.

As if reading my thoughts, he said, 'Janice and I, well, no one else was involved, but I guess we broke up because we didn't have too much in common once our daughters grew up.'

'So who instigated it?'

Luckily he didn't seem to mind the question. 'She did. I was never home, she said. But when I was home, I got in the way. Or I was too macho, tried to take over too much. Or I made everything a mess.'

'Sounds a bit unreasonable.'

'Yeah, well, maybe I am kind of untidy by her standards. She likes everything to be perfect, always plumping the cushions – you know the type?'

I smiled ruefully. 'I certainly do.'

'I was relieved Janice made the first move because I'd been on the point of doing so myself, but I didn't want to hurt her. We'd been kind of leading independent lives for some time, and since the girls were settled, I'd been thinking they could probably cope with the idea of their mom and I going our separate ways. I'd only hung on in there so long because of them.' He drank some wine. 'Well, there may have been other reasons, like reluctance to admit failure, that kind of stuff. I guess I don't like failing.'

'Who does? It's sad, all the same.'

'Yep, but divorce happens. Maybe we don't try hard enough in North America.'

'Happens everywhere. As I should know.' Then thinking that sounded too light-hearted, I asked, 'So how did they take it, your daughters?'

'Well, they're both married. Sure, in an ideal world they'd like their parents to be together, but they know Janice and I had problems and they understand. I was with the girls in London recently and they're cool about it. Or so they say.'

'Good,' I said, still attempting to sound neutral. He hadn't said anything derogatory about her, but I'd taken quite a dislike to soon-to-be ex-wife Janice.

'My elder daughter asked me if I had a girlfriend.'

'So what did you say?'

'I told her maybe. If I get lucky.'

He was looking at me with great approval, as if I were the

most marvellous, most amusing and intelligent and beautiful woman he had ever seen. It was very flattering, especially after Philippe's more or less permanent negative critical scrutiny. Although by this stage I had rather forgotten about Philippe.

'You're not eating,' he said. 'Shall I have them bring something else?'

I said I wasn't really hungry, so he called for the bill with that calm, authoritative air he has. Normally bill-bringing takes hours in France because new diners' stomachs take priority, but this evening it appeared quickly, as if the head waiter had recognized Joe's authority too.

Hand in hand, we walked along the harbour looking at the boats. Then we turned towards the sea. We'd missed the sunset, but the night was warm and, away from the restaurants, increasingly quiet apart from the waves slapping gently at the wall below us. The winds had dropped and the salty darkness, illuminated by occasional lamps along the quay, was soft and romantic.

I stumbled on a cobblestone. Without speaking, he put his arm round me and we wandered out along the path beside the breakwater towards the lighthouse. I couldn't speak either as I was holding my breath.

As soon as we were alone, he drew me to him and kissed me, so sweetly, so tenderly and then so passionately that I swayed on my feet, clinging to him.

A few hazy minutes later he said, 'Let's go.' Still with his arm round my waist, he led me to my car.

On the way back to Hendaye, neither of us spoke. Now and then his fingers touched my right hand as I drove, and every time they did so I was electrified, as if it were a great intimacy.

'Look,' I forced myself to say eventually, 'I can't have an affair. Not now. I've made such an awful mess of my life. I can't chuck away everything I've built up in France. I've got to stick with what I've got. You see, there's Philippe. He'll be here soon. Now that we're more or less engaged, it's too late. My job, my life is here. There's Alex to think of. I'm not free, really. I'm sorry if I led you to . . .'

'That's OK. No pressure. We'll just see each other whenever we can and see how it goes.'

'But, you see, I'm a waste of your time.'

'I don't think so, Clio. I don't think so.'

When we reached the esplanade, he said he'd walk the rest of the way alone. He didn't demand that I join him in his hotel room; he didn't demand anything except another long, exploratory kiss.

'See you on the beach tomorrow, my love,' he said after a while.

'Yes,' I murmured shakily, and drove slowly home.

Ten

Next morning I was up early, and as soon as Alex had trotted off to sailing school, I rushed to the shops to buy some food for his lunch and do various other practical things that had completely gone out of my head yesterday. Later I would go down to the beach and spend a lovely hour or two with Joe. No harm in just chatting to him.

On my return I was irritated to see a navy Renault with Paris number plates parked in the space allocated to our flat. Typical lawless French, I thought. I was just backing temporarily into the area by the wheelie bins when I realized whose car it was. Yikes, Marie-Clementine, dear Philippe's dear sister. She'd said something ages ago about swapping Hendaye weeks with one of the cousins since Philippe and I had selfishly bagged the end of July to the beginning of August, but I hadn't been listening, mainly because I never intervene in these complicated timeshare disputes, which go round and round in circles for months.

Sure enough, a few moments later she came bounding down the steps.

'Clio, *comme je suis heureuse de te voir*, – 'Ow 'appy I am to see you.' She kissed me three times and hugged me as if we were the greatest friends in the world. Marie-Clementine is all thin, sharp edges, which doesn't make for a cosy hug.

She warbled on about how she'd managed to drive down before the weekend rush, staying the night en route with Aunt somebody or other near Bordeaux, and the roads were miraculously empty on the route she took, and wasn't it wonderful that cousin Natalie's flat downstairs was free. Of course, being on the ground floor, it didn't have such a nice view, wasn't as cool and airy as ours, or as well equipped, or as well modernized, but it did have the garden, etc, etc. We must have lunch together, dinner, go swimming, go sailing. It would all be such fun, and the boys were longing to see Alex. How was dear little Alex?

I told her about the sailing course and she said she must go

round to the *club nautique* at once to book the boys in for next
week and would I take them down to the beach for her while
she did that and while she unpacked because – she lowered her
voice – cousin Natalie was not the most wonderful housekeeper
in the world and therefore a thorough cleaning would have to
be done before Marie-Clementine could think of installing herself
and her family in the flat, which, she mentioned again, was not
by any means as well modernized as the one that belongs to our
family. *Our family.* So she, too, is at last beginning to see me as
part of it. I think.

Naturally I agreed to take the boys.

'And I invite you and Alex out to dinner tonight,' she said,
squeezing my arm.

I couldn't think of any excuse not to accept this kind offer.

I was late getting down to the beach in the end as I had to wait
until Marie-Clementine had unpacked the boys' swimming gear
and found the sun cream, the buckets and spades, and their surf-
boards. Then she had to give them lengthy instructions not to
go out of my sight and to do everything I said the moment I
said it.

Lucas and Max are nice little boys of eight and ten, and they
both swim like fishes, so I didn't anticipate any difficulties.
Nevertheless, I knew I would have to keep an eye on them in
the surf and it was the very last thing I wanted to do. I wanted
to keep an eye on Joe.

Standing on the top of the steps looking over the beach, I
couldn't see him anywhere. Lucas and Max were dying to swim,
so we just dumped our beach bags in the nearest empty space
between the sunbathing bodies. Clutching their little boards,
the boys ran to the sea, with me puffing after them. Fortunately
the rollers were just large enough for gentle surf runs, but not
so large as to be any kind of danger.

Apart from a few experts down the other end of the beach,
surfing here is fairly amateur. The standing-up, pro surf bums
mostly operate further north at places like Biarritz. Here in
Hendaye it's family stuff with brightly coloured polystyrene mini
body-boards, much smaller and lighter than a surfboard. The technique is you stand waist deep, waiting for a wave. If the right

one comes, you fling yourself stomach down on to the board, and if you have timed it right, you're pleased if you get a run of 10 or 20 yards. It's not serious Hawaii stuff.

All the same and despite the lifeguards, I stood in the shallows watching the boys, just in case there was some mysterious undertow or sinister paedophile around.

'Is this something else you haven't told me?' said a voice in my ear.

I jumped. 'Oh, hi, Joe,' I gushed. Watch it, I told myself.

'No, they're not mine.' I explained the origins of Lucas and Max.

A glamorous French girl in a minimalist black bikini gave him the eye as she passed us on her way to swim, but to my gratification he appeared not to see her.

'I got kind of impatient waiting for you,' he said with a devastating smile. He was looking at me as if he wanted to eat me up and it was most unsettling.

'I know. Sorry. I wanted to come sooner.' I told him about Marie-Clementine's non-stop conversation.

He smiled at my description of her. 'So where are we going tonight?' he asked when I drew breath.

He took it pretty well when I told him about my date with Marie-C, but it was clear he was disappointed, flatteringly so. 'I couldn't leave Alex alone again, anyway,' I said.

'Tomorrow, then? Have lunch with me.'

'I don't know if I can.'

'You can. In fact, you must. I have a business proposition to put to you.'

'Seriously?'

'Absolutely,' he said with a twinkle. 'I am a very serious man.'

And a damn persistent one, I thought.

At that point I had one of those panics that all nervous mothers or minders have at some stage. I just couldn't see Max and Lucas. Talking to Joe, I had taken my eye off them for a moment and I couldn't pick them out in the crowded sea, which at that time of day was crammed with wet-haired children bobbing about.

Alarmed, I began to rush along the edge of the water.

'What do they look like?' yelled Joe, running beside me.

'Dark, plump and very pale-skinned,' I replied frantically.

We must have searched for more than five minutes – although it felt like an hour – when I heard a distant shout of 'Clio, Clio, coo-coo!'

I spun round and there was Marie-Clementine dashing across the sand towards us like a marathon runner.

Oh my God, I had lost her children.

'Clio, my dear, those naughty boys, they come 'ome without you, no?'

My panic increased. 'No, I can't find them. They must be all right, but . . .'

'No, no, they come back to the apartment. The strap of the surfboard of Max is broken and he wanted to change it for another one. I told them they were very naughty not to tell you.'

I smiled in enormous relief, but Marie-Clementine wasn't looking at me. She was gazing speculatively at Joe.

'*Bonjour*, madame,' he said in his peculiar-sounding but fluent Canadian version of French. 'I am Joe Dryden, a client and business colleague of Clio's.'

Marie-Clementine looked him up and down with a suspicious but approving eye. 'So you too are a journalist? Or tour guide? Or . . . ?'

'I am an entrepreneur,' he said smoothly. 'And I think Clio should set up her own business, but it is all under discussion at the moment.'

I tried not to look too stunned at this load of old flannel.

'You Americans, always business, business. In France we leave business behind on 'oliday,' boomed Marie-Clementine.

'I'm Canadian,' he said with a patient smile.

Marie-Clementine was unabashed. 'All you Anglo-Saxons, the same thing.'

I looked at my watch and said quickly, 'I must go. Alex will be back soon.'

'Don't forget our lunch tomorrow,' said Joe brazenly.

'Right.' I fled, leaving the two of them staring after me.

I don't know if Marie-Clementine had anything to do with it, but that evening Philippe rang up and announced that, instead of arriving on Sunday, he had decided to take Friday (tomorrow) off to avoid the weekend traffic. He would get up early and do the eight- or nine-hour trip in one day, so he could be with me in the evening.

'What a nice surprise,' I said insincerely, feeling like a two-faced bitch, which indeed I was.

So I only had one more day with Joe. He had come all this way to see me and I had nothing to offer him, not even time. In true womanly fashion, I was suffering a mega dose of guilt. I was being semi-unfaithful to Philippe in coveting another bloke, I was wasting Joe's time because it wasn't going to go anywhere, and I felt bad for taking my attention off Alexander.

But the mischievous gods were having fun with me. They decided to play on Joe's side for a while.

Alex screwed up his face. 'Mu-um?' It was clear that he wanted to ask me a big favour. 'You know cousin Carole?'

'Uh-huh.'

'Well, there's this boy Jean Leclerc in my sailing class whose parents are related to Carole and his dad has a really big, mega-safe yacht and they want me to go on a sailing picnic tomorrow straight after the class and I was like, "Wicked, but I'll have to ask Mum," and he was like, "My *papa* is a champion sailor so your *maman* won't mind, and anyway, my baby brothers are going because it's going to be dead calm." And I was like, "Give me your dad's phone number so Mum can ring him up." If they're related to Carole, they must be related to Philippe, mustn't they? So that's OK?' Alex has already learnt the importance of family ties in France.

'Probably,' I said. 'Seems like everyone's related to Philippe, if you ask me.'

Sensible, middle-aged Monsieur and Madame Leclerc were very proper and respectable. They called round to see me, took me to the harbour to inspect their fine boat, told me the weather forecast was for light winds and promised to have Alex back by four.

So naturally I said, yes, of course. How kind of them. I was delighted that Alex had met such a charming family.

Indeed I was.

That gave me the whole day to explain to Joe, calmly and sensibly, that it was all over. Not that we were having a 'relationship', so therefore there wasn't anything to finish. I would just say that at my age and stage in life, and with my dubious history, I didn't want to play any silly games.

The walk I chose for us in the Basque hills was not the greatest, scenery-wise: a steep, hot cart track that didn't seem to lead anywhere. We were surrounded by squadrons of unpleasant flies, and there was nothing much to look at apart from high hedges and empty fields. I could look at Joe, of course. Always a treat, though he was wearing the baggiest shorts on record since World War Two and a battered pair of trainers. Joe's casual attitude towards clothes was part of his charm as far as I was concerned. Such a change from Philippe, whose wardrobe is so immaculate it depresses me.

Of course, I confess I had put some thought into my own gear that day. I was chic in a sporty off-white ensemble – I wanted to look good on our last date together, so Joe would remember me kindly and all that.

I'd taken him up to the hills to avoid the crowded beach and, of course, Marie-Clementine. Not that there was anything to hide, I told myself.

I was conscious every step of the way that I must broach the subject of Philippe's arrival and hence goodbye Joe. Finally I managed to stumble out something along those lines.

'Don't worry,' he said calmly, as if I'd announced a lost hankie. Sometimes Joe's laid-back attitude irritates the hell out of me.

A long, shimmering silence.

Then he touched my arm. 'How about a swim in the hotel pool? When it's a fine day, no one uses it at lunchtime.'

I thought I'd get some more dramatic reaction to my announcement about the end of our non-affair than this. We'd wasted half of our last day driving up to the hills and now he wanted to get back to the town. Without so much as a kiss.

I have to admit, though, that the vast indoor thalassotherapy pool was gorgeous, with numerous contra-currents, 'body-sculpting' underwater jets and little jacuzzi whirlpools. As he predicted, it was virtually empty, the only other swimmers being two large French ladies doing a solemn breaststroke.

'We need to talk,' he said.

I caught my breath, various possibilities flashing through my head. He was either going to say, 'I'm bored shitless with all this prissy prick-teasing. I agree it's all over. Let's forget it, huh?' or, 'Let's run away to sunny Spain together and live happily ever after in a lemon grove.'

No, that was too unlikely. Maybe it would be, 'Let's go upstairs to my room for a first and last round of red-hot sex. Then we'll call it quits.'

Instead he said seriously, 'If you like the work, you should start up your own tour-guide business.'

Taken aback, I spluttered, 'But I'm not good at money and tax and things. I like to be employed. It's more peaceful. I'm not into stress.'

'You need to be more positive and can-do, Clio,' he said, sounding like a self-help guru. He was right of course. I'm very lazy and feeble about accounting and stuff that doesn't interest me.

So I asked him where I was supposed to get my clients from without spending a fortune that I didn't have on advertising, and he said he knew any number of Canadians who would use my services and surely I knew some tame French accountant who could help me with the figures. I admitted I did. Philippe would probably help me set up the business, he thought. Again, I admitted he probably would.

Joe said he reckoned I could handle simple finances if I put my mind to it since I wasn't stupid.

'Thanks,' I said, splashing the water with my toes and floating on the chair of foaming bubbles. I was secretly admiring his muscular arms. Seemed more interesting than business.

'So will you think about it?'

'What?'

'Setting up your own business, angel face.'

Angel face? Shrugging my shoulders, I promised to do so and then he asked if he could be my first client. I could take him on a tour of anywhere I chose at the end of September, a private tour.

I grinned and said that I didn't trust myself or him on a private tour.

'Why not?' His attempt to look hurt and surprised was comical.

I took a deep breath. 'You may expect more than I can deliver.'

'I won't.'

'Are your fingers crossed?'

'Maybe.'

After a good-natured, flirty argument on the subject, I found myself agreeing that towards the end of September I'd take him on some trips around Paris, strictly daytime tours only.

'I told Marie-Clementine we were going to talk business and that's our meeting finished,' he said, gazing at me bright-eyed. 'Now we should celebrate our new partnership.'

I looked around the pool. We were completely alone. Even the fat ladies had put on their white towelling bathrobes and disappeared. 'What partnership?'

'Business-wise. Forrester's Tours of Fantastic France dot com or whatever.'

'Of course.'

'I'm serious, Clio. I'm going to find you some clients.'

'OK.' I smiled, not really believing him. 'So what's in it for you? What's going to be your share of this great new business venture?'

'Nothing. I'm doing it for love,' he said.

I raised my eyebrows and splashed around a bit. 'No strings?'

'No strings.' But then he said enticingly, 'There's some champagne in my room. It's nice and cool up there in the air-conditioning.' He put his arm round my shoulders and drew me towards him in the water.

Smiling, I shook my head. 'Joe, I can't.'

He held me closer. 'Just a small, quick glass?'

With difficulty I repeated, 'No, sorry.'

'A kiss, then.'

A long, erotic kiss it was, half lying, half floating together on the edge of the pool.

'The attendant, the hotel staff, they'll arrest us . . .' I spluttered, laughing.

'They're still at lunch. Anyway, this is France,' he said.

We drew apart and then kissed again.

'Come up with me,' he said.

'No,' I began, but he put his finger on my lips. Before he changed my mind for me, I tore myself away and swam towards the steps. Pulling myself out of the water, I said, 'The champagne'll keep, won't it?' I bent down to pick up my towel.

'Yes,' he said, standing in the pool and looking up at me. 'We'll drink it another time. Clio, I have to tell you something.'

'What?'

'You have a pretty nice ass.'

'Goodbye, Joe,' I said firmly, trying not to laugh.

He smiled. 'Call you in September.'

When Philippe finally arrived after midnight that night, I pretended to be asleep, but long after he'd flopped into bed beside me and begun to snore heavily, I lay awake thinking of Joe. His persistence, his determined and romantic wooing was going to my head, or more likely my loins, but I was too old for falling in lust and it was too late to risk what I had. I care for Philippe, of course I do. And he must care for me because he had talked about marriage . . . Not that marriage is essential in life, but as Ma said, I'm not much of a catch and I'm not getting any younger.

All the next day I thought about Joe, even during Marie-Clementine's hearty lunchtime barbecue. Alex looked so happy in the middle of this extended family group, and Philippe was on excellent form, laughing with all his relations. I watched Alex as he boasted about his intrepid sailing trip with the Leclercs. Philippe was listening patiently, an amused expression on his hand-some face.

''Ow lovely to 'ave the family all together', as Marie-Clementine so rightly said.

No decent, mature and sensible woman would or should want to break up this secure world. The incident on the beach where I'd temporarily lost Max and Lucas made me see the dangers of inattention. I should focus on what is important.

After Alex had gone to bed that night, Philippe was carefully casual. 'Marie-Clementine said you met a friend, an American businessman. What a coincidence that he should be here.'

Good old Marie-Clementine, I thought. I was clearing the dirty dinner plates that tonight both my son and my betrothed had managed to ignore. 'Oh, you mean Joe. He's Canadian.' On this occasion I was glad of the fact that Philippe isn't a great one for helping with the chores, so he couldn't see my face as I began to stack the dishwasher.

Subterfuge and economies with the truth are not generally my scene, but in this case a frank confession would serve no purpose. No point in causing a drama and having a fight over nothing. My more or less harmless non-fling with Joe was over. I had made up my mind. Definitely.

Philippe continued, 'You don't see too many Yanks or Canadians in Hendaye. Is he French- or Anglo-Canadian?'

'Anglo- or Irish- or something, but Joe's very keen on France.'

'Really?'

'Yes.' I warmed to my theme. 'I haven't made any decisions about it, but he wants me to set up my own tour-guide business. He reckons there are plenty of Canadians who need to come to France to see the battlefields before people have forgotten the world wars. Oh, and he wants to promote the French culture to English-speaking Canadians. Seems to think it will help Canadians understand each other, as well as Europeans.' I wasn't actually making this up – Joe had said something along these lines.

'Very admirable,' said Philippe dryly. 'And is he also to have a financial interest in this great business venture of yours?'

'Amazingly, no. He just wants to promote France, like I said.'

'I wonder why. It sounds too good to be true.'

I clattered the plates loudly and turned on the tap to rinse the vegetable dish. 'Yes, I wondered that myself. Maybe he is hoping to do some networking in France or be president of some Canada-France society or get a medal from the Queen or the *Légion d'honneur* or something.'

'So he doesn't want a percentage?'

'Doesn't seem to.'

'Or maybe he wants a share of something else.'

'Such as?'

'Maybe he wants a share of you.'

'You're joking!' I said gaily. 'He's far too serious and obsessed with business. Not my type.' I poured the dishwasher powder into the machine, spilling it all over the place. Perfectly true, he isn't my type; I just fancy him like crazy.

Philippe said smugly, 'Yes, Canadians can be a little dull and bland, even more so than you English.'

'We can't all be as super-intelligent, deeply cultured and good-looking as the French. Or as phenomenally stylish.'

He smiled. 'True.' Philippe does have enough sense of humour to recognize irony when it hits him in the face. 'I suppose he wears lumberjack shirts, this Canadian?'

'All the time.'

'Ah, the strange Anglo-Saxon dress sense – they must have inherited it.'

'Enough insults,' I said.

Even if he didn't actually dress like a lumberjack, I have to admit that Joe's wardrobe was a bit hit and miss. His clothes often look rumpled, sometimes rather old and baggy like today, almost verging on the anorak. But then wasn't it Herrick the poet who wrote about sweet disorder? He's always been a comfort to me, that Herrick chap.

I didn't mention these random thoughts to Philippe. 'Would you like some coffee or a *tisane*?' I asked sweetly.

He allowed me to make him some mint tea. Coffee is *out* at the moment, apparently. Philippe is always changing his mind about what one should eat or drink in order to be healthy.

I settled down beside him and waved my nice brown arm under his nose. 'What do you think of my suntan?'

'Not bad. Improves your look, but you still need to lose some weight. In a bikini, one notices the *rondeurs* in the wrong places.'

'Rude bastard!' I said in a friendly manner. Not a very good subject for discussion, I thought, but better than Joe. 'I saw this new diet in *Top Santé*,' I went on. '*Le ventre plat* in four weeks. Maybe I should try it.'

All French health magazines promise a flat stomach if you follow their latest regime, and every week I buy one or other of these mags at our local news-stand, but my tum remains just as round. Funny thing, that.

He picked up his teacup and took a sip. 'You know my colleague Sandrine? Well, she's much older than you, but she has lost seven kilos at Weight Watchers. Said it was easy too. You should see her. She looks infinitely better, far more chic and elegant. It is difficult for a woman to look good if she is overweight.'

'Seven kilos, that's brilliant.' With some tough mental arithmetic, I worked out that this was more than fourteen pounds, a whole stone.

'You should try it, the Weight Watchers,' he said. 'Shall I get Sandrine to telephone you?'

I leapt up. 'Look, bossy boots, I'll go on a diet as and when I want to, and I don't need you and bloody Sandrine to tell me what to do.' I have to confess that I wasn't as indignant as I sounded. He criticizes me so often that I don't really notice it, water off a duck's back and all that. All the same, I stormed off to bed.

He joined me rather too shortly after, and when I felt his hand creeping over in my direction, I professed to have another headache. With any luck I'd have *les règles* soon, the best female excuse for avoiding sex, but I couldn't put the poor bloke off indefinitely, of course. We were meant to be engaged, after all.

He didn't persist tonight. Maybe he was feeling the heat. Or maybe he was brooding about our conversation.

Before we went to sleep, he murmured, 'So are you serious about this business venture, setting up on your own?'

'Shouldn't think so,' I said drowsily.

'I agree. In my opinion, it would be too much responsibility for you.'

'Mm.'

'Not your thing at all. I can't really see you running a business. It's not as if you have great organizational powers.'

'Mm.' I pretended I was nearly asleep, but this time I felt genuinely indignant.

Eleven

Back in Paris after the holidays, I had an email:

> Hey, Clio,
>   I have some prospective clients lined up for a tour of
> Normandy in the fall, say October or November. Can you
> take them, or shall I contact Insider Tours? If I do the latter,
> I will insist you be reinstated. Meanwhile see you for the
> tour we arranged end of September. What dates?
>   Sincerely,
>   Joe

Hardly passionate. I admit I was disappointed.
   I thought about my reply for about ten minutes, then I mailed
back:

> Hi, Joe,
>   I can take you on a tour of Paris any week after 15
> September. As for clients in October or November, I'll get
> back to you as soon as I can.
>   Bfn,
>   Clio

Bfn. I didn't know if he'd understand 'Bye for now'. On second
thoughts, I decided it was a pretty silly phrase, but unfortunately
I'd already clicked 'send' so couldn't change it. This is always
happening to me. The trouble is, once you make a decision in
life, it's so hard to alter it. That's why I hate to make up my
mind. One thing about blokes I really like is their ability to
make a decision, even if it isn't the right one. For instance,
Philippe is very strong on what he wants to eat at dinner, what
wine he wants, what clothes and furniture he should buy, what
dress I should wear. He takes on the decision-making role in
our relationship, style-wise at any rate, and that leaves me free

to concentrate on creativity, motherhood and domesticity, or, some might say, on being a doormat in New Woman's clothing.

So I sat and stared at my computer screen and then I made a list of pros and cons.

Pro setting up a tour-guide company: I'd be a businesswoman and hopefully make money doing work I enjoyed. I'd achieve self-esteem and girl power and all that. Woman power, rather.

Half pro, half con: I'd be dependent on some kind of business relationship with Joe, to start with.

Con: I have financial responsibilities and accounting worries.

I looked at the list and the pros seemed to be longer than the cons, but then on the other hand, a business relationship with Joe might lead to the brink of a non-business relationship that would not necessarily be in my own, or Alex's or Philippe's, best interests.

I chewed my biro. I checked my emails. I paced around the flat. Was I the business type? Not really, let's face it. But Philippe had been so dismissive about my prospects that 'I'll show him' was a factor. I wasn't taking over the chairmanship of Shell, was I? I'd be the smallest company you could imagine. In fact, what was the difference in being a freelance journalist and running a one-man band? Not much.

A feisty, modern professional woman sitting as a fly on the wall would be unimpressed by this wimpish dithering and lack of go-getting attitude, but, in my own defence, I'd say that I wasn't brought up to be confident, nor had my dud marriages done much to bolster my self-esteem. The facade of self-assurance I'd acquired in recent years had been painfully won.

The next couple of days were occupied with getting Alex back to school, but then who should telephone but Elaine.

'Clio, you don't have a new job lined up for the fall, do you?' she asked without preamble.

'Not as such, but . . .'

'Then you're in luck.' Elaine was her usual Piggy patronizing self.

'I am?'

'Yep. You remember Mrs Hooper?'

'Kay? Lovely wife of not altogether lovely Melvin? Yes, of course I do.'

'Well, she seems to have persuaded Mr Hooper that you weren't so bad after all, and since I have a whole lot of new clients now, I'd like to have you join us again.'

'Oh?' I kept my voice neutral.

'But of course you'll have to sign an agreement that you'll abide by the guidelines and be courteous.'

'Actually, I was always extremely polite to the punters, sometimes under great provocation.'

'There you go again, always arguing. Can't you just apologize graciously?'

'Excuse me, Elaine, but I'm a bit lost here. What am I supposed to be apologizing about?'

'Never mind, never mind. You just don't get it, do you?'

'Don't get what?'

'That I am calling to do you a favour.'

'Mm. So these new clients you're talking about, they aren't Canadian, are they?'

'No, why?'

'Just wondered.' What I'd been wondering was had Joe become fed up with waiting to hear from me and sent his tourist friends to her.

'Clio, just get your butt over here and we'll talk about your fees and your expenses. Same fees as before, actually, but the new system with expenses will take me a while to explain. There have to be three copies of every receipt – it's all quite detailed. Mr Hooper is very thorough in that way. He likes to keep an eye on things. In fact, he'll be passing through Paris any day now and he wants to talk to you personally. He recognizes that you have fine knowledge of your subject, but he still feels you need to have a better attitude towards your clients regarding punctuality and politeness.'

Up yours, I thought. I took a deep breath. 'You know something, Elaine, I clean forgot to tell you, but I am setting up my own company. So, delightful though it would be to see you and Mr Hooper again, I shall have to forgo that pleasure.'

'What d'ya mean? What kind of company?' spluttered Elaine. Wish I could have seen her face.

'Oh, you know, same old thing, travel, guided tours. It should be great being my own boss. In fact, the advantages are becoming more and more obvious by the minute. Bye, Elaine. My kind regards to dear Mrs Hooper.'

Quickly, I put down the phone. Carried away by the excitement of the moment, I emailed Joe and told him I was available for the Canadian tourists anytime in October or November. I would boldly go it alone, I said.

This decision might be small stuff for a lady tycoon, but it seemed like a giant step for me.

Philippe was extremely dubious and managed to think up several scary possible snags, some of which had occurred to me and some that had not.

'What about the safety aspect? What if they are rapists or psychopaths, these clients?'

I said I was sure Joe wouldn't send me any nutters. I was expecting most clients to be married couples.

'Ah, yes, this person Joe. What do we really know about him?'

'I told you, he's a staid, upright Canadian businessman, but I don't know who his great-grandmother was, if that's what you mean.'

Philippe waved his arms in a Gallic way. 'Suppose he sends you clients that don't pay?'

'He won't,' I said. 'So far they are friends of his, members of some kind of social club, I believe.'

'They may be con men or Mafioso looking for European prostitutes.'

'Don't be ridiculous. Mostly they're coming to look at war graves and battlefields.'

'What if they are dissatisfied with you?'

'They won't be,' I said crossly. 'Look, I know what I'm doing, OK?'

At that point the alarm on Philippe's watch buzzed. He likes to time the tumble-dryer so he can take his shirts out at the correct moment. Fortunately he doesn't trust me to iron them properly and so this is one domestic chore he always undertakes.

'I'm still suspicious of the motives of your Canadian,' he called over his shoulder as he hurried off to the kitchen.

'Don't judge others by your own standards,' I said airily.

* * *

Joe was efficient. He mailed back to say that he had already lined up six or seven couples who wanted tours of around five days each, and another pair who wanted two sets of three days. This would take me practically to Christmas. The various couples then contacted me direct and I had no great difficulty in organizing the dates and tours. They all sounded friendly, charming and easy-going.

I had a brief but lovely phone call from Joe, who announced he was arriving in Paris next week, so we could finalize the tour arrangements together. I said I was looking forward to these business consultations. You bet I was.

My mother made one of her rare phone calls. 'Is that you, Clio?' She always asks that, as if she doesn't recognize my voice.

She then went on at breakneck speed – so as not to waste call charges – to say that she'd had a piece of luck, though her friend Daphne hadn't . . . The National Health was a disgrace, wasn't it? Even the French have better hospitals, she'd heard. Daphne had been collecting vouchers for a Eurostar ticket to Paris that she couldn't use because she'd had a fall and broken her hip, her leg, big toe, whatever.

The upshot was that my mother had been given the vouchers and bought a last-minute ticket at half-price.

'Oh, that's nice,' I said with sinking heart. 'So when will you be coming?'

'Wednesday at four o'clock. Can you collect me at the station? I hope it's convenient,' she added as an afterthought.

'Fine,' I said. 'You mean the day after tomorrow?'

'Yes, dear.'

The day after tomorrow. Dammit, I was supposed to meet Joe on Thursday and take him around the Musée d'Orsay. Plus Philippe was not going to be too delighted that his least favourite female was about to arrive.

'Philippe, you know about give and take in a relationship, that sort of thing?' I began towards the end of dinner. I had tactfully cooked an especially delicious meal of scallops with a cheese and wine sauce, all served up in a pretty pale green painted dish. Strawberries and crème fraiche, also presented with unwonted elegance, were next on the menu. 'Live and let live,' I added.

'*Quoi?*' Philippe raised his expressive black eyebrows.

'I've decided to offer you a deal.' I took a large gulp of wine. 'I will absolutely promise to go to Weight Watchers for at least three months . . .'

'Excellent, so long as you take it seriously,' he said warmly.

'And in return?' Sometimes he can be quite quick on the uptake.

'In return, you don't make a scene when I tell you about our new house guest. You treat her as politely as you can, and you prevent me from wringing her neck by being especially nice to me. You also get in some extra bottles, or rather crates of wine to calm my nerves.'

'Hardly good for the diet regime. But may one know the name of this guest, although one has one's suspicions?'

I grinned. 'Do you agree to the bargain?'

'It all depends on the guest and how many kilos you promise to lose.'

'Three,' I said, reckoning that was about half a stone.

'If, as I suspect, the guest is your mother, then it will have to be six.'

'Five kilos, and yes, it is Mother and you have to be as nice as pie to the old bag.'

'*Mon Dieu!* Five kilos, then, but making another condition – that I don't have to sit down to dinner with her every single night. How long is she staying?'

'Oh, about a week, I expect.' Come to think of it, Mother hadn't said.

Fearing I would renege on the deal, Philippe drove me to Weight Watchers that very night. He isn't the best driver in the world – he tailgates, he cuts in, he shouts at other drivers, he races up to a crossroads or traffic lights, then slams on the brakes at the last minute. He was doing a great deal of brake-slamming that night, but for once I held my peace on the subject. My mother's impending arrival meant Be Nice to Philippe Week.

I'd chosen English-speaking Weight Watchers because I couldn't face the idea of queuing with a whole lot of skinny young French girls wanting to slim down from a size 8 to a size 6. Because of the one-way system, Philippe dropped me at the end of the street, and as I walked along following behind a pair of Brits with plump Marks & Sparks-clad bottoms, I smiled to myself. I was clearly in the right place and, mirror, mirror on the wall, who was the fattest of them all? Not me. Hurray!

Ashamed of myself, I caught up with the M&S girls, who were young and pretty, and also living with Frenchmen, it transpired. We had a giggle together as we stood in the queue in the strange underground church hall. Apparently one French husband weighed his wife every morning and then drew up a diet sheet for her before he went to the office. Another had bought his girlfriend slimming pills that had kept her awake all night. At least Philippe is not that obsessive.

Our leader in the battle of the bulge was an American called Pixie. Speaking in a charming Southern accent, she looked like a Barbie Doll but, that apart, I couldn't help liking her. 'How much did y'all wanna lose?' she enquired of me, pencil poised to add up the kilos.

After being weighed on electronic scales – yikes, can they have been accurate? – she had us sit in a circle and introduce ourselves. 'My name is Clio and I am a foodaholic,' I felt I should say. Most women announced they were there to raise their self-esteem. Blimey, I thought. How the feminists would disapprove. I just want to appease my boyfriend and get into a few more of my clothes. That's what I told myself, anyway.

When I got home, Philippe demanded to know my weight, poured over the diet booklets and promised he would be with me every step of the way. Hell's teeth, I thought. The whole thing seemed such a hassle that I had to have an extra whisky to drown my sorrows. Philippe looked up whisky on the Weight Watchers chart and said that since I'd had a generous double, I'd have to count it as two points out of my daily twenty.

'Never mind,' he added when I growled at him. 'You will be nice and slim for my mother's party next month.'

'Oh, yes,' I said unenthusiastically. Camille was planning a huge bash to celebrate Edouard's seventieth birthday and their forty-fifth wedding anniversary. She'd been talking about it for months. How could I forget?

'It might be an opportunity to announce our engagement.'

I nearly dropped my whisky glass. 'I don't think we should be too hasty. It might spoil Camille's big day, you know, if we . . .'

He frowned. 'Are you being sarcastic, Clio?'

'No, no, but she needs to get used to the idea of your divorce first, once you have fixed it. She really won't want any extra worries,' I said quickly.

'Ah, yes,' he said.

'Anyway, I think we should get Mum's visit over with first.'

'Will you tell her?'

'Tell her what?'

'About our engagement.'

'Oh, no. Not yet.'

He looked relieved, I thought.

By the time I found myself at the draughty, stale-smelling Gare du Nord waiting for my mother to arrive, I was starving from excessive consumption of lettuce and not in the best of tempers. The only thing that was keeping me going was the thought of seeing Joe. I'd phoned him to say that my mother would be around for a while and he'd taken it calmly, as usual. He said he was looking forward to meeting her and why didn't we tour the sites together, all three of us. Why not? I'd agreed rashly.

I stood by the barricade thinking, why doesn't he mind more? The fact that he was so laid-back about Ma seemed to show that he wasn't that interested in me personally. All that flirty stuff was just routine for him, as for many guys. It was just business after all. Which was just as well. Maybe I'd better ask him to lay his cards on the table. Why was he helping me?

The yellow-faced Eurostar hissed into the station and it seemed as if about three hundred passengers had passed me by before I finally saw my mother. There she was at last trotting down the platform: grey-haired, tidy and respectably dressed in a natty navy blue pleated skirt with matching blazer. She was dragging behind her one of the biggest wheelie suitcases I'd ever seen. Not a good sign.

I kissed her powdery cheek, noticing sadly that she looked older, though still a nice-looking woman in a faded sort of way, just as long as you ignored her disapproving expression. No, that was unfair, her face did brighten when she saw me, and equally,

I was glad to see her. It was just that I dreaded the next few days.

'Smart case,' I said, for want of a better opening gambit.

'Daphne's. She lent it to me. I told her I didn't need it because I've got some perfectly good suitcases of my own, but she said mine were too old and too heavy, not having wheels, and with these Paris platforms – far too long, aren't they? – I suppose she's right. I wouldn't have wanted to get a porter. I'm sure you pay through the nose for those French chappies. Doesn't anyone want to check my ticket? Aren't there any customs? I think your hair's too long, dear, and have you dyed it? You used to have such pretty curly hair when you were a little girl.'

In the car park she continued, 'Is this your car? My goodness. Fancy you having a car like this. I didn't have a car of my own at your age.'

'There's the Opera House,' I said, as we drove along Boulevard Haussmann.

'Very nice. What a lot of people there are in the streets. Far too crowded for my liking.'

'It's a capital city,' I said, turning towards the river. 'See how pretty the shop windows are.'

She snorted. 'Pretty prices too, no doubt.'

'Place de la Concorde,' I commented a little later, negotiating through the snarled-up traffic around the famous landmark.

She stared at the obelisk. 'Fancy naming a square after a botched aeroplane.'

I smiled although she hadn't been joking. 'Look, there's the river.'

Even she couldn't find anything derogatory to say about the Seine and its graceful cream stone bridges, though Pont Alexandre had rather gaudy decorations and that gold dome over there was a bit vulgar, she thought.

'Les Invalides – that's where Napoleon's tomb is. Shall we go and see it?'

'Certainly not,' she said.

She was more interested in the underpass where poor Princess Diana met her untimely end. She might go there and lay a wreath. Oh dear.

Turning away from the river, I pointed out the charming

stately apartment blocks of the sixteenth arrondissement. 'See how harmonious they are, all the same colour, all the same height.'

'That one's not harmonious, that modern one behind the trees. It may be the same height, but otherwise it's not the same as the others at all, quite unsightly really.'

Absolutely typical. Unerringly, she's picked out the only ugly block of flats in the whole street.

I've suddenly realized who she reminds me of: Camille, of course. Philippe's ma and mine may come from completely different cultures, but they are sisters under the skin. I pray they never meet.

'I forgot to ask you, Ma, how long are you staying?'

'Two weeks, dear. The tickets are for two weeks. I don't really want to stay that long, but I'm afraid I can't change them.'

Mother was in full flow again during dinner. Philippe looked bored out of his mind, my nerves were on edge, and it was only day one of the grand visit.

'Rosalind and Michael went to the Garden Party again,' she said smugly. 'Your sister is a very lucky girl, isn't she, Clio?'

'Why a gardening party?' asked Philippe.

Ma didn't realize she was being teased. 'The Queen's *Garden Party*. It's the kind of thing we do very well in England, with our royalty. You probably don't have social occasions like that here, what with having chopped your king's head off whenever it was. Rosalind and Michael are asked every summer. It's a bit crowded of course, but they love it. Rosalind says the Queen has some very nice penstemons in the herbaceous borders at Buckingham Palace.'

'Isn't that nice,' I murmured before Philippe said something less polite.

'What are penstemons?' he asked.

'Flowers.'

There was a silence. 'Does Roz wear the same hat each time?' I ventured. An inane question, but I was desperate to fill the gap.

'No, no, dear. Michael buys her a new one every year. He's a very generous man and a wonderful husband.'

This was bullshit, I knew. Actually, Michael is fairly stingy, or prudent, as he would say. I could have pointed out that Roz pays for her own damn hats, but I didn't like to spoil Ma's story.

'She wore ice-blue this year,' said Ma, 'with navy accessories.'

'Gosh,' I said. I couldn't help it. I was now as bored as Philippe looked. I wish he would try a little harder with her. 'How's Roz's job, by the way?' I asked, hoping this would be more interesting than her clothes.

We then had a twenty-minute dissertation about how successful Roz was as a teacher of English at the local posh girls' day school. What a perfect mother she was, despite her high-powered job, and what an excellent housekeeper too – you wouldn't believe how spick and span their house in Putney looked. She'd just painted the master bedroom a nice magnolia, though of course they called it something different these days, oyster glow or blossom blush or something.

She was just moving on to distinguished Michael and the wonderful grandchildren when Philippe suddenly stood up, scraping back his chair. 'I have a meeting. A colleague from Geneva is making a flying visit and he has very little spare time,' he said.

An imaginary meeting invented on the spur of the moment, I guessed, as this was the first I'd heard it, but I just nodded my head and said, 'Of course.'

Ma wasn't taken in. 'You have to watch it, Clio, when a man starts to go out after dinner,' she said after he had slammed the door behind him.

'He doesn't do it often,' I said defensively.

She shook her head. 'Looks a bit peaky, doesn't he? All this rich French food, these big lunches, can't be good for you. And breathing in all this pollution in Paris. You can almost touch the dirt in the air, can't you? Must be difficult to keep things clean. By the way, I noticed your window sills are a tiny bit grubby, Clio. Need a good scrub, don't they? I'll give you a hand with some spring-cleaning while I'm here. Luckily I've brought my pinny and rubber gloves with me, just in case.'

Twelve

Joe was there waiting for us outside the museum. My heart did a double-flip, and then another as his expressive weathered face broke into a wide smile when he caught sight of us.

Initially petulant and disapproving at being told he was joining us, my mother went all girly as she shook hands with him and then started gushing on and on about nothing – Clio this, Paris that, the weather the other. I don't know why he has this effect on women, even old bats like Ma. It must be to do with his bright-eyed charm because basically, though tall and broad, he's not that handsome. Philippe, on the other hand, is seriously good-looking, slimmer, almost as tall and much better dressed in that cool, understated French way. Still, handsome is as handsome does, as Ma would say. She certainly doesn't fancy Philippe.

I have my own method of showing people around the Musée d'Orsay. If they are seriously interested in art history, then they get the full monty, starting at the ground floor and going on until they drop. But I take the average punter straight up to the third floor to see the Impressionists and their successors. Many people are more than satisfied with the Monets and Renoirs, the Degas and Van Goghs, and all they want to do after that is have lunch and go home to put their feet up.

My mother was definitely going to be a third-floor-only woman, so if Joe turned out to be a stayer, I'd have to abandon him to see the rest on his own.

'Did you say it used to be a railway station, this place?' asked Ma, gazing around as we made our way in. I could see she was trying not to look too impressed by the elegant marbled loftiness of the building.

I explained that it was converted into a museum in the mid-1980s and was a showcase for the years 1848 to 1914, roughly speaking, a bridge between the Louvre and the Musée d'Art Moderne.

'Isn't she clever?' said Ma to Joe, her head on one side.

I could have throttled her. It's not as if she normally behaves like this. Usually, the one thing you can rely on is that if other people are around, Ma will be faintly disparaging about me. She goes through a would-be humorous litany of all my faults, past and present, plus, if she's on her usual form, a series of double-edged remarks about my appearance.

She'll nudge the listener and say, 'What do you think of Clio's new dress? A bit skimpy for a woman of her age, eh?' Or, 'You can tell Clio's been living the life of Riley in Paris, all that rich food. Can't be good for the waistline, can it?' Or, 'Did you say you'd had your front teeth done, dear? Much better colour now. Mind you, I bet you paid a pretty penny. Shocking price, dentists.'

Fortunately when we reached the Impressionists, she was as amazed and thrilled by the originals of the great paintings as all visitors are. This distracted her temporarily from her flirtatious confidences to Joe and any digs at me.

In fact, for a while she wasn't embarrassing at all. She did say something about recognizing *Whistler's Mother* from a TV ad, but otherwise refrained from comment, apart from, 'Oh, look, Joe, the poppies,' and, 'Oh, look, Joe, the water lilies.' Why it was necessary to draw his attention to them in this proprietorial manner, I didn't know.

'I love the turkeys,' I said, waving my arms towards Monet's huge white birds. I was having a problem keeping my little group together because Ma was jumping quickly around the gallery like a child in a sweet shop, whereas Joe wanted to study each painting and hear such learned comments as I could muster on them.

Finally, despite her sensible shoes, Ma complained about her feet and plonked herself in one of the tiny sitting areas. I found her a museum guide sheet to read and left her to it.

'Great lady, your mother,' said Joe, taking me by the arm and leading me back to the Degas room.

'In very small doses. Thanks for being so patient with her.'

'No, I like her, quite a character.'

I raised my eyebrows. 'Really? She certainly likes *you*, anyway.'

'It's great she's so proud of you.'

Sometimes North Americans can be a bit earnest, can't they?

'Rubbish,' I said. 'As far as she's concerned, I'm still a wayward and rather inadequate little girl.'

'I don't agree at all. It's obvious to me she thinks you're great but she doesn't want you to know. She watches you secretly – her eyes shine when she looks at you. Like mine do, but for different reasons.'

'You're so wrong about my mother, but I guess flattery will get you everywhere,' I said with mock flirtatiousness. He really does lay it on a bit thick, but somehow I don't mind.

'I'm so right,' he said with a confident smile. 'You and she, well, I guess you have a communication problem.'

'Joe, you and I are going to have a communication problem if you don't lay off the psychobabble,' I said lightly. 'Now d'you want to hear about this painting?' I waved at *The Absinthe Drinker*.

'Absolutely. But first, when am I going to see you alone? We have to talk about your clients.'

'They're all organized, thanks to you. But yes, we do need to have a chat.' I added quickly, 'Don't be offended, but I feel – and, well, Philippe feels – that I should give you a percentage of my takings if you introduce the tourists to me. Just to put our relationship on a proper business footing.'

He grinned, but said nothing, leaving me to flounder on. 'What do you think would be appropriate?' I asked desperately.

'No way. I won't take any money from you. What *is* appropriate is that you should have dinner with me one night, when your mother has gone.'

'But I can't. Philippe, um, he's not convinced that your intentions are entirely above board.' As soon as I'd blurted out the words, I thought they sounded not as amusing as I'd hoped, in fact hopelessly uncool and coy.

He smiled even more broadly. 'OK, you can tell him I'm researching the travel business in Europe from the Canadian point of view.'

'You mean you're writing a book?'

'Kind of. And as you're both a tour guide and a travel writer in France, you can give me some pretty good pointers.'

'Thanks,' I said. But I felt oddly deflated. Stupidly, I'd wanted him to admit he was chasing me about and helping me because he fancied the pants off me. Literally.

'Why didn't you tell me about this book in the first place?'

His eyes twinkled. 'Well, it doesn't do to be too open in the literary world. Otherwise someone might steal your idea.'

'I see, but I wouldn't dream of stealing anyone's ideas.'

'I know that, Clio, which is why I'm confiding in you.'

I still had the feeling he was teasing me and I wasn't sure that I entirely believed in this book.

He touched my hand again. 'So when will you have lunch with me, if dinner is out of the question?'

'Trouble is, she's here for a fortnight.'

His face fell. 'Really? That's too bad. I have to leave in ten days. Some business to tie up.'

I didn't ask what or why. His wanderings were a mystery to me and seemed to indicate a lack of stability.

We walked slowly around the gallery together and he listened and looked with great attention. It was flattering, I admit. I also admit that, far from diminishing, the frissons between us had revved up a gear or two. Now that Ma was temporarily out of the way, he wasn't just looking approvingly at the paintings, he was gazing at me too with long, long looks. It was going to my head again, just when I thought I'd managed to file him away into the category of 'interesting but not for me'.

'I wonder if that severe-looking attendant guy over there would arrest us if I kissed you,' he said suddenly.

Flushing, I stepped back. 'Joe, you're crazy. This is a museum, a public place.'

'OK, OK, chill out. Just a suggestion.'

'Not a good one.'

'So when?' His mischievous, expectant expression was hard to resist.

Fortunately at that point I suddenly saw Ma bearing down on us. 'Have you seen the Van Goghs?' she trilled. 'They've got the church – it's just like the one Rosalind has on her kitchen wall – and there's that bed and the haystacks. Fancy you not mentioning that, Clio.' She wagged her finger. 'We'll have to get a new guide.'

'We haven't got to that section yet,' I said narkily. 'Maybe you'd like to take over, Mum.'

'Good idea. Come along, Joe. I'll show you what's what. Clio's too slow. Always was the over-thorough type.'

She's equally capable of saying I'm too slapdash when she's in the mood, and both accusations would be true.

With a surreptitious wink at me, Joe followed in her wake. 'Well, I don't agree there, Mrs Forrester,' he was saying. 'I reckon that Clio judges the pace pretty well.'

Soon after that Ma flaked out and said she absolutely had to have a coffee and a sandwich.

'Why don't I take you both to an early lunch? I believe there's a restaurant here,' offered Joe.

But Ma said no, she just wanted a snack and, she added with a not-so-innocent smile, why didn't we young things do a bit more of the museum while she rested in the café. Young things, indeed!

Before she changed her mind, I dragged Joe off and took him all the way down to the ground floor. We looked at some of the sculptures and then at some early Monets and one of my favourite paintings, *The Spring* by Courbet. This shows a naked young girl sitting on a rather uncomfortable-looking rock in the middle of a wood. She has her back to us, her left hand is trailing in a small waterfall, and her toes are in the stream. I like her because, though her waist is narrow, she has an enormous bottom and cellulite-dimpled thunder-thighs. Nevertheless she is still utterly beautiful and I find that reassuring.

On second thoughts, maybe this nude wasn't the right painting to be studying. Moving away, I told Joe about de Maupassant's description of his visit when Courbet was painting *The Wave*. 'He said there was just this large bare room with a dirty, greasy, fat man who was using a kitchen knife to smear paint on the canvas . . .'

'A kitchen knife?'

'So he said. And Courbet just went on shoving the paint on to the canvas and then peering out of the window at the storm, which was so close that the sea was lashing the house. While he was painting, he'd swig a few draughts of cider and then return to his work. Very prosaic, wasn't it?'

'Amazing.'

'Of course, Courbet was a Realist, in the painterly sense.'

'Of course,' echoed Joe.

'Interesting, don't you think, how the Realists and the Impressionists were disapproved of originally? Courbet was criticized because he painted poor and ugly people, instead of romanticizing his subjects, although not in this case, of course,' I said.

I was trying to distract Joe from whatever amorous intentions he might have. On the long journey down the escalator, I'd again convinced myself that I really didn't want to get involved. What was the point?

'It was *A Burial at Ornans* that caused a lot of controversy,' I continued breathlessly. 'Shall we go and look at it?'

'Amazing,' he repeated.

'Are you listening to me?'

'Absolutely . . . Clio.'

'Mm?'

'Are there any exhibits that no one ever visits in this museum?'

I thought for a moment. 'Well, I suppose the cinema and early phonograph section isn't always that popular.'

'The early phonographs room, that would be so interesting,' he said in a deadpan manner. 'Do we have time to check it out before we collect your mother?'

'Well . . .'

'Just for a minute,' he said with an appealing smile.

Obviously he wasn't going to try and shag me over the show-cases, so up we went again. Anyway, with any luck there'd be a party of French schoolchildren lurking around.

There wasn't. The room was deserted, apart from the spy camera. Even the attendant seemed to have gone for his lunch.

I started to babble on about Edison and the Lumière brothers, but he put his hands on my shoulders and turned me towards him.

'Joe, we'd better go,' I whispered.

'In a moment.' Then he kissed me in that wonderful tender and passionate way of his and all sorts of resolutions I had made melted away.

There were voices approaching and suddenly he let go of me and said, 'We'd better find your mother. We'll finish this another time.'

I laughed happily like a silly schoolgirl.

Then guilt kicked in and I thought, there aren't going to be many other times.

★   ★   ★

On the way home, Ma said, 'I like that Joe.'

'So I noticed.'

'Good manners. Unlike some . . .'

I fiddled around with my bus ticket. 'Come on, Ma. You have to make allowances for Philippe.'

'There's no excuse for rudeness, dear.' With a loud, disapproving sniff, she turned and stared out of the window. 'What does "*Eglise Americaine*" mean?'

'American Church,' I said patiently.

'Fancy. You certainly get all sorts in Paris, don't you?'

No answer to that, I thought wearily.

I could try to explain why the French find the English rude and abrupt, and vice versa, but there was no way Ma was ever going to understand. Better to hold my peace.

Philippe wasn't in the best of tempers, but I put it down to my mother. In the last few days I'd been mentally blaming her for everything. Finally, when she'd gone to bed, he said, 'Had a call from your friend before you got back from the shops this evening.'

'Mm? Which friend?' I said, tidying up the salon and plumping up the cushions. Philippe thinks it's important to leave the room in immaculate condition before we go to bed and of course he is right. It's just that normally I'm not in the mood for housework at this stage of the day.

'Monsieur Joe, your so-called business partner.'

'Right,' I said, straightening the pile of magazines. To my shame, Ma had bought *Hello!*, which of course I only read in secret in the hairdressers. Nervously I picked it up and then put it down again underneath a copy of *Interiors*.

'I invited him to stay on and come to our engagement party at the end of the month, but he said he had to leave Paris. That's why he was phoning.'

'Our engagement party – what d'you mean?' I asked as coolly as I could.

'You know, *chérie*, we said we would make the announcement at my mother's great reception.'

'But I thought you'd changed your mind.'

'Yes, but now I am of the opinion that my first plan was a good one.'

'I see.'

'Pity your friend couldn't come, wasn't it?'

I pushed the chairs so that they were at right angles to each other, as Philippe prefers. 'Yes, what a shame.'

Why hadn't Joe called me on my mobile? Then I remembered I'd been deep inside the supermarket, where there was no signal.

I could have said aloud, 'Actually, Philippe, I kissed Joe in the Musée d'Orsay and I've kissed him before, so maybe you and I shouldn't get married after all.' Kate Winslet, playing one of those impetuous young girls she portrayed so well in the past, would definitely have come clean about it.

But I wasn't eighteen and I didn't want to hurt Philippe if it could be avoided. I admit – and this is not so noble – that I was also paralysed by the thought of being left with nothing, an impoverished, lonely single mother, just as I had twice in the past. Various of Ma's favourite axioms were swirling around my head: the grass is always greener on the other side of the fence; don't change horses in midstream.

OK, I wasn't head over heels in love with Philippe, or I wouldn't have been flirting with Joe, would I? But Philippe was my man and had been for a while. Just because someone different and more exciting came along, there was no reason to bolt. Even if my fancy or lust for Joe felt like love, I'd learnt not to trust those kind of feelings.

'When did he say he was leaving?' I asked carefully.

'Oh, very soon. He mentioned something about emailing you when he got back to Canada . . . Now, you have shut the kitchen window, *n'est-ce pas?*'

Later, when Philippe had gone to sleep, I crept up on to the roof terrace with my mobile. I stood there for a while shivering, staring at the Eiffel Tower and the stars, and then I came down again. I didn't phone Joe because there wasn't anything I could say.

Philippe would probably change his mind again about announcing the engagement. It may just have been a ploy to get rid of Joe. In which case it looked as if he had succeeded.

Next day I had another unwelcome surprise. Alex telephoned and said that he wanted to go skiing with his father at Christmas.

'At Christmas?' I echoed, horrified.

'No, I mean New Year, not Christmas. You don't mind, do you, Mum? Only they'd like me to go with them. I mean, I want to spend Christmas with you and Philippe, and the cousins and everyone, but after that you wouldn't mind, would you?'

'Of course I wouldn't,' I lied. 'It would be lovely for you, darling.'

'Dad says he was going to ring you about the arrangements. You don't mind, do you?' he repeated anxiously.

Harry did ring and of course I agreed. Naturally Alex wanted to go skiing and it would be horrifically selfish for me to say no. I did mention to Harry – in a carefully pleasant and friendly way – that I thought we should discuss holiday arrangements first before talking about them to Alex, and in an equally friendly manner he said that yes, sorry, he would in future. Could have been that Samantha talked about it by accident.

I did wonder why Harry and Samantha had started wanting Alex around more these days. Originally it seemed that she was much happier if he was out of the way either at boarding school or with me in Paris, so that she and the baby would have Harry's full attention. But towards the end of the phone call Harry said, 'Alex is so good with Flora,' and the penny dropped. Now that the nanny had gone, my son was an ideal babysitter for his little half-sister and therefore a popular holiday guest.

I didn't want to share this revelation with anyone. Alex must be pleased and reassured that his father wanted to see more of him. Harry and I get on fine at this distance, and though Alex has divorced parents, at least we're divorced parents who are amicable with each other and I wasn't going to spoil this relatively good friendship by being difficult. Not rocking my various boats seems to be a major preoccupation these days. Trouble is, I caused too much wreckage in the past by not accepting the status quo.

Now the main aim of my life has to be to create as stable an environment as possible for Alex. Which doesn't leave room for love affairs with wandering gypsies like Joe.

All the same, I was checking my emails day and night until

finally I received one, which just said, 'Sorry to miss your engagement party. Hope the tours go well.' After giving me the email
addresses of some more prospective clients, he ended, 'I'll be out
of touch for a while, so don't reply. Joe.'

Thirteen

It was Camille who accidentally stymied Philippe's plans for announcing our engagement at the forthcoming Great Family Happening. He came home about three weeks before the party with a worried and guilty look on his face. Finally he came out with it.

Taking my hand, he said, 'My mother has . . . Well, she is a traditional Frenchwoman, as you know.'

I waited.

He cleared his throat. 'And a traditional Frenchwoman likes to have all her extended family around her, particularly on special occasions.'

'Naturally,' I said in a reassuring voice.

'She has been planning this soirée for many months and it is very important to her.'

'Well, of course, that's why I keep saying we shouldn't try and steal any of her limelight by announcing anything,' I began.

'Not only that, but there is something else.' He was looking extremely put out. 'The fact is, she has invited Françoise and she has accepted.'

His first wife, still his only wife, in fact! I almost laughed. It was so typical of Camille. 'Well, of course, she's still friendly with Françoise,' I said calmly. 'One can't blame her. Françoise was part of your family for ages, much longer than me.'

'You don't mind? But I feel it would not be correct to make public our engagement if Françoise . . .'

'I agree. It wouldn't be fair on her.'

'That is very generous and sensitive of you, *chérie*. *Mon Dieu*, I have always admired the English *sang-froid*, but you are *extra*.'

Telling me I was '*extra*' was a big compliment.

I grinned. 'Good thing you bought me that new dress, though, and that I lost some weight.'

'You are much prettier than Françoise. One could say you will be the belle of the ball.'

Blimey. A middle-aged belle. Another over-the-top compliment.

And if not exactly pretty, Françoise is chic, slim and quietly intelligent. Unassuming and worryingly nice, too. She's older than I am, five years older than Philippe in fact, and if one were to be catty, one might say her face is prematurely wrinkled, not helped by the fact that she appears depressed, a little nervous even, most of the time. This sad look of hers makes me feel guilty, even though I wasn't the cause of their separation.

Part of her sad look must be due to her childlessness, of course. Philippe doesn't discuss the problem or whose 'fault' it was. Maybe they were both sub-fertile. He has always claimed he never wanted children anyway, which is a relief because I certainly don't fancy any more at my age, even if it's fashionable for older women to give birth these days. Besides, I'm not sure our relationship would be strong enough to stand the strain, especially as he'd hate the fact that babies and toddlers are so loud and messy. In many ways, a ready-made child is ideal for him and possibly one of the reasons he likes me. He often says he is more than satisfied with the job of being part-time father to Alex, who is old enough to be interesting. I find this pride in Alex natural and gratifying, of course.

Camille was telephoning her dear son every half-hour with last-minute worries about the marquee and the catering and moving the grand piano somewhere. Then there was the band and all its works. If Philippe wasn't summoned on the telephone, it was because he was already there at the house involved in yet more arranging. He'd been going there for weeks. Poor Edouard must have been hiding somewhere out of reach.

We were to have some of the distant relations to stay. Marie-Clementine and Anne-Sophie, plus all Camille's neighbours, had also been roped in to put people up. In fact, it was hard to imagine that there was anyone left in the whole of Saint-Cloud who was not dancing to Camille's tune.

Aunt Isabelle was typically scathing about the whole thing and had refused to help her sister in any way. She had not the least intention of filling her flat with boring cousins from the provinces. In fact, at one stage, after a petulant quarrel with Camille, she had announced to me that she wasn't even going to attend.

'Oh, but you must,' I said. 'Who will I have to talk to?'

Aunt Isabelle sighed. 'Alas, my dear, you are right. One must be there. Otherwise dear Camille will say I am jealous of her. Although why one should want to celebrate forty-five years with a dull dog like Edouard I cannot imagine.'

'But he's a sweetie,' I said. 'A kind, reliable, tolerant man, who's brought her home the bacon every day for years and years.'

She smiled smugly. 'I have always preferred caviar myself.'

Miraculously shoehorned into the half-acre garden, the huge tent was magnificent, all swathed with yellow and white drapery, with yellow and white flowers galore, in vases, on pillars, on pedestals, everywhere. There were over a hundred guests who all had places allocated to them at round tables, just like a wedding. Camille was in fine form, elegantly coiffed and bejewelled, wearing black, of course, as were almost all the women. The men were in dinner jackets, black tie, tuxedos, whatever you like to call it. I'd chosen to wear white, just to be different and to show off my tan. In the distance, I caught sight of Françoise, who, to my chagrin, had also chosen the white option, quite becoming on her pale olive skin, I have to admit, but maybe her décolletage was too scrawny for a strapless dress – especially around the neck and accompanying salt cellars. I know, I know, Françoise doesn't bring out the best in me.

To my surprise and delight, Mary was there. I'd forgotten that she and Camille had met ages ago at flower-arranging classes, organized by a ladylike social group where upmarket Frenchwomen get to meet diplomatic wives and vice versa. This is the sort of posh pastime that's just up Camille's street.

We hugged each other, Mary and me. She'd been away on leave since July, so there was plenty to talk about: Miss Piggy, the summer holidays, the children, my new mini tour-guide agency.

She did ask me about Joe, but I said it was strictly a business relationship. Mary raised her eyebrows, but before she could pursue the subject, I asked what she'd done with her husband.

'Oh, Tim and half the embassy are at some conference in London, so Camille said I could bring Virginia along to keep me company. Kind of her, wasn't it?' Mary waved her hand in the direction of the bar, where voluptuous Virginia, tightly sheathed in red, was gazing into the eyes of two short, prosperous-looking Frenchmen, who were drooling over her frontage.

I smiled at this vision. 'Shouldn't she be babysitting?'

Mary sighed. 'Well, actually, I've got a wonderful new Filipina now and I was rather hoping that Virginia would take the hint that she's no longer necessary and leave, but apparently her relationship with Paolo is at a critical stage. I do wish she would either bugger off and live with him permanently or throw in the towel and go back to England, but Tim still says we have to be patient with her, blood is thicker than water and all that.'

I was faintly surprised that decorous Mary should use the term 'bugger off', but then Virginia does tend to arouse strong feelings. 'Why doesn't she get a flat on her own in Paris? I'd have thought it'd be much handier for illicit liaisons.'

'She can't afford it. She does stay with Paolo when his wife is in Brussels, but when she's had a falling-out with him, she comes back to us and moons around the apartment all day.'

'She's certainly not mooning around now,' I said, looking over my shoulder at Virginia, who was still in full vamp mode.

Mary laughed. 'Trouble is, she's good company most of the time and the children adore her. I do wish she could get a job, though.'

'But then you'd be stuck with her for the duration.'

'Oh, I wouldn't mind. Anything to get her out of the house. Besides, if she gets a job, she might get a flat.'

Poor Mary, why is she so patient? Bet she would like to have got rid of her so-called nanny months ago. Pompous old Timbo has a lot to answer for.

Virginia had now shaken off the drooling Frenchmen and was advancing towards us.

'Clio, sweetie, you look simply marvellous. Have you lost lots of weight?'

I told them about my bargain with Philippe – if he put up with Ma, I'd go to Weight Watchers. Virginia roared with laughter. She can be charming, no doubt about it. People who laugh at one's smallest joke are irresistible. Encouraged by this audience, I told them about Françoise and pointed her out. Virginia said she thought she looked like a tired and bony old witch. Unfair because Françoise is not a witch at all. I didn't much mind about the tired and bony.

'So how is Philippe?' asked Mary.

'Oh, fine, fine.' I wasn't going to talk about our supposed engagement in front of Virginia.

'What the hell is his bloody first wife doing here, anyway?' demanded Virginia, who wasn't keen on wives in general, obviously. 'Thought they were separated.'

I explained.

'Stupid cows, the lot of them,' snorted Virginia. If she was referring to Camille and co, I had to agree with her.

Towards the end of dinner it transpired that Camille had planned a surprise – a musical interlude, starring her family. Philippe hadn't told me a word about it, so I was as astonished as everyone else. We all listened politely as Marie-Clementine sang, accompanied by Philippe at the grand piano. So that was why Camille had it moved into the marquee at vast expense. Marie-Clementine had composed a special birthday lyric for her father, which was touching if a bit mawkish, and her voice was thin but good. Then Anne-Sophie had her turn, her notes flattish and less certain, though since I am not musical, maybe I shouldn't judge them. After this excitement Philippe made a short, correct speech, and we all raised our glasses to Edouard and then to Edouard and Camille.

I thought that would be the end of the cabaret, but to my amazement, Camille beckoned a shyly reluctant Françoise out of the crowd and Philippe and his supposedly estranged wife sat down together on the piano stool. After a second Françoise stopped simpering, lifted her elegant fingers and began to play duet after duet with Philippe, classical stuff to start with and then modern pieces.

I stood transfixed. At first I was unable to tear my eyes away from them, but then, twisting Aunt Isabelle's ring round and round my finger, I began to stare hard at the vase of flowers at the far end of the piano. The yellow roses were vibrating with the thump of the keys, just like my nerves. Philippe and Françoise must have been rehearsing to play so well together and it seemed as if they would never stop. Every time they paused, there was applause and, just when I thought it must finally be over, they began again, piece after piece after piece.

The guests, who had originally been seated, were now in a large circle round the piano. I had been trying to back away but somehow found myself standing, far too conspicuously, at the front of the group. Aunt Isabelle made a sympathetic face, but Camille had her eyes fixed on her son and Françoise like a proud impresario.

Then something caught my eye, something slinky and red. Virginia was moving in the crowd behind the piano, still clutching her coffee cup. She was gradually pushing her way forward, as if to get a better view. Then all of a sudden she tripped and somehow or other the coffee cup was thrown forward, spilling its contents down Françoise's white dress.

There was a collective gasp. Françoise screamed, Camille screamed, I screamed, and Philippe leapt up and down. In the commotion, I pushed my way through towards the piano, where Virginia could be heard booming, 'Frightfully sorry. Lucky it must've been almost stone cold, wasn't it? Put loads of milk in it.'

'Milk? Milk and coffee?' Françoise stuttered, staring down at the huge brown stain. '*Quelle catastrophe!* The dress, it is ruined.'

'Frightfully, frightfully sorry,' repeated Virginia, who looked more triumphant than apologetic. 'You aren't hurt, are you?'

'No, I am all right, but I must leave, I must go. Oh *mon Dieu*.'

'Yes, take her home, Philippe,' ordered Camille.

'No, no, I have my car,' said Françoise bravely. 'Philippe must not leave the party.' Gathering herself together, she made a pretty good exit in the circumstances.

A while later, when the furore had died down and the dancing had begun, I caught up with Virginia on her way to the loo. 'Did you do that on purpose?' I whispered.

'*Moi?*'

'Yes, you.'

Virginia winked. 'What a shocking accusation. What a nasty, suspicious mind you have.'

'Don't I just.'

'Naturally it was a complete accident, but then again, she had it coming to her, the possessive, mealy-mouthed bitch.'

I grinned. 'Poor Françoise. She's OK, really.'

'You're such a hypocrite, Clio. You hate her guts.'

'I don't. I really don't.'

'Bullshit. The only place for an ex is in the rubbish bin. You'll never get anywhere if you don't remember that.'

I shook my head. I couldn't explain the mixed emotions swirling around my head to myself, let alone to Virginia. But yes, she was right, I had been horribly jealous of Françoise tonight, so where did that leave me? A shameful mess, as usual. This jealousy must mean I loved Philippe, mustn't it?

'Anyway, you owe me one,' said Virginia, staring at herself in one of Camille's gilded mirrors.

I laughed. 'Right.' Then as an afterthought, I added, 'By the way, Virginia, I thought you liked your coffee black.'

'Yes, but didn't want to scald her, did I? Anyway, white coffee makes a much better stain.'

Fourteen

It was only a few days later that Virginia called me. 'I hear you're setting up a travel company. Taking on any staff?'

'Not yet,' I said cautiously. 'Thing is, I don't need an office because I can do it all myself on the computer, and with the mobile I'm always in touch.'

'I wasn't thinking of office work,' she said, a trifle haughtily. 'You know I've got a degree in art history?'

I said I didn't, adding that she had so many qualifications and talents that it was hard to keep track of them.

'Absolutely. Well, I reckon I'd be a bloody good guide if you gave me a bit of training. And I'm pretty quick on the uptake.'

Not to mention popular with male clients, I thought. 'Look, I can't promise anything because I've only just started up. How about working with Mary? At Insider Tours, I mean.'

Virginia made a rude noise. 'We-ell, I did go for an interview, but I didn't see eye to eye with that stupid megalomaniac bitch Elaine. You wouldn't believe it, but I overheard her tell Mary she thought I was a foul-mouthed slut, quite a bit ruder than you and that was saying something. I quote.'

I grinned. 'That's too bad.' I could see they wouldn't be a marriage made in heaven.

'Anyway,' continued Virginia, 'I've got heaps of reference books, I'm reading up on the history and the battlefields, and Mary is giving me a few pointers, so I'm all raring to go, once you need me.'

'Right,' I said. 'But I'm sorry I can't promise anything. Wouldn't want to let you down. If anything better comes along, you'd better take it.'

'No, no, sweetie, you're bound to grow and grow, and when you do, think of little me.'

'Right . . . Virginia, been meaning to ask you, why *did* you bomb Françoise the other day?'

'Singleton solidarity, my darling. We Other Women should stick together.'

I wasn't sure that I wanted to be in some kind of sisterhood of 'other women' with Virginia, but it didn't seem worth explaining yet again that Philippe and Françoise had been legally separated well before I came on the scene.

And who was I to moralize?

It so happened that Virginia was right about my business. Thanks to the distant Joe, now in Canada, I was almost overwhelmed with clients and when a couple of sixty-something widower friends of his turned up in Paris when I was too busy to cope with them, Virginia seemed like a natural escort.

I called them afterwards to ask how they had got on with her and it sounded as if the guy was trying not to laugh. 'Wonnerful, wonnerful gal. We loved her. Didn't we, Fred?'

'We sure did,' I could hear the other one say.

'Where did she take you?' I asked cautiously.

'Oh, the Eiffel Tower, Notter-Daime, the Moanay collection, you know. She was cute, real knowledgeable too. She took us to some great restaurants, didn't she, Fred?'

'She sure did, Buster.'

'Clio, we were real satisfied with your associate,' he chortled. 'Real satisfied, weren't we, Fred?'

'We sure were.'

'So will you use my travel company again and recommend it to your friends?' Pushy, I know, but I'd read a book how to sell myself and I was trying out the spiel they recommended.

Buster chortled again. 'Clio, we love your travel company and your guide Virginia. We will sing her praises all over Canada, won't we, Fred?'

'Hallelujah,' said the disembodied Fred.

Great, I thought. So next time some chaps came on their own, I'd send her again. I had the feeling that women wouldn't be so enthusiastic about her. Naturally most of the men who wanted guided tours were middle-aged or older, and so would be respectable and not expect more than Virginia was willing to put out, always presuming there was a limit.

To be on the safe side, I did say casually to her one day that

Miss Piggy, who was a pro whatever one might think of her, had a rule about not getting too close and personal with male clients, and that I thought that this was pretty sensible because we needed bona fide tourists. As two women on our own, we had to be ultra careful of the agency's reputation because we didn't want to attract sad or dangerous blokes looking for the wrong sort of escorts, did we? Not that Joe was likely to send us any sickos or sex maniacs, but one never knew.

'Course not, boss lady. I promise to keep my legs crossed at all times,' said Virginia.

I was more or less reassured. Virginia could be perfectly sensible if she chose, as Mary said.

Virginia was also competent on the computer, so I was able to pass on most of her own bookings for her to deal with direct. Meanwhile, I wasn't finding the paperwork or accounts too much of a problem, though they took more time than I'd anticipated. Sums were not my forte. It wasn't quite so bad once I'd started, but getting down to the accounts required major willpower and major willpower is something I can't always invoke.

The work was piling up, with guiding, the office and my journalism, such as it is, and the hotel articles for *French Fantasia*. Poor old BB, editor of the latter, was being pushed further and further into the background. Luckily I had some reserve articles from the back of the drawer that, with a few phone calls, I could revise and send him, and he seemed perfectly content with my contributions, just as long as he could edit them and shred them to pieces until they were a sad, turgid dirge. But if that's what rocked his socks . . .

As well as emailing, Joe phoned now and then, purportedly on business. During one early conversation he asked me how Camille's party went. I described the event briefly and was obliged, under interrogation, to confess that Philippe had not announced our engagement. 'Interesting,' said Joe. 'Very interesting.'

Then a while later he phoned to say he was making a flying visit to Paris again soon.

'Great,' I said breezily. I'd already thanked him a million times for his help with clients.

'Hope to see you,' he said.

'Absolutely.' But I refrained from gushing. 'Anytime, except I'm busy when my son's here the last week of October.'

'Darn it, that's when . . . Never mind I'll try and change to November.'

'OK, see you whenever.'

'Maybe you could take me on a private tour for a couple of days.'

I smiled. 'Not such a good idea.'

'Yeah, yeah, I know you don't think we should consummate our relationship just yet. OK, I'll wait until you're ready.'

'I didn't mean . . . I mean, I don't want to discuss this on the phone,' I said wildly.

'Sure, better to discuss it in person,' he said, laughing. Then he rang off, the bastard.

It was most unsettling. Yet again I told myself firmly to concentrate on other things like my work, and Philippe. Proper family things.

Meanwhile, of course, the most important family thing was Alex. Harry and Samantha were keen to have him for the school exeats, but I had staked my claim for the late-October half-term, when he was coming to Paris. I had arranged my work so I could devote the entire week to him and I couldn't wait. Virginia had agreed to cope with the tourists during this period. She was becoming more and more useful, taking on responsibility and using her initiative. As Mary says, she has her good points. Alex likes her, as all children do. Perhaps one should rely on their judgement.

It still sometimes strikes me that, despite my messy life, I have done one brilliantly clever thing and that is produce my son. In the days when he was a baby, lying plump and edible asleep in his cot, I would stand over him and just gloat.

Admittedly he is less gloat-worthy now, especially if we're quarrelling about his dress sense or the state of his room, and there is no question of watching him while he is asleep. It would seem like an intrusion on an adult. But my heart still glows with pride when I catch sight of him for the first time waiting for me outside the school.

Sometimes at the beginning of the holidays it takes him a while to shrug off his school persona and become Alex again. This makes me sad. Should a child of his age have to split his personality like that? But then I remembered I used to do this myself, even at day school. With my contemporaries I'd giggle and speak in playground slang, with teachers I'd be formal and mousy, and at home I'd revert to intimate family ways and generally bounce around more, though my mother didn't approve of high spirits. 'Showing off' was just about the worst thing you could do.

I suppose we're all different with different people. It's just more noticeable in a boarding-school child, because the constrained good manners instilled by the school are more apparent at the beginning of the holidays; then gradually Alex becomes his normal relaxed and bubbly self. He is still good-natured and easy to handle, but I wonder sometimes how Philippe is going to cope with a teenager.

Philippe is strict with him, which is OK, but during half-term they had a misunderstanding, which worried me and boded ill for the future. It concerned the dog. Gigi came to us when Aunt Isabelle was making one of her rare trips to London and her staff had been given the weekend off. Philippe dislikes dogs, particularly large, obstreperous, undisciplined ones like Gigi, but of course he was prepared to make an exception for a pooch belonging to a frail old aunt. If Isabelle were a less-well-off aunt, it might have been another matter.

Gigi, a dog of character, has firm likes and dislikes. If there's one thing she hates more than anything else, it is cats. You've only got to mention the word '*chat*' and she'll go berserk, leaping about and barking her black curly head off. There are other things she disapproves of, like cyclists and men with ladders, but cats are definitely top of the hate-list.

She's such a fool that one can't help teasing her at times. Alex loves her, but he is also fond of hissing, 'Cats, Gigi! *Cherches le chat!*' in her ear for fun. Trouble is, on the last day of half-term he did it once too often and Gigi, in her frenzied search for the invisible cat, raced round and round the apartment and finally knocked over one of Philippe's precious ornaments. My son, being basically a goody-goody, was horrified and apologized profusely, saying he'd never tease Gigi again, but Philippe, cold with rage, sent him to his room.

After a white-faced Alex had gone upstairs, Philippe and I had a major row, but because my policy is that adults should stick together about discipline, we conducted it in furious whispers. I said Alex was too old for such a punishment, that he was genuinely sorry, anyone could see that, and that I'd pay for the ornament.

Philippe said it was irreplaceable and I couldn't afford it. So then, trying to remain calm, I suggested maybe Aunt Isabelle could pay half, since Gigi is her dog.

'Out of the question,' he snapped.

'Anyway, please go and tell Alex you forgive him,' I said, still in as reasonable a voice as I could manage. 'It's his last night here; the holidays end tomorrow.'

'But I don't forgive him.'

'Then you should. It was an accident, for God's sake.'

'It was entirely preventable if the dog had not been teased . . .'

'I know, I know, but he won't do it again. He's a perfectly sensible boy and if you can't see that . . .' I stopped.

'If I can't see what?' he asked dangerously.

'Then you damn well don't deserve him,' I finished with a glare.

'Clio, if you didn't idolize and spoil that child, and if you weren't quite so obsessive, then—'

'He is *not* spoilt,' I snapped, forgetting to whisper. 'You just haven't got a clue about children, have you?' I nearly said something along the lines of it's a good thing he and Françoise had been infertile, but I managed to stop myself being that bitchy.

He was glaring at me. 'What I do know is that for a boy to grow to manhood, he needs to get away from his mother.'

'That's rich coming from you – you're still tied to Camille's damn apron strings.'

'What bullshit you talk,' he shouted. Then without another word, he left the flat, slamming the door behind him.

I went to fetch Alex. Though I said he was forgiven, he kept repeating how sorry he was every five minutes. Finally I gently told him to stop. 'Save your breath for Philippe,' I said.

But Philippe did not come back until after Alex had gone to sleep and had left for the office before Alex woke up.

It took me weeks to persuade Philippe to send Alex a postcard to school saying all was forgiven, and this gave me pause for thought.

Fifteen

I didn't much like the look of the next tourist client who turned up at Charles de Gaulle Airport, but I told myself not to be prejudiced just because he had a pale red beard and strutted cockily as he walked. As he introduced himself, he gave me a long appraising stare, which I ignored, the way you do.

His name was Neil – Neil the Gnome, I decided. He had sharp blue eyes under sand-coloured eyebrows and sparse sandy hair surrounding a high balding forehead. About my own height, thinnish but wiry-looking rather than weedy. Aged around fifty, I reckoned. And, though much thinner, horribly like my second husband.

On the long journey on the autoroute, we chatted politely enough and I asked him how he knew Joe.

'Joe?'

'Joe Dryden, our agent in Canada, the one who finds our clients for us.' I know it was poncy calling him 'our agent', but I wanted to sound businesslike.

'Oh, yeah. No, I don't know him.'

'I thought you put his name down as a contact or reference.'

'May've done, because I found out about you through a coupla friends of his.'

'That's interesting,' I said casually. 'Which friends?'

'Buster and Fred.'

I was reassured. Buster and Fred were members of Joe's golf club or something like that.

We were doing the World War Two battlefield tour of Normandy, the one I had originally meant to do with Melvin and Kay, and Joe, of course, all those months ago. Unlike back then, today I was careful to act in an ultra-professional manner. Something about Neil the Gnome put me on my guard. It wasn't just his resemblance to Gerald. Maybe it was the way he stood too near me, or the randy spasmodic stares, as if he was still weighing me up, as if he fancied his chances.

We spent some time in the Mémoriale in Caen and he seemed to be genuinely interested, moved even by the terrible film footage and other aspects of this huge, modern war or anti-war museum. I hurried him through lunch – choosing the snack bar at the museum because I didn't feel like parrying his smutty remarks over a long French restaurant meal. Not that he had made any smutty remarks as yet, but I had the feeling that his repartee with women would consist of sexual innuendoes. He was that kind of person.

Munching his cheese baguette, he did ask if I had a boyfriend.

'Yes, I'm engaged,' I said.

'That's nice. So is he good to you, your boyfriend?'

I raised my eyebrows and said coolly, 'Of course, and we're getting married soon.'

'So when's the happy day?'

'In two months' time,' I lied.

'Lovely, lovely. So where are you going for your honeymoon, eh?'

'Not decided yet.'

He leant forward and smirked, showing his sharp teeth. 'I could make some suggestions.'

I changed the subject to ask him if he had any family connections with World War Two. Yes, a relation who had landed at D-Day in a glider, he said. Then after the war his family had emigrated to Canada, where he was born. This was a much better subject for discussion. He agreed that he would like to visit Pegasus Bridge and the landing beaches, especially Arromanches, where he wanted to see the remains of the floating D-Day harbour and yet another museum. As we drove around this quiet, rather ugly part of the Calvados coast, his interest and historical enthusiasm were such that I began to warm to him slightly, but only very slightly. There were still too many leers and sneaky glances for me to feel entirely comfortable.

'Doesn't call you on your mobile, does he, your boyfriend?' he remarked at one stage. 'Are you sure he isn't cooling off?'

I laughed gaily and changed the subject.

I couldn't really avoid having dinner with Neil that night in Bayeux. Yes, we were going to do the tapestry tomorrow. All the tourists want to see it and I didn't mind going myself for the umpteenth time. It's so intricate that one always notices something new.

I dressed dowdily that evening in a loose, high-necked top, plain jacket and mid-length skirt, all in silvery grey. If I looked ninety, that was the intention. I came down a little early and sat waiting for him in the bar, clutching a glass of white wine, determined that Neil the Gnome wasn't going to buy me a drink.

He'd chosen amazing gear to wear for dinner: a dark pink shirt with olive trousers and a mid-blue jacket, plus pink hankie to tone with the shirt, all of which clashed horribly with his hair. This technicolor ensemble looked very odd in a formal hotel restaurant in France in November.

I guessed he'd already started on the minibar as he was loud and garrulous even before dinner began. He ordered oysters with much raising of the eyebrows. 'Are they really an aphrodisiac?' he asked with a would-be naughty twinkle.

'No idea,' I said shortly.

'Now isn't that strange? I would have thought that an attractive woman like you would have plenty of ideas.'

I distracted him by asking what he wanted for the next course and invited him to choose the wine.

'You choose, my lovely. You're the kind of woman who knows what she wants. And I bet you get it.' He paused, head on one side.

It was all routine stuff for me and I can't think why I was getting so irritated. I can usually deal perfectly well with unwanted advances. Most blokes take the hint after a couple of polite, almost imperceptible put-downs. Neil didn't. He moved his chair a little closer to mine and he was even trying to play footsie with me. Finally, I kicked him on the ankle.

'Stop it, Neil. You're being stupid and obnoxious, and you've had too much to drink.'

He wagged his finger. 'Love it, Miss Whiplash. Way to go.'

'What about your wife?'

'We're separated. My wife is a cold person and we don't live together any more. She treated me real badly. I need a warm woman who understands me. Someone like you, Clio.'

I stared at him in disgust and tried to turn the subject back to the delights of Normandy, but Neil kept up his stupid flirtatious banter.

'How long ya bin with your boyfriend? Philip, did ya say his name was?'

'Philippe. Oh, it's a few years now.'

'So you're, like, kind of ready for the three-year itch? Four-year itch? Any old itch?'

'No, we're getting married, as I said.' I spoke evenly but I felt uncomfortable. Joe? Was he just an itch?

'Love's dream, or just convenience? Phil-eep seems to have taken a long time to make up his mind. People can get cold feet that way.'

I didn't reply.

'So what does he do, your Phil-eep?' Again he stressed the final syllable in an exaggerated manner. 'Does he have a good job?'

'Yes.'

'Right. Guess you better hang on in there, Clio. But when the mouse is away . . .'

'Neil,' I said icily, 'I don't wish to discuss my personal life with you. Now let's talk about something else.'

He refused to be distracted for long. I must have mentioned Alex earlier because he asked me who his father was.

'My first husband.'

'Excellent! Like, how many husbands have you had?'

'Twenty,' I said.

A fatal joke because he roared with laughter and asked me silly questions until I thought I would throw up.

After the salmon main course I'd eaten enough food and endured enough of Neil. I asked the hovering waiter to put my share of the dinner on my hotel bill. Then I told Neil I was leaving.

'Having an early night, are we?' He stood up quickly, knocking over his chair. The waiter rushed forward to pick it up.

'I am. I have a headache. Suggest you have a dessert and some black coffee. See you in the morning.'

'My, my, didn't think you were the kinda girl who'd have headaches.'

'Not usually, but you've given me one. Goodnight, Neil.' I swept out, feeling that I couldn't have made my feelings any plainer.

I was just going to sleep when there was a loud banging on the door. 'C'mon, Clio, open up.'

I stumbled out of bed. 'What's the problem?' I hissed, keeping the door shut.

'Open up and I'll tell you.'

'Better if you phone me,' I said firmly.

'What?'

'Phone me, OK?'

'Okey-dokey. If that's what turns you on.'

I heard the sound of heavy footsteps and keys turning in the lock of the room next door, as did probably half the hotel, though with any luck most people would still be at dinner. The phone beside my bed then rang and reluctantly I picked it up.

'You're a beautiful woman, Clio, and you've got class. I like that a lot.'

'What's the problem? Why are you ringing?'

'I think you know why I'm ringing.'

'Neil, why don't you get some sleep?'

'I need you, Clio.'

'No, you don't,' I snapped. 'Goodnight.' I put the phone down but immediately it rang again. I felt I had to pick it up. 'Yes?' My voice was ultra forbidding.

'Me again. Look, why are you being so darn stubborn? I'm tired of all this playing around. If you put out for Buster and Fred, why not for me? I thought you liked me.'

'Look,' I said furiously, 'you have the wrong idea. Totally.'

'Oh, I get it. I don't mind paying extra if that's the problem.'

Bloody hell. 'Neil, shut up *now* or I'll call the hotel manager.'

'You wanna threesome?'

'Piss off,' I said, and put down the phone, but after a few minutes it rang again.

'Clio, Fred and Buster said you were *so* warm and friendly. It's not fair. If you don't come round pretty darn soon, I'll bang on your door till you do.'

'Listen, you arsehole, if this doesn't stop, I'm calling the police. They don't like drunken foreigners here.' I slammed the phone down.

The word 'police' seemed to have got through to him and there was silence. Wide awake and on edge, I sat waiting for the phone to ring again. There was no way he could break the door down, and if he started another row in the corridor, I could call the manager. That would be hideously embarrassing, though, and I could never come back to this hotel again.

After a long and restless night I got up at 6 a.m., wrote out a cheque to Neil for the full amount he had paid me for his tour and stuck it in a hotel envelope. Then I packed my case and marched downstairs to pay my bill. I left a note of apology to the manager with the surprised night clerk, and another note to Neil saying that the trains in France were good, here was his refund, and I didn't want to hear from him again.

Still in a rage, I drove back to Paris alone. Neil was a total prick, but he must have heard some sleazy rumour from Buster and Fred, and who'd been their tour guide? Not me, of course, but good old Virginia.

It might have been better if I'd waited a day before phoning her, but then patience is not always one of my virtues and the episode had left me with a bad taste in my mouth.

Ever since husband number two, I've had a sense-of-humour failure about any kind of persistent unwanted sexual advances. Gerald couldn't bear to be refused, and he was also a drinker. It was after one of his long, drawn-out benders that he broke my nose. I've put it all behind me, that low period in my life, but sometimes people remind me of him, as I said, people like Neil.

Maybe I didn't handle the call to Virginia too well. I told her that the hideous slimeball Neil seemed to think I was a call girl and who had he got that idea from but Buster and Fred, and what the hell had she been doing? I thought we agreed that—

She said something along the lines of 'For God's sake, calm down. Don't get your knickers in a twist. It was only a bit of fun.'

'Did you have to have sex with *both* of them?' I asked.

'Well, I was a bit tired after the orgy with the museum curators and then five of the waiters in the restaurant, so in fact I confined my services to Buster and the mean bastard didn't even leave a tip on the mantelpiece,' she said coldly.

'Very funny. This is serious, serious for the agency's good name,' I said.

'Up yours, Clio. Don't be so fucking judgemental.'

'I'm not in the least judgemental. Look, I don't give a toss if you shag every bloke in Paris, just so long as it's not in my time.'

'People in glasshouses, pots and kettles and all that, you pompous cow. You're hardly a nun yourself. Two husbands and a Frog, and from what I heard about our special agent in Canada . . .'

I took a deep breath. 'Joe is just a friend.'

'That's what they all say.'

How the hell did she know about Joe? 'Virginia, we're getting off the point. I thought we agreed no sex with clients.'

'Yes, but you issued this prim little directive about not mixing business with pleasure *after* the horse had bolted, after Buster as it were. Since then I have been as pure and spotless as the driven snow. Not that it's any of your bloody business.'

'That's where you're wrong. It *is* my business, literally.'

Virginia snorted. 'Oh, for God's sake, grow up. You ought to have learnt how to deal with a randy bloke by now. You sound like a maiden aunt. This is the real world. Anyway, don't tell me you've never shagged a client.'

'No, I damn well haven't.'

'Not even Joe?'

I was taken aback for a second. 'Totally not your business. But certainly not him. Anyway, he's not a client.' Shit, I thought. Really shouldn't have answered her, the nosy bitch. Then I added priggishly, 'Besides, there's Philippe.'

'Crikey O'Reilly, sorry I spoke.' Then luckily she laughed, which broke the tension slightly. 'Look, I'm sorry you had a bad time, OK? I promise I'll be a good little girl and I'll never, ever have sex on duty again. Unless Mel Gibson employs us.'

Despite myself, I grinned. 'Maybe I'm overreacting.'

'Yeah, and maybe if Neil had been a dishy hunk instead of a vile beardy-weirdy, you wouldn't have turned him down.'

'Virginia, don't push your luck.' Although of course I couldn't sack her because it wasn't that easy to find a replacement and she knew it.

'Only joking, sweetie. Only joking. Come round and have a cup of tea with me and Mary when you're in a better mood. Then we can be best friends again.'

'Oh, OK,' I sighed. But I wasn't entirely sure about the best-friends bit.

I was still worried about Neil. I had an uneasy feeling that if he ever came back to Paris, he'd come and bother me, not because he fancied me but because he wanted to get his own back for being dumped in the middle of Normandy by his tour guide. For a while every time the phone went, I jumped and I even felt nervous calling up my emails. Ridiculous because what could he do to me? I was in the right.

One dark evening I had a scare. Someone, a bloke with light-coloured hair, was following me at a distance along Rue de la Pompe. After going to the cinema with a girlfriend, I'd just got off the bus. I glanced back quickly at the man, who did vaguely resemble Neil but I couldn't be sure. I hurried along, quickening my pace. I usually feel safe in Paris, but tonight my skin prickled on the back of my neck.

I turned the corner, but the stranger walked on, ignoring me. I sighed. What a fool. Even if it had been Neil, he wouldn't do anything terrible. Pull yourself together, Clio.

It was quiet, work-wise that week. Joe hadn't managed to send any more punters. Pondering the fact that he hadn't been in contact for a while about his proposed visit, I decided that in this current lull I should catch up on my disorganized domestic life, like the overflowing laundry basket, the messy kitchen shelves and other failings that Philippe moaned about. I also had several articles to write for BB and *French Fantasia*.

After a couple of restless days at home I decided to go and mend my fences with Virginia. As arranged, I called round for a cup of tea at Mary's posh apartment. She herself was out, but Virginia was there, plus the children, plus the new lovely Filipina, so it was with difficulty that I managed to engineer a private chat.

The conversation started fine. I admitted I'd probably been overreacting about the Neil incident. Then I mentioned that the rest of the winter was going to be pretty quiet. There weren't going to be that many bookings between now and March, but of course I'd pass on to her what I could. Meanwhile if she had the chance of another job, permanent or temporary, then she should take it.

Virginia stared at me angrily. 'So are you giving me the push?'

'No, of course not. It's just that there isn't so much work during the winter months. One could hardly expect there to be.'

'I've done a lot of bloody hard work, hours of reading to learn up all this guiding stuff.'

'Yes, I know. And of course we'll still have people coming to Paris to see the galleries and do some Christmas shopping. It's just that there aren't so many and I can't guarantee the work.'

Her dark eyes flashed again. 'So you're laying me off.'

'Kind of. Well, no. I'm just warning you that, apart from the Christmas holidays, there may be less work.'

Turning her back on me, she stomped over to the window. 'Great,' she said sarcastically. 'That's all I need.'

At that point my mobile rang. It took me a few seconds to recognize the voice; it was Aunt Isabelle's Greek butler, Nicos, sounding even more incoherent than usual.

'Your aunt . . . She fall . . . Hospital . . . Sick . . . Dog . . . Worry . . . No good . . . Doctors.'

I had to ask him to repeat himself three times to discover that Aunt Isabelle was in hospital, something was broken, and she needed me immediately. That's what I thought he said, anyway. He speaks in a curious mixture of French and English, which makes him hard to understand on the telephone.

'Is it an emergency?' I demanded.

'*Oui, oui*, yes, emergency.'

'She's not dead or dying, is she?' I faltered.

'No dying. She OK. *Elle désire vous venez* come see her.'

I wasn't much reassured. Leaving Virginia to stew in her own juice, I rushed out and took a taxi to the hospital.

To my great relief, I found Aunt Isabelle lying in a private room in the lap of medical luxury, not dying, not seriously ill at all, but with a broken hip, in shock and not in the best of tempers. Apparently the butler and the maid simply could not understand what she needed. There was a long list of things they were supposed to bring from her apartment that would make her life bearable, but they had forgotten half of the items.

'What happened?' I asked.

Isabelle made a face. 'You know how Gigi is sometimes a little naughty on the lead?'

'Mm.' The dog, though charming, was totally untrained and undisciplined, but this was not the moment to mention that. A little naughty indeed.

Reluctantly she explained it was the dog's fault. Gigi had wrapped her lead round Isabelle's legs and Isabelle had taken a tumble. I made sympathetic noises and refrained from pointing out that it could also have been something to do with the lunatic high heels she always insisted on wearing.

It was all extremely inconvenient, she said. Could I please go back to the apartment and make sure that Nicos was looking after the dog, that its food had been properly prepared and that walks were taking place as scheduled. I was to make sure that only Nicos walked Gigi, as the maid could not be trusted to manage such a powerful animal. Isabelle was counting on me, she repeated.

All this fuss about the dog didn't disguise the fact that Isabelle was in some pain. It was clear that her pain and worry would be lessened if, as well as checking on Gigi, I were to fetch from the apartment the essential items she needed for her stay in hospital: her make-up including her Dior Bio daily-renewal anti-free-radical eye cream, her La Prairie placental neck elixir, her Givenchy *eau de parfum*, her nail polish – a selection of the transparent pinks (red being not *comme il faut* for hospitals), her new bristle hairbrush, her best night attire – the Swiss cotton ensembles rather than the silk, she thought – plus certain specific books I would find in the bookshelves and her engraved correspondence cards for thank-you notes for the flowers people would send her. I'd find them in the drawer of the smallest desk.

'Before you go, Clio dear, pass me the menu. I have not had a moment to choose my meals for tomorrow.'

I read the choices out to her: *salade niçoise, sole meunière, filet mignon* and other pleasant-sounding possibilities.

Naturally Aunt Isabelle's suite was equipped with a private telephone line and I rang Philippe to explain what had happened and that, with all these commissions for her, I would be late home. Properly concerned, he said I was to tell her he'd come and see her himself that very evening.

With all this commotion, and toing and froing to the hospital, it wasn't until the next day that I realized I had stupidly left my mobile behind at Mary's. So, feeling like a headless hen, I dashed round there to collect it.

The polite Filipina let me in and handed me the phone and a note from Virginia in her scrawling childish handwriting:

> Hi, Clio!
>
> Checked out your messages on yr mobile in case you had any business calls. Only one. It was Joe saying he's in France today. Unexpectedly. He's booked a room in a hotel on the Loire tonight and wanted a tour guide. I couldn't get hold of you at the hospital, so have gone myself. As he's been such a help to the firm, I knew you wouldn't want me to let him down. Will explain you're busy with Philippe's family.
>
> Love,
> Virginia xox

Sixteen

'Are you still angry about Françoise?' asked Philippe.

'Not especially. Or have you been to piano practice with her again?' I snapped. It's pretty unusual for him to notice what kind of mood I'm in, but I suppose he did feel guilty in the aftermath of Camille's party.

'No, of course not.'

I grunted. 'Anyway, as far as I'm concerned, you can play duets with her anytime you want.'

He spread his hands in a Gallic gesture. 'I do not want.'

'Fine, OK, whatever.'

'But you are not fine – you seem to be *distraite* and, if one may say so, in a disagreeable temper.'

'Sorry,' I muttered.

He was right, of course. In fact, I had forgotten all about Françoise. I was conscious only of the rampant jealousy that was curdling my brain with horrific visions of Joe and Virginia lusting around the Loire. Try as I might to focus on other things like my so-called journalism or poor Aunt Isabelle or Philippe, I could not.

Joe was only human. He liked women, that was clear. And Virginia vamped men for breakfast, even old or freaky ones, so she would certainly go all out for a mega-hunky specimen like Joe.

And offered Virginia, the epitome of sexual allure, on a plate, how could a red-blooded man turn her down? Answer: he couldn't. Well, an ultra-faithful married man might. Or a man madly in love with someone else. But what about a madly in-love man who'd been turned down time after time by the someone else he fancied? Anyway, Joe had never mentioned being in love with me, let alone madly.

Virginia said she proposed to tell him I was 'too busy with Philippe's family' to go to the Loire. He'd think I sent her. So the message 'Clio says get lost, Joe' would come through loud and clear. He was absolutely bound to console himself with her, even if he did still fancy me a little.

'Are you listening?' asked Philippe.

'Sorry, what?'

'I said madame la concierge was complaining about the noise from the building behind. You know, across the back courtyard, where they are converting those service flats.'

'Stupid woman, she's not happy unless she's moaning about something,' I said absently.

'She's right this time. They are not suitable for the *seizième*.'

'Dear me, no,' I said, unwilling to get into a pompous discussion on what was or wasn't suitable for our refined area of Paris.

Later he interrupted my thoughts again. 'Did you hear what I said about Aunt Isabelle?'

'What about her?'

'*Mon Dieu*, Clio, wake up. I said that she needs you to take some more of her lingerie to the hospital. She doesn't like to ask me or Nicos.'

'Of course. I'll phone her.'

'She is very grateful to you.'

Pulling myself together, I smiled. 'No problem. I love Aunt Isabelle.'

'It was she who said you appeared worried about something and she wondered if you were tired by all these hospital visits. She feels I should take better care of you.' Philippe laughed to show that it was just an old lady's fancy. As far as he was concerned, he was a wonderful partner and I was damn lucky to have him.

'I'm fine. It's just a work thing. I'm behind with my stuff for BB and so on.'

'If one may make a suggestion, to make your life easier you should try to improve your concentration. I see you wandering around the apartment staring out of the window when you should be writing. If you were focused, you would achieve more. One minute you will be preparing the vegetables, then you forget about them and make a telephone call, and then you turn to your writing and still the vegetables are all over the kitchen.'

I sighed theatrically. 'Sorry, Professor Higgins. I will try harder.'

He took off his glasses and polished them. 'It seems you try to keep too much in your grasshopper mind. Why not make a list of things you should do in order of priority and tick them off one by one?'

'Why not indeed?' My voice was spiky.

'There is a diary programme on the computer that would help you.'

'Bollocks to the computer,' I said, and stomped out of the room.

But of course he was right. I must learn to make lists and not lose them, tick items off and generally try to turn myself into an organized, high-achieving person.

Top of my new agenda: 1) tell Philippe to get stuffed; 2) punch Virginia in the face; 3) snog Joe.

Or I could change that to 'make love with Joe'.

Either way, I decided not to write this particular to-do list down. Especially as it was wishful thinking.

It wasn't clear to me how many days Virginia and Joe were spending in the Loire in this cold month. Not many chateaux would be open this late in the year, so that would give them more time for other activities. I could call either of them on their mobiles, but I didn't, of course. I have some pride.

Eventually, five days after her original note, Virginia phoned me.

'Any new work for me?' she asked in a happy, friendly manner.

'Not at the moment. When did you get back?'

'Oh, recently, recently.'

'How was it?' I couldn't prevent myself from asking. 'Must've been a bit cold, the weather.'

She chortled. 'Hardly. Not cold at all. What a hunk! You didn't tell me. Very, very glad I went. Had the most fab time and he's so generous, Joe. Paid for everything. I tried to stand him the odd drink on your behalf, but he wouldn't hear of it. So I'm not submitting any expenses except my petrol.'

'Fine,' I muttered.

She raved on about hotels and chateaux and the river. Then she said, 'He asked after you.'

'Oh?' I hoped I managed to infuse this with casual insouciance.

'Yeah, and I told him about you and Philippe. What a lovely couple you were.' Her voice was full of laughter.

I remained silent, breathing hard. Then I said, 'So it went OK?'

'Brilliantly, brilliantly. Good thing he isn't a client as such, though, because one or two of Aunty Clio's strict little rules may just have been naughtily broken.'

I could contain myself no longer. 'So you shagged him?'

'Curiosity killed the cat, but I may have done. I just may've done. And boy, did you miss out on something. How shall I put it? Something outstanding, dear Clio.'

I almost choked. 'How nice for you.' I somehow managed a frosty sarcasm.

'It most certainly was. And if Paolo's going to Brussels for Christmas, I'm thinking of checking out London, since Joe's going to be there. Have to see how I feel.'

'Let me know when you come back, then. Bye for now,' I said in a strangled voice. Then I put the phone down.

When I had simmered down from a million degrees Celsius, I thought of calling or emailing Joe, but then I didn't have anything to say at present, or rather I had plenty I could say but nothing that should be said. After all, why shouldn't he shag Virginia? They were both more or less single, consenting adults and all that. And why should I mind? It was totally, absolutely nothing to do with me.

I could call him.

No, I couldn't. Or . . .

I could call him about the business, but there weren't all that many bookings yet for the new year. Presumably things would pick up again in the spring, I could say in a nonchalant voice. But did I trust myself to sound casual enough?

He might contact me, though. I checked my emails all the time and kept my phone close by, carrying it around in my pocket. But calls were never from Joe.

I had to turn off the mobile, of course, when I visited Aunt Isabelle in hospital, where she was holding court, with most of Paris in attendance. Next day whom should I find at her bedside but dear Camille, plus, amazingly, frigid Françoise, both dressed in the height of conservative fashion. In black, naturally.

Neither of them looked thrilled to pieces to see me, but having kissed Isabelle with pleasure, and Camille without, I put a brave face on it and kissed Françoise. In France everyone kisses everyone hello on both cheeks all the time, and if there are only three women in the room and you normally kiss two of them, then you really have to kiss the third if you know her. Not that my lips actually touched Françoise's face; it was definitely an airy, 'mwah, mwah' kind of greeting. I wondered what the heck she was doing here. Isabelle always maintained she couldn't stand her, saying she was a constipated hen.

In her usual chilly manner Camille asked me how I was and we all made a few polite noises. Aunt Isabelle was looking bored and tired, I thought.

Then the devil got into me. 'Françoise, how's the dress?' I asked. 'Did you ever get the stain out?'

She told me in great sad detail about all the exclusive dry-cleaners she had taken it to and how they had thrown up their hands in horror, saying it was a catastrophe.

'Maybe you could dye it a nice coffee colour to match the stain,' I suggested helpfully.

No one seemed to find this idea amusing, not even Isabelle. Camille said it wasn't a subject for levity and Françoise was lucky not to have been injured and who was that dreadful Virginia girl?

I explained that she was related to Mary's husband and Camille sniffed and said that it was surprising that such a girl should come from a good family, but then, of course, almost inevitably many good families had a black sheep.

'Ah, yes,' said Isabelle, with a renewed glint in her eye, 'I should like to encounter this Virginia. We femmes fatales should stick together, particularly if we are black sheep as well.'

I laughed and promised to bring her along one day. Camille and Françoise remained stony-faced.

Then, to my embarrassment, Aunt Isabelle chucked them out, saying that she was tired and she had some little jobs for Clio.

'But I am only too delighted to help you with anything you need. What are sisters for?' said Camille in an uncharacteristically coy manner. 'And Françoise, I am sure she too would . . .'

'I am used to Clio,' said Aunt Isabelle, 'and she knows my ways. Now you two must depart, Camille, or you will be stuck in rush-hour traffic at the Pont de Saint-Cloud.'

Camille looked as if she'd swallowed a wasp with vinegar sauce.

Noses in the air, she and Françoise donned their almost identical black fur-lined macs, gathered up their Hermès handbags and swept out.

After they had gone, Isabelle told me not to worry. 'It is quite impossible that Philippe would want to return to such a limp woman as Françoise, so one can disregard the Machiavellian plans of my dear sister.'

I smiled and said I wasn't in the least worried, but she looked at me sharply.

That night after rather too many glasses of wine at dinner I told Philippe I'd seen his mother and Françoise. 'If it weren't for me, would you go back to her?' I asked. Rash, but I had to know where she stood in case I was being a dog in the manger.

'Certainly not,' he said without hesitation. 'She and I have separated permanently. We have nothing in common except music, and that is not enough.'

'But your mother and Françoise, seems to me they sort of still hope that . . .'

'Clio, my dearest, I am a grown man. I love my mother, but her views are unimportant.'

Hm, I thought.

'And as for Françoise, I know I should be firmer with her about the divorce but she keeps saying that she is not well and can we postpone the next meeting. Indeed, she does look pale and ill at times. One doesn't want to be unkind or cruel.'

'Absolutely,' I said. 'If she is ill, then you should wait . . . no hurry.'

He made love to me that night, in gratitude for my patient, understanding nature. I complied absent-mindedly, wracked with guilt that my so-called understanding nature was mostly focused elsewhere. Then I lay awake thinking about Joe and whether or not he would ring and whether or not I should ring him.

At last Joe did call, and a careful tiptoe conversation it was.

'Sorry you couldn't come to the Loire,' he said.

'Me too.' There was a silence, which I filled with a neutral 'But you had a good time, I gather?'

'Great,' he said pleasantly.

'Right.'

'How's things with you?'

'Fine,' I said, twiddling the phone cord.

'Good.'

'And you?'

'I'm OK,' he said.

I cleared my throat. 'Not so many clients for the new year, though.'

'Only natural. Business is bound to pick up in the spring.'

'Hope so. Thank you so much for your help.' I thought of telling him about being harassed by Neil the Gnome, but what was the point? Least said soonest mended, as my mother would say.

'You're welcome,' he replied, polite as ever. 'OK, I'll mail you in the new year if I hook some more tourists.'

'Wonderful, thanks so much.'

'It's sort of early, but happy Christmas, then.'

'Happy Christmas,' I responded parrot-fashion. 'Where will you be for Christmas? Are you going to be in Canada?'

'No, the daughters want me to come to London, so I guess I'd better do as I'm told.'

So Virginia wasn't inventing it. He will be in London. With her.

I couldn't speak for a moment as an icy hollow hit my stomach.

Filling the gap, he continued, 'And you'll be spending Christmas with Philippe and his family, I guess?'

'Yes and my son, he'll be here too,' I managed.

'That's nice.'

'Yes, right, then. Well, season's greetings and all that. Bye, Joe.' Before I said anything even more lame and stupid, I put the phone down.

Seventeen

Christmas came and went. Alex enjoyed himself with the cousins in Saint-Cloud, and despite excessive consumption of Yuletide champagne, I managed to be polite to Camille. Françoise was not present on this occasion, but Philippe spent some time on the telephone to her a couple of days later, an event which I politely ignored.

The next major hurdle to overcome was a visit from Harry and Samantha, plus wayward little Flora, who were all due to stay the night en route for the Alps. When Harry first suggested this plan as being the most convenient way to collect Alex for the ski holiday in Val d'Isère, I gushingly said I thought it would be a wonderful idea. I prided myself that I was being ultra sophisticated and civilized in welcoming my ex and his wife under our roof.

Philippe wasn't enthusiastic, I admit, but I persuaded him it would be reassuring for Alex to see his divorced parents together again on good terms. Then later, when I announced Alex would obviously have to sleep on the sofa because Harry and Co would be in his room, Philippe made a major scene, growling and fussing that he didn't want his apartment to become a doss house for all my stray connections, especially dissolute former husbands. By pleading virtually on bended knee and renewing my promise to lose yet more kilos at Weight Watchers, I prevailed. At the time I hardly noticed that, as usual, Philippe referred to the flat as *his* rather than ours. Technically he's right, of course. I contribute to the housekeeping, but the flat belongs to him, so maybe I have no right to regard it as my home.

Not wanting Samantha to discover any signs of sluttishness, I spent hours spring-cleaning before their arrival. As she was arriving after dark and leaving at dawn, with any luck she wouldn't have time to do a thorough Ma-type inspection.

As I anticipated, it was a sticky visit, but mercifully brief. Philippe behaved like a primitive male whose territory had been invaded, eyeing Harry in a hostile manner and saying little. Samantha, dressed in jeans and a frightful snowflake-patterned jumper, looked pale and on edge.

I was not at my best either. Trying not to mind that my son was about to be taken from me, I was jumping around like a nervous flea in case something went wrong or someone said something unforgivable in the tension of the moment. Only the smooth, urbane Harry and the two children seemed to enjoy themselves. Or rather they did until Flora threw a tantrum because she wasn't allowed to sleep downstairs with Alex instead of on a folding bed squashed into her parents' room.

'Never again,' stormed Philippe after they had gone. Harry was a languid buffoon, Samantha a boring frump, and as for the brattish Flora, even by low Anglo-Saxon standards, she was the worst-behaved child he had ever set eyes on.

Still trying to be patient for the moment, I said that Flora was only a baby really, so one had to be tolerant, but he'd scored a zillion Brownie points with me by putting up with them.

'Scoring so-called Brownie points does not interest me,' snapped Philippe. 'What interests me is leading a civilized life in a pleasant environment, without being encumbered by all your idiot ex-husbands and other appalling relations.'

Of course, I then mentioned his appalling relations and the row went on for some time.

In the aftermath, I decided that my New Year's resolution was to entertain more of Philippe's family. Aunt Isabelle was now out of hospital, and to cheer myself up after Alex's departure, I invited her to dinner, plus, to entertain her, Virginia and her lover, Paolo. Aunt Isabelle was always saying she'd like to meet the femme fatale Virginia, and I had a less noble ulterior motive: I wanted to assess Virginia's love life, post her fling with Joe. I didn't suppose for a moment that she would have confessed all to Paolo – not her style – but it would be interesting to see them together, to gauge the body language and vibes between them.

Quite apart from that, I genuinely wanted to get to know Paolo better. He's a fifty-something Italian, smallish but good-looking, and as he is cultured, highly intelligent and full of charm, no one, not even Philippe, could complain about uncivilized guests. And I knew Philippe liked Virginia, despite her coffee-pouring activities. All men do.

Flapping around to the best fishmonger, greengrocer and cheese shop – Philippe is always trying to impress on me the fact that a true Parisienne doesn't shop at supermarkets – I prepared what I hoped was a reasonably delicious meal.

It's Philippe's habit on these occasions to arrive back from the office and pace about criticizing the menu, the table decor, the flowers, the arrangement of the furniture and anything else that meets with his disapproval. Today was no exception. When he discovered I'd made artichoke soup – the Jerusalem variety – he asked me to explain.

'*Soupe aux topinambours*,' I said, rather proud that I had managed to find them.

He threw his hands in the air and said French people ate nothing but this soup in the war and its aftermath, therefore one simply did not think of offering such a lowly dish to guests, particularly guests old enough to have been affected by the post-war years like his beloved aunt. I said that having spent hours and hours peeling the wretched artichoke roots, I was damn well going to serve the soup regardless.

'And why are we having sole?' he enquired. 'Two pale-coloured dishes one after the other, the meal will not look well balanced.'

I said I was bearing his beloved aunt's teeth in mind and that shut him up, apart from a warning that I mustn't overcook it.

'Philippe, *please* stop nagging. You'd better ration my wine until dinner's cooked, though, in case I screw up.'

'I most certainly will,' he said without smiling.

Then he made me really worried by announcing that he thought Paolo had some kind of special dietary requirements.

'Oh my God, why didn't you say so before? I didn't even know. Virginia would surely have told me. What sort of things can't he eat?'

'No idea,' said Philippe, and leaving me to fret, he went upstairs to shower.

After all that drama Virginia arrived very late and on her own, raving about taxi problems. It was quite an entrance. Despite the cold January weather, she was wearing high-heeled pink mules, tight black trousers with a sequin rose appliquéd on the right buttock, and a short, pale pink cashmere cardigan buttoned only halfway up so that above there was an excellent view of her substantial cleavage, and below fetching glimpses of her midriff.

Just as well she hadn't come on the metro in that gear or she might not have made it. Philippe couldn't take his eyes off her and Aunt Isabelle, who had already had two glasses of champagne in the interim, looked highly amused.

Distraught that my small dinner party was minus a crucial guest, I asked what had happened to Paolo.

Virginia waved her champagne glass. 'A last-minute meeting in Brussels. Sorry I didn't let you know,' she said airily. 'D'you mind if I have a fag, sweetie? Been trying to give up, but tonight I'm feeling too frazzled to cope.' She rummaged around in her expensive-looking and no doubt deeply fashionable handbag.

I turned to Philippe. If there's one thing he hates, it's smoke polluting his precious apartment, but, unperturbed, he smiled and leant forward to take her little gold lighter from her. I thought for a moment he was going to confiscate it, but no, he was acting the gentleman, all ready to light her cigarette. In a typical flirty gesture, Virginia cupped his hands and gazed at him under her eyelashes as he did so. One couldn't help admiring her brazen-bitch technique.

As soon as dinner began, Virginia said, 'Fantastic soup, sweetie. Just like my old mama used to make as a special treat. Clio's such a superb cook, isn't she? What a lucky chap you are, Philippe.'

'Yes, indeed, but I sometimes fear her skill in the kitchen is detrimental to her waistline,' he said pompously.

Feeling more cheerful after the champagne, I grinned. 'Rude bastard. Anyway, whatever you say, I've lost quite a bit of weight.'

'Sweetie, you're perfect as you are. Please don't lose any more,' said the slinky Virginia.

I recounted some Weight Watchers stories and she roared with laughter in that flattering way she has.

Then she told Aunt Isabelle she absolutely adored her jacket and asked where she got it from.

'Oh, it's only Saint Laurent ready-to-wear from Frank et Fils,' purred Isabelle.

Virginia put her head on one side. 'Isn't that the most gorgeous shop? But don't they have the scariest saleswomen in Paris?'

Aunt Isabelle then explained the assistants weren't in the least frightening if one knew how to handle them – undoubtedly true in her case, in view of the money she spends – and a girly discussion took place. It wasn't quite the intellectual evening I'd planned for Philippe, but far from looking bored, he followed the small talk with an amused expression on his face.

He didn't even frown when the sole roulade turned out to be dreary and tasteless, despite the time and cash spent on it. Maybe he is mellowing at last, I thought.

At the end of the evening he had to drive Aunt Isabelle home and naturally enough Virginia was offered a lift too, although Mary's flat is in the opposite direction. With a great deal of faffing around and saying that would be oh-so kind, she accepted.

I was relieved to have a chance to clear up the kitchen on my own, as Philippe frets about the mess I make when I cook and also maintains that certain precious things can't be put in the dishwasher. Personally, I'm so shattered at the end of a dinner party that I chuck almost everything in, shut the door and hope for the best.

I hadn't looked at my watch when he departed, but it seemed to take him a surprisingly long time, especially in view of the fact that late at night one can whizz from A to B in compact central Paris in about fifteen minutes. A weird thought entered my head. He couldn't possibly be romancing Virginia, could he? Then I pulled myself together. Even Virginia wouldn't dream of shagging on her employers' chaste diplomatic sofa. Anyway, I knew Mary was at home tonight because I'd talked to her earlier.

I chided myself for having a twisted, jealous nature. The poor man was probably in fact doing a little chore for Aunt Isabelle, since she likes to take every opportunity to have us all dancing attendance.

I had just turned out my bedside light when the front door opened and I heard him moving around downstairs. He sounded as if he was opening a bottle, presumably brandy, and pouring himself a glass. Then he seemed to be clattering about in the kitchen, no doubt doing all the things I had left undone, or not done properly. Oh, well, bully for him. A few minutes later I fell into an exhausted and wine-enhanced sleep.

Next day I was ashamed of my nasty suspicions when he mentioned having to take Gigi the dog for a late-night pee-pee at Isabelle's request. Moreover he said I'd been a brilliant hostess and that, apart from a little disappointment with the sole, I'd produced a meal that was almost to French standards.

'Gee, thanks, what an accolade,' I said, half sarcastic, half amused. But I was pleased nonetheless. His compliments are so rare that one can't help being flattered.

It was a few weeks later that Philippe surprised me again. We were drinking our usual sensible healthy herbal tea after dinner when he announced baldly, 'I've been offered a good job in Geneva and I have accepted.'

I gaped. 'You didn't say.'

'Nothing was certain until today. One was not permitted to speak about it.'

'Not even to me?'

'No, sorry.'

'So that's why you've had all these late meetings . . . But my job . . . Oh, I suppose I could do it from there, but it's a long way from Normandy.'

'In fact, I think it's best you should live here, so you can both do your work and look after the apartment. I shall return to Paris at the weekend, or you can come to Geneva if you're free.'

I stared at him. 'I could . . . but I often do guiding at the weekend.'

'True.'

'Right,' I said, my brain working overtime. 'So you don't want to rent out this flat?'

'Certainly not. I would not want strangers here.'

'And you don't mind being on your own in Geneva?'

'Not at all.'

'Right. I see. OK.'

'I'm independent by nature and so are you, Clio, and we shall be all the more pleased to see each other when we do meet.'

I smiled cautiously. 'It all sounds very civilized, the way you put it.'

'It is,' he said firmly. 'Now if you will excuse me, *chérie*, I must telephone my mother and tell her the news about my job. You know how she enjoys the success of her children.'

I clutched his arm. 'Oh, yes, great news, congratulations, of course. I was so surprised . . . You said it was a good job. Do tell me about it, please.'

'Later, but thanks for your good wishes,' he said dryly, and left me sitting there.

A nasty, chilly, bucket-of-cold-water feeling told me that not only had Joe ditched me but now Philippe was about to do the same, though possibly in a long, drawn-out way. And it was only what I deserved.

Panic-stricken thoughts raced through my mind. What would happen if I was kicked out on to the streets? Could I afford a flat on my own? Yes, of course, but not here in the *seizième* or any other part of Paris where my friends and Alex's lived. Alex would hate living in a garret in the zillionth arrondissement. He'd want to spend all his school holidays with Harry and Samantha in their lovely house with their lovely puppy, and I'd never see anyone except my clients. Even my clients would prob- ably stop coming because Joe wouldn't send any more, so my tour-guide company would go bust. I could probably survive on the pittance I earned from writing for *French Fantasia*, but basic- ally my whole life would be shit.

Pull yourself together, calm down, Clio, I told myself firmly. You are meant to be a new woman, an independent woman, as Philippe said. You'd soon find some more profitable work. It is totally non-PC to be so man-dependent. In fact, it will be good for you to stand on your own two feet again. Definitely.

You haven't got a fatal disease and nor has Alex, nor are you living in a war zone or a famine zone or any other kind of Third World hell, nor, by global standards, are you destitute or friend- less. Alex is your son, he loves you and would never desert you entirely, however grotty and dreary your lifestyle was.

Besides, Philippe hasn't actually thrown you out.

If the worst came to the worst, you could even go back to your mother. In her retirement village.

That last thought didn't particularly cheer me, and despite the hearty self-pep talk, my little world felt shaky to the point of dissolving into smithereens. Ridiculous. Smithereens can always be glued back together with the right attitude.

Can't they?

Eighteen

I survived, of course. I soon got used to Philippe's absence, though I was often alone, especially as there wasn't a great deal of work on offer. I didn't fall apart, far from it. In fact, I felt more relaxed now that my man was out of town, and when Philippe did return to Paris for the weekend, I was faintly pleased to see him, but I realized that my heart hadn't grown much fonder.

I had yet to visit him in Geneva. Apparently the fog was bad there in winter and I wouldn't enjoy it, he said.

I had my friends to keep me company some of the time, of course. Virginia was often away – a part-time job in London, I gathered – but I saw plenty of Mary. Kind-natured Mary was a prop and stay to me at this difficult time. She was thinking of training to be a counsellor or some kind of psychotherapist next time they were posted back to England, she told me. Though Tim wasn't keen on the idea.

'Why not?'

'He thinks I'll get depressed if I see sad people all day long. Maybe he thinks I won't be any good at it.'

'Of course you'll be good at it. If it's what you want, then give it a go. It doesn't do to take much notice of men.'

'You're a fine one to talk.'

I grinned sheepishly. 'Yeah, well, do as I say, not as I do.'

I reckoned counselling was just up her street, though I had the suspicion that, despite her travels, she'd led rather a sheltered life and so might find her patients' problems a shock.

'So can I practise my listening skills on you?' she asked one evening after plying me with food and wine.

'Always happy to have an audience,' I said, settling back. Her fat, chintzy sofas are so comfortable that one can't help relaxing – makes me feel I am home in England.

She wanted to know about my parents, all that stuff. I told her my mother had been widowed at a young age, hence her toughness. Mary said nothing.

'Aren't you supposed to ask me whether I was abused by my mother's boyfriends?'

'I think one is just supposed to sit and listen, but were you?' asked Mary, agog with anxiety.

'No, absolutely not, because she didn't have any boyfriends. Or rather none that she brought home. Maybe men were put off by her prissy, mega-strict view of life.'

'Mm.'

She was obviously waiting for me to say more about my mother, so I burbled on for a while about her and my childhood inferiority complex about my clever sister – 'divide and rule' could have been my mother's motto. I dislike raking over all that stuff. It's depressing to dwell on jealousy and other flaws in one's own character.

'How do you get on with your sister these days?' she asked earnestly, fiddling with her pearls. She was, as usual, conventionally dressed in a neat skirt. Like me, though, she doesn't quite achieve that understated Parisian chic. Mary works in a local shelter for the homeless and she tells me that even the most decrepit destitute Frenchwomen manage to look good. It's the way they arrange their little scarves, even if the scarves are second-hand and tattered.

'My sister?' I went on. 'OK, really. We hardly see each other, though. Thing is, we don't have a huge amount in common. She's a successful teacher and mother of three, respectably married to a senior civil servant, and I'm, well, I'm not in the same league.'

Mary smiled. 'Thank goodness. *Vive la différence.*'

To distract her from my mother, I began to talk about Harry. People often want to know how a tame woman like me managed to have so many husbands. Of course I'd told Mary the abridged version before, but now, after several glasses of Tim's claret, I was in the mood to retell the story with all the trimmings. I told her about how in my early twenties I'd worshipped Harry from afar, staring at him across a crowded room at London parties several times (he was my flatmate's cousin) and then finally he noticed me.

'You see, I was very flattered that such a gorgeous man fancied someone as ordinary as me. Then, after a suitable number of dinners out, he took me to bed and it was heart-stoppingly wonderful, though I didn't have much clue in those days.' I had another large swig of wine. 'Well, maybe heart-stoppingly wonderful is putting it too strongly, but when you're innocently in love, sexual prowess doesn't matter. Well, maybe it doesn't matter, anyway.'

I was thinking about how Harry was the trigger-happy type, but I didn't really want to go into this subject with Mary, who was looking a bit puzzled at this point. I wondered a bit about her sex life with the pompous workaholic Tim. He's the kind of bloke who would have to note it down in his diary: 'Shag wife on Thursdays at 11 p.m. Schedule in another session at the weekend if she looks peaky.'

I dragged my mind back to the conversation. 'Then Harry went off to work in America and didn't write to me once.'

'How awful.'

There was a long pause while I sat remembering how I used to rush back from work, longing to find a letter on the doormat, how I used to sit by the telephone begging it to ring and it never did.

'And?' prompted Mary eventually.

'Then he came back and I fell in love all over again and we got married in a rush of heat, even though in my heart of hearts I knew it was a mistake.'

'But why?'

'Because, as I told you, I have a stupid jealous streak and someone like me should never marry an ultra-good-looking chap like Harry, the kind of sexy bloke women chase.'

'But if he was the faithful type . . .'

'He wasn't. That's the point about Harry. And if you marry that kind of bloke, you have to do a Hillary Clinton or a Mary Archer and rise above it like a lady, or play some similar games of your own. If you don't fancy either of those alternatives, you have to get a divorce.'

'So you did.'

'Yes, eventually,' I sighed.

'Do you ever regret not taking the silent, tolerant option?' asked Mary gently.

'No, because you need to be very noble or hugely self-confident – I knew I wasn't either of those.' I shook my head again. 'Maybe I've had too much to drink.'

'No, no,' said Mary. 'I'm sure it's good for you to get this off your chest.'

Poor girl, I thought. But to humour her, I went on to tell her about husband number two and how he seemed so sweet and kind until I married him and then overnight he turned into Mr Hyde or rather David Copperfield's stepfather, an egotistical bully.

Her eyes widened. 'You mean . . . Did he beat Alex?' she asked, even more concerned.

'No, not Alex, thank God, just me. And then only when he was drinking too much.' After a pause I went on blearily, 'That's why I divorced him so quickly – just in case he turned on Alex.'

'Didn't you notice anything wrong before you married him?' she asked, obviously forgetting the neutral, uncritical approach.

'Fact is, I wasn't thinking straight. Gerald lived nearby during the divorce from Harry. Very sympathetic, very fair, or so it seemed – my judgement must have been up the spout. Where Harry was rich and brash, Gerald was poor but sweet, I thought. I just couldn't tell what he was really like. Kind of rushed into it. I was very lonely and I wanted a father for my child. Gerald seemed like the answer to my prayers. You see, I left Harry when I was pregnant with Alex. Not very good timing.'

Mary blinked. 'Pregnant? How awful.'

'Yes, I cried a lot, and generally behaved like a moron.'

She shook her head. 'How long had you been married to Harry?'

I told her seven years but he didn't want a baby to start with, and I was happy working away at my editorial job on a house magazine and then rushing back to cook his dinner like a good little wifey.

'And?'

I took a deep breath. 'Well, you see, I had a little difficulty getting pregnant and all those medical tests put a strain on our marriage. Then I found out Harry was still playing away – it had happened before and he'd said he was sorry, he loved me and me alone, and promised to be faithful for ever more if I would just forgive him. Old story. Anyway, sure enough he was caught out again, cavorting with a friend of mine, so I decided to hell with that in a bucket, I'll divorce the bastard. Then, having made this mammoth decision,

I discovered the amazing fact I actually was pregnant. I went ahead all the same, with the divorce. That's it, really. Apart from going off my trolley and marrying Gerald of course.'

'Oh dear.'

'As I said, I don't think I was always the wisest judge when it comes to men. Harry was too handsome for his own good, so I chose an ugly man next and he turned out to be a bastard too. To have chosen one dud husband may be regarded as a misfortune; to have chosen two begins to look like carelessness.'

She smiled wryly at this old chestnut of a joke. Then she asked, 'What about Philippe?'

I sighed. 'I'm playing that by ear.'

'But how did you meet him?'

So I told her briefly how he picked me up at a conference and how attractive and original and sophisticated he seemed. And how grateful I was he didn't mind about my murky past. And how even more grateful I was he liked Alex. I'd been on my own for ages and he seemed to be the answer to a single mum's prayer. A handsome, solvent, Alex-appreciating Frenchman, who was I to turn him down?

'Mm,' said Mary doubtfully.

I didn't want to enquire what she meant by that particular 'mm'.

'Your turn now. How did you meet Tim? Did you say you were a secretary in the Foreign Office?'

So with shining eyes she told me all about being posted in the same embassy as Wonder Tim, how clever and successful he was, a rising star in the fastest of fast tracks. How thrilled and flattered she was when he proposed. He told her at the time that he'd decided she would make an excellent diplomatic wife.

It was hard to tell whether she was joking or not. Poor Mary. I could just imagine Tim evaluating her performance in various ladylike jobs before popping the question. Did he give her French tests, or an exam on which knife and fork to use?

Glancing around at her dark, formal apartment, I took another swig of wine. 'Isn't it a bit scary, entertaining all those VIPs?'

She sighed. 'Yes, I do find it rather a strain. Tell you the truth, I'm a nervous wreck at times. But of course I have help. The new Filipina is lovely.'

'Virginia must be hugely helpful too.'

Mary giggled. 'Don't be sarcastic, Clio. Actually, y'know, she'd be much better at the hostess job than I am. She isn't scared of anyone. In fact, she's so confident people often think she's the lady of the house, not me. They come up and thank her after our parties here, and if I'm standing nearby, they ask me to get their coat.'

'Rubbish,' I said. 'That can't be true. If Virginia was a diplomatic wife, she'd probably have caused a major international incident by now. She's not the most discreet person in the world, probably seduce a female prime minister's husband or something.' I shook my head. 'But why didn't she get married when she was young? Must have had plenty of offers.'

'Life is never easy for the beautiful,' said Mary sagely. 'Too much choice. Tim says she set her heart on some upper-crust young blade when she was about twenty and he let her down. Never got over it, apparently.'

'So to console herself she's shagged every man she's met ever since?'

Mary grinned ruefully. 'Only half of 'em. You know, it's a relief she's away so much at the moment. I really wish she'd leave for good, but she still seems to want to base herself here. Tim just says we must look after her, but it's not as if she's a teenager.'

'That's for sure. But, like I said, why doesn't she get a flat of her own?'

'She likes to spend all her money on her wardrobe,' said Mary darkly. 'And she doesn't seem that good at earning it, anyway.'

'Ah, yesh.' I was beginning to slur my words. 'Look, sorry I'm not giving her any work at the moment. Business is a bit quiet. But what's this other part-time job of hers? Hardly seen her. Maybe she's miffed with me. Wouldn't even say whether she'd be available once the tourist season starts.'

Mary screwed up her eyes. 'God knows. She's always being cloak and daggerish about where she's going. I don't want to be uncharitable, but I reckon she's got another married man.'

'What about Paolo?'

'I don't think he's ever going to leave his wife for her. Maybe she's trying to make him jealous, or maybe she's bored with him.'

'So she's got her claws into some other poor sod?'

'But she hasn't completely given up on Paolo. Whatever she's doing, she's playing a very deep game.'

'Maybe her new lover is a politician or even royalty? And she's going to take him to the cleaners with a bonk-and-tell article in the *News of the World*.'

'Very likely,' smiled Mary. 'Very likely. A randy celeb. Probably that chap who was supposed to be shagging half of London.'

We both collapsed into childish giggles.

'I'll make it my life's work to find her Mr Right,' I burbled, clutching Mary's arm. 'Then you'll be rid of her.'

We giggled again. Realizing I'd had at least two glasses of wine. too many, I gathered myself together and departed.

On the way home, I wondered why some women worry so much about what their man and everyone else thinks of them, and why the Virginias of this world manage to sail through life without giving a damn. We should all be more like her, I reckon.

Then I had another blinding glimpse of the obvious. Alcohol always makes me philosophical. I'd had a really good evening with Mary, a major gossip, a great time. If Philippe and Wonder Tim had been around, there would have been hours of pompous discussion and she and I would've just sat there looking polite.

Even on my own with Philippe, though, why was conversation never that relaxed? Or with any other man? Blokes were good for sex and nothing else, I told myself blearily. But I knew it wasn't true. If ever sex could be set aside for a moment, one could have a great chat with a laid-back bloke who listened, a bloke like Joe. He was well informed and intelligent, but he made me feel witty and amusing rather than an inept dumbo. Probably all part of his line. With girlfriends you know where you are, I thought, as I tried to fit my key into the lock. With blokes, well, it's a mystery.

Another friend in my new half-single life was Aunt Isabelle, who was demanding a lot of attention, as usual. She had another fall one afternoon, not a serious one, but the servants were out shopping and so she called me round to get her upright again. Not an easy task now she's put on yet more weight. I tactfully wafted my constant Weight Watcher diet into the conversation, but Isabelle appeared not to catch my waft.

Talking of the family, Marie-Clementine kindly invited me round to lunch on my own, but, in Philippe's absence, his parents ignored me. Not that I minded. Not seeing old Camille was a major plus in my new solitary lifestyle.

The only thing that disturbed me about living alone was sleeping alone. I thought I would welcome a nice big bed to myself, but I did miss Philippe's gentle snoring – more than I missed him, in fact. I slept less deeply and was jumpy about strange noises in the night, even though nothing could possibly happen to me up here on the top floor. Unless of course a mad Quasimodo crept across the adjoining rooftops. It could easily be done with all the ledges and parapets. When my mind started to haze over into that sort of scenario, I'd give myself a sharp pep talk.

I soon became accustomed to travelling on my own in the Paris evening, though again I was irrationally nervous. Once or twice I thought someone was following me home from the bus stop, but it was all in the imagination, I knew.

Pull yourself together and get on with your work, Clio.

I talk to myself a lot these days.

Not having any tour-guide clients, I was working on an article on golf in France for BB and *French Fantasia*. I wanted to do this from the point of view of non-golfing spouses, so I was writing about what other facilities, attractions and sights there are near the various golf hotels. Quite a bit of this research was available on the Internet, or from my notes and on the phone, so I didn't have to travel to dreary golf courses in midwinter. It wasn't the most fascinating work I had ever done.

I was deep in dull thoughts about golf when I bumped into Elaine in full Miss Piggy mode trotting along the Champs-Élysées.

'Clio, it's been, like, *ages*,' she said, swooshing back her hair, now more red than blonde and far too long for a woman of her age. She was wearing a coat with a furry collar, possibly real fox. A nice coat, basically, except that she doesn't have a neck, so she looked like a sow that's been beheaded, stuffed and hung on a plaque on the wall.

No, that's too unkind, even for Elaine.

'So what are you doing at the moment?' she said.

'Shopping.' I wished I was sporting a carrier bag with more cachet than Virgin Megastore's where, in a sad lone-female manner,

I'd been buying an exercise video to tone my hips'n'thighs and bum'n'all.

'Yeah, I can see you're shopping, but what about your cute little travel business? Like, how is it going?'

'Quiet,' I said shortly.

She smiled patronizingly. 'That's the way the cookie crumbles. See you around.' And off she swept.

One morning soon after that I had a call from her.

'You know, Clio, it's good I ran into you the other day. I might have a little freelance job for you. Sounds like you kinda need one.'

'What?' I asked, trying not to sound desperate.

'Well, I have a client who wants to be driven to Geneva tomorrow. They'd like a French-speaking person, and the guide I had lined up got sick with the flu and all my regulars are away or busy, so I thought of you. You may not know too much about Geneva, but you can get a book, can't you? The way I remember it, you got most of your spiel from books, anyway. So what d'ya think?'

'Well, yes, OK in principle. Why not? How about the pay, though?'

'Oh, same as before.'

'But how about a rise, considering it's short notice? I mean, I'll have to spend all day and night reading up about Geneva.'

She paused for a second and I could imagine her fighting with herself, longing to tell me to get lost. 'OK,' she said. 'I'll up the rate.' She then suggested a much better fee than I expected.

'And the client?' I had a sudden illogical dread that the person might turn out to be a mad sex maniac like Neil the Gnome.

'Well, it just happens to be your friend Mrs Kay Hooper. Mr Hooper has a business meeting here and she thought she'd like a little side trip while he is busy. She has a friend in Geneva she wants to visit, but she's nervous about travelling on her own on trains or planes.'

Of course, I was delighted to be going to Geneva because I'd see Philippe and that was a good thing. It must be.

Nineteen

Philippe wasn't in when I called to tell him the good news about my visit and I was obliged to leave him a message on his answerphone. He didn't get back to me until just as I was leaving home to pick up Kay, so I had no time to talk.

Dear Kay, she was still kind and sweet and almost over-appreciative of the smallest thing one did for her.

'This is just wonnerful. Such a pity my husband can't come on this lovely trip with us.'

Hm, I thought.

'You'd never find a great restaurant like this on an American highway,' she said of the motorway café.

'They're not nearly as nice in England either,' I said.

Then she told me about all the excellent meals she'd had in England and weren't the pubs cute and she just loved our bed-and-breakfast places. Obviously Melvin had been on an economy drive, I thought. She looked just the same, with her glasses and her tennis shoes and her lovely smile.

My assignment consisted of driving her all the way to Geneva and then depositing her at a friend's flat near the Hilton. This long trip took most of the day, though the jams getting out of Paris were not as horrendous as usual.

Kay chirruped merrily during the journey, telling me I was a brilliant driver and I didn't make her nervous, and I was a cute person with a lovely personality and how lucky she was that I was free. Melvin was working real hard at the moment and she had this brilliant idea to visit with her friend Jessica who . . . and on she went.

I don't know Geneva well, but by some miracle I found Jessica's apartment block in Petit-Saconnex without difficulty. I deposited Kay, promising to take her on a tour of the museums in a day or two. Tomorrow she had just so much to discuss with Jessica she didn't know where on earth to start. Anyway, she added coyly, I must surely want to spend time with my boyfriend.

During the journey Philippe had sent me a voicemail on my mobile saying tersely that he would be home at five thirty and so I could arrive anytime after that. He would be out of his office all day at meetings, so I wasn't to try and contact him sooner.

He didn't sound overwhelmed with delight to hear that we would soon be reunited, but I put that down to the stress of all those meetings plus his new job. He has been in a keyed-up, tense mood whenever we've met lately. It must be relocation stress, culture shock and so on. Not that the Geneva culture is hugely different from the Parisian. If anything, according to Philippe, the pace of life is slower in Geneva, so he ought to be more relaxed.

Since I'd managed to drop off Kay much earlier than expected, there was over an hour and a half to fill before my rendezvous with Philippe at, or rather after five thirty. Not enough time to go and look at shops, even if I had the energy after the long drive. I decided to suss out his flat, park the car as near as possible and then go and sit in a café until he rang me to say he was home.

Luck was with me again today. I found his address at 82 Rue Schaub easily and, miraculously, a parking space only 20 yards from his doorway. A nice location on the right bank of the lake, conveniently near the Palais des Nations and the other international organizations where all his work took place. It was getting dark and chilly, and I looked longingly up at the building. Again Philippe had chosen an attic flat, he'd told me.

To my surprise, I saw a light at the top window. Maybe his flat was at the back and the light was shining on the landing. Yes, definitely, that must be the case as it had now gone out.

Shivering in the cold Geneva dusk, I had one of those annoying blips that happen when you're tired. My car keys were in my hand one minute and then the next they had disappeared. I fumbled in my pockets and then in my handbag. Dammit, pull yourself together, Clio. I took off my gloves and searched again, and of course they were somehow in the pocket of my jeans, not my coat.

I looked up again and saw a woman in a black mackintosh coming out of number 82 and hurrying away. The mackintosh had a hood, maybe fur-lined, which was pulled down around her face, but the woman vaguely reminded me of someone I knew. For some reason I walked after her towards the lake, but when I turned the corner, I couldn't see her, or any cafés for that matter. I hesitated and then, retracing my steps, trudged back in the general direction of the Palais des Nations until I came across a rather uninspiring little bar, where I sat self-consciously sipping a *café renversé* and studying the *Tribune de Genève*. I don't know why I dislike being alone in a restaurant or bar. I ought to be used to it by now.

Skimming through the not deeply interesting local news, a wild thought occurred to me: Françoise had a black fur-lined mackintosh. Ridiculous, I told myself. Thousands of Parisiennes and no doubt thousands of Genevoises wore black at all times of day and night, so why the hell should I think Françoise might be in Geneva? I ticked myself off for paranoia, or rather insane Othello-type jealousy.

When at last I found myself being embraced by a reasonably enthusiastic Philippe in his charming rooftop apartment, I tried to put my suspicions to one side, but I couldn't help noticing that his windows did overlook the street. Nor could I prevent myself from looking for signs of female lotions and potions in the bathroom cupboards. There were none.

He had somehow managed to find a miniature version of our Paris flat, though the ceilings were much lower and there was a certain amount of Swiss wood about, which gave the place a faint Alpine-chalet look. To counteract this, presumably, he had acquired some ultra-modern furniture, chrome and black leather, a white carpet and some severe black-and-white abstract prints.

'Lovely apartment. And very clean and tidy. You are a wonder, Philippe.'

He smiled smugly. 'Ah, but I do have a *femme de ménage*. A Bulgarian girl, rather attractive.'

I sighed to myself. The cleaner, of course. With a fake fur hood. 'Which days does she come? Am I likely to bump into her?'

'Oh, she has a peculiar routine. Never comes at any set time, but I don't mind. One cannot be too particular in a rich city like Geneva, where good household help is as rare as gold dust. My landlady organized her.'

'That's good. Is she nice, your landlady?'

He laughed. 'Not in the least nice, but she's quite efficient. An overbearing Swiss-German. She's inclined to visit the flat while I'm at the office, which irritates me. She claims she is checking up on maintenance items, and in all fairness she does get things done. Be careful though – she appears without warning, and if she doesn't get an answer from the doorbell, she lets herself in and pokes around. I came naked out of the shower one morning to find her standing there.'

Twirling my wine glass, I smiled. 'Exciting for you both. So did you take advantage of this opportunity?'

'It'd take a braver man than I am. A dangerous woman – she probably eats her mates afterwards.'

Quite a good joke by Philippe's standards. I didn't ask him if his landlady or the cleaning woman had a black mackintosh, nor did I mention the light I thought I'd seen in his apartment. It all seemed too stupid.

He made love to me that night in a polite, mechanical kind of way and in a polite, mechanical way I responded. We don't kiss these days, but maybe that's inevitable. Is this really what I want? I asked myself yet again.

Again my lesser self took the upper hand the next day. As soon as he had gone to the office, I snooped around the flat. Those looking for trouble sometimes find it, as my mother would say, and I did. Behind the laundry basket in Philippe's smart white and chrome bathroom lay a scarlet Dior lipstick. The cleaner or the landlady must have expensive taste, I reckoned. Then I told myself to stop being paranoid. Any female guest powdering her nose might have dropped it. I was just being a prying, unworthy, distrustful bitch.

Or I was a realist looking for an excuse to leave Philippe before he dumped me. Either way, I wasn't proud of my behaviour.

The lipstick could stay where it was. I didn't want to tackle Philippe about it, just in case I saw a flicker of guilt in his face. Irrationally, I didn't want to have my suspicions confirmed.

Next morning I went to pick up Kay from the apartment block in Petit-Saconnex and to my dismay who should be in the marble entrance hall alongside her but Melvin. Looking more than ever like a less jolly version of Father Christmas, he managed to arrange his face into some sort of smile, so that was an improvement.

'Hi, Clio. Great to see ya. Now, where are you taking us this morning? Guess you don't know too much about Geneva, huh?'

'Mel's business meeting was postponed,' murmured Kay, clutching her husband's hand and giving it a little squeeze.

'I am taking you to the Old Town,' I said firmly, since it was the only area I had mugged up on.

Of course Melvin got the map out and showed me where to go. The darned Swiss were no better at driving than the darned French, he reckoned. I dropped them off by the cathedral and had to search around for twenty minutes before I could park. By the time I returned, Melvin was pretty impatient, having decided that the interior of the church was uninteresting and not nearly as good as Notre-Dame.

'But it's quite different. Protestant churches in Switzerland are generally relatively plain compared with Catholic ones.' He didn't want to hear all that. He didn't approve of the cobblestones and didn't think it was safe to walk on them, and it certainly wasn't safe for Kay to climb the 157 steps to the top of the pointed tower. So duly we did the archaeological foundations tour under the cathedral, but he was only faintly interested in the fourth-century mosaics.

Hoping it would appeal more, I walked them to the nearby Maison Tavel.

'Didn't I mean travel?' asked Melvin. I didn't.

Kay enthused about the Tavel family's mediaeval house, but Melvin thought it was kind of boring. He'd seen a million old houses turned into museums and he sure didn't want to waste time looking at another. Maybe I could find more interesting sights.

'Now, dear, Clio's only had, like, half a day's notice of this tour,' put in Kay.

I remained polite for her sake. 'I believe there's an interesting 3-D model of 1850 Geneva in the attic, showing its fortified city walls and things.'

Mel was really fascinated by this. Maybe he was a scale-model freak. I was silently congratulating myself on finally finding something that appealed to him when he received a call on his mobile.

'Yup,' he barked. Then, his red face growing more and more

serious, he listened. 'Right, I'll be there. But I have to get a taxi. My driver is busy looking after Mrs Hooper.'

His driver? Me, I suppose.

And off he went with a barked, 'Thanks, Clio. You did a good job.'

Wow!

Kay looked worried. 'He's been having business problems, makes him kind of grouchy sometimes,' she confided. 'You won't tell anyone, will you? Especially Elaine.'

'Of course not. What sort of problems?' I don't know why I asked as I couldn't care less about Mel.

She hesitated. 'Someone is trying to steal the business, he thinks.'

'You mean a takeover bid or something?'

'I'm not sure, dear. I don't really understand, but I guess we must keep very quiet about it, OK?'

'Sure,' I said. 'My lips are sealed.'

'It makes Melvin cross, because he loves the travel business, and Insider Tours has been a disappointment. I just want you to understand he never had anything personal against you. He thinks you're a lovely woman.'

I doubted that, but as Kay was looking so distressed, I changed the subject and took her down to look at the museum kitchen, which she found satisfactorily fascinating.

When we finally got back to the car, I saw I had a massive parking ticket. Typical Swiss efficiency.

Kay dived into her handbag and gave me a fistful of Swiss francs to cover it. 'Better not tell Melvin,' she whispered conspiratorially.

I wonder what else she hadn't told Melvin, poor woman. I was thankful that I didn't see him again during the rest of our stay.

It was only on the way back driving through France that I realized I had forgotten to ask Philippe for a key to his Geneva apartment.

Twenty

Home in Paris after my tour with Kay, I was walking back from the metro at about nine one cold, damp February evening when I heard a male voice in my ear.

'Hi there, Clio. Good to see you again.'

I jumped and spun round. My heart sank to my new Italian boots. It was Neil the Gnome, in a black coat and Cossack hat that definitely didn't suit him.

'Oh, hello, Neil,' I said, clutching my umbrella. What the hell was he doing here?

'Come and have a drink with me,' he said, eyes glittering under the street lamp.

'No, thanks, very kind but I have to get home.' I don't know why I was being so polite to him.

'Why? Your boyfriend is in Switzerland, I heard.'

I stared at him. 'How do you know?'

'Oh, I have my sources.' He rubbed his hands together in their leather gloves. 'So how about tomorrow?'

'How about tomorrow what?' I asked frostily. Somehow the hat made him look even more like husband number two than ever and that made my flesh crawl.

'Like, come to dinner tomorrow, come to lunch tomorrow, or the next day. You name it, I'm free.'

'I'm busy at the moment.'

'Not true. I heard you're not busy at all.'

'Well, I am.'

Who had he been talking to?

'I guess the truth is, you have plenty of free time. In fact, I can even see your flat from where I'm staying – isn't that nice?'

'Wh-what do you mean?' I stuttered. 'I never gave you my address.'

'Yes, you did. To send the deposit for my tour. I'm renting a top-floor service apartment in the block behind yours. Like, the entrance is in the next street, but my apartment looks right over yours.'

I didn't even notice they'd finished converting those flats, let alone started letting them out. It was all coming back to me. The concierge had been disapproving, I remembered – any kind of hotel was not normally permitted around here, she'd said with a sniff. She had spoken to the workmen, the rooms were to be nicely presented, etc, etc, but they might attract the wrong type to the *quartier.*

The wrong type was now in front of me. And who had been talking to him? The concierge herself, I bet, nosy old bat.

Neil went on, 'Like, I saw you cooking in your kitchen the other night. You should be more careful to close your drapes, you know. There are some strange people around.'

I felt sick. I didn't know if he was lying or not. In theory, of course, people can see across the courtyard into our flat, but it would have to be from a pretty high window. 'How long are you staying in Paris?' I asked.

'Long enough for you and me to get to know each other. I guess we didn't have such a good start, but . . .'

'Neil, I'm engaged to be married, OK? I don't want to get to know anyone else.'

He clutched my arm. 'So if you're engaged, why isn't your boyfriend here?'

I pulled away and said sharply, 'It's cold, it's dark, and I just felt a drop of rain. I'm sorry but I can't go out with you.'

'It's not going to help your business if you don't.'

I stared at him. 'What d'you mean?'

'You don't wanna get a reputation for walking out on your clients, do you? You dumped me and left me in the middle of nowhere. You don't want any kinda bad reputation at all, do you, Clio? There are lawyers who might be interested in my case.'

'Yes, in the sexual harassment aspect. Goodbye, Neil,' I said, and walked away as fast as possible without running.

Footsteps followed me. I reckoned he wouldn't actually do anything terrible, not on a Paris street, but it wasn't a pleasant experience. There's a short cut you can take down a quiet road, but I walked the long way round, the busier way, where I was sure there would be people.

As I approached the flat block, I glanced quickly round. I couldn't see him, but on an inspiration I fumbled in my handbag for my mobile. I could pretend to be calling the police if he caught up with me again.

The street door of our block is not locked until 10 p.m.; this street door lets you into a small courtyard and the main entrance, which is opened by a four-digit code. I punched in the code at record speed and slammed the door closed behind me.

I was hopping from one foot to the other waiting for the lift to arrive when I turned and jumped as I saw Neil standing out there in the courtyard staring at me through the glass entrance door. He couldn't open it, of course, but I was suddenly afraid one of the other residents might arrive and inadvertently allow him to follow them in. People are quite careless in our block.

I scrabbled in my bag for my mobile. When Neil saw me pretend to make a call, he waved his hand insolently and then walked away. I heard the heavy outer door clang shut behind him.

As soon as I was safely in the flat, I poured myself a large glass of wine and gulped half of it down in one go. Then, cursing myself for being paranoid, I drew all the curtains at the back of the flat very carefully so that not a chink of light would shine through. Not only was the kitchen overlooked at the back, but also my bedroom and bathroom. Rear-window syndrome, I thought, trying to jolly myself along, but I was both furious and rattled by the idea of Neil spying on me and he knew it.

It was after midnight when the telephone calls started. It was Neil. He wasn't obscene, just very persistent.

'Clio, you know you like me. You're just playing hard to get.

'It's such a waste, Clio. You and me would be so good together. Try me.

'Clio, I love your hair and your legs.'

Yuck!

'I wanna be your man. I wanna be your man.' The latter was half sung, half hummed. It would have been amusing if I'd felt less besieged.

Each time I just slammed the phone down without speaking. Finally I put the answerphone on and unplugged the handset by my bed, but I could still hear the endless messages being recorded downstairs.

I forgot he had my mobile number. Similar drivel. So I turned it off. Oh my God, I'm going to have to buy a new mobile if this goes on. It did. It went on for three days. I kept having to delete all my messages, but of course I had to check through them in case there were any business calls. There weren't. Neil had flooded the phones with his stupid garbage.

I thought of calling the phone company or the police to change the number. I tried France Telecom first, but they said that as it was in Philippe's name, I couldn't change anything without his permission, so I dashed off an email.

He mailed back:

> Clio,
>   You are overdramatizing the matter. I do not wish to change the number. Just wait and this man will get bored and go back to Canada. You should be more careful with your clients, as I said.

Charming.

Then someone let Neil into the block, but by some miracle I opened my flat door on the chain when he knocked.

'Go away,' I hissed through the gap in the door, 'or I'll call the police.'

'But, Clio, I need you.'

'You need to get the hell out of France before you end up in jail,' I shrieked and slammed the door.

That night I managed to silence the bell of the answerphone and so the flat was eerily quiet. I vowed that if he called the next day, I would pick up the phone and give him hell. Then I would, I really would call the police.

Twenty-One

Next morning the red light on the answerphone was blinking away. Six messages, all from Neil. I deleted them one by one. At around eight thirty, just as I was having breakfast, the phone rang. I snatched it up. 'Look, you bastard, they're putting a tap on this line today! And once the French police get hold of you, you're in big trouble,' I screamed all in one breath. I was lying about the tapping of course.

There was a silence and then a polite male voice said, 'Clio, sorry it's kind of early. Is this an inconvenient moment? Only you weren't answering yesterday.'

Oh my God, it was Joe.

'I'm sorry, really – how awful. You see, it was this bloke, this stalker, he keeps on ringing me all night and I . . .'

'What stalker?' he asked sharply.

I told him.

'But can't Philippe deal with him, for Christ's sake?'

So I explained about being on my own.

Joe sounded shocked and concerned. 'Then I'm coming right over today. Reckon I can deal with this jerk OK. Should be with you around eight. Gotta whole load of meetings this morning unfortunately. I don't know what train I can get. Depends.'

'Train? From Canada?' I asked stupidly.

'I'm in London. See you soon.'

Unable to concentrate on writing that day, I began to clean the flat, frantically hoovering and dusting. I even took all the stuff out of the kitchen drawers and cleaned them. I smiled grimly to myself. At least this drama was having one good effect.

The phone rang. Unwisely I snatched it up.

Neil again. 'Clio, it's me, in a call box. If you involve the police, it's really going to screw up your little tour-guide business. Like, think no clients at all. Not when my lawyer is finished with you.'

Bastard. I slammed the receiver down without responding.

I cleaned some more around the flat, savagely scrubbing the bath with more vigour than it had seen for months, or years even.

Then I caught sight of a grim-faced harridan in the mirror. Me, looking a pallid, spaced-out, freaky mess. Help, said the frivolous side of my nature – never very far away – what if Joe cancels a meeting and gets a plane or an early train? So I dropped my cleaning gear, showered, washed my hair and preened myself generally. And yes, I thought about fancy bras and pants, and about dressing myself from head to toe in fetchingly sexy but not too sexy garments that might just be removed at some stage or other. I didn't want to get too close to Joe, but I had to be prepared in case of momentary weakness.

I don't know why it was necessary to change four times before I was satisfied with my appearance. Even then I kept returning anxiously to the mirror. Having finished tarting myself up, I was unable to concentrate on anything. I tried to type but I couldn't. I was too clean to do any more housework. Nor could I go out in case Joe was early.

The phone didn't ring at all. Even Neil didn't call. Maybe because he was watching me instead.

Five o'clock, six o'clock, seven o'clock came and went. Maybe Joe had changed his mind. Well, he'd said eight, hadn't he? So should I call him to find out exactly when he'd arrive? He was probably stuck in a taxi queue at Gare du Nord or a traffic jam. Or he wasn't coming at all.

It was around seven thirty when someone knocked on the door of the flat. Not the door phone, the flat itself. I jumped out of my skin. 'Hello?' I whispered without opening the door.

'Hi, Clio,' said Joe's lovely voice. 'The entrance downstairs was open, so I . . .'

I didn't mean to fling myself into his arms straight away, but that was what happened. Then there was a long kiss that made it difficult to imagine keeping the resolutions that I'd made about no close encounters. If I was thinking at all at that stage, it was that resistance was going to be pretty well impossible, but suddenly in the heat of the moment he stopped and, putting both hands on my shoulders, pushed me away a little.

Absolutely right, I thought, taken aback. We mustn't get carried away.

Then he smoothed my hair, sat me on the sofa and poured me a large glass of red wine from the expensive-looking bottle he'd brought with him. I was made to retell the Neil story from Bayeux to now.

'OK,' he said. 'Neil is toast, or he soon will be. But for now, have you eaten?'

I shook my head. 'Not for days,' I said.

He didn't even raise his eyebrows at this overdramatization of what was not a great crisis. 'So we'll go out to dinner.'

'Bit early for Paris,' I said. 'How about a takeaway?'

'I was thinking of a good restaurant.'

'It's hard to explain, but I'd rather not go out.'

'OK, eating in could be a neat idea. Then if Neil calls, I can bust him quickly. And you can stop worrying.'

Eating in would also mean spending time alone with Joe, which would be both dangerous and lovely. Dangerous and lovely? Why not?

'Yes,' I said breathlessly. 'How do you like Thai? There's a takeaway down the road.' I didn't add that I'd occasionally bought food there and pretended to Philippe that I'd cooked it myself. Pathetic, I know, but sometimes it was difficult to meet Philippe's high standards of perfection, and oriental cuisine is so different from French that he's prepared to accept lower or different standards.

'Tell you what,' said Joe, standing tall and masterful, 'how about you walk alone to the takeout place? I'll follow at a distance. Then if this Neil guy approaches you in the street, I can be there right beside you.'

'You mean, like police entrapment? How dramatic!' I felt suddenly powerful and heroine-like.

So to look extra bold, I put on my cherry-red coat, which Philippe hates because it's not sophisticated. Then I took the lift down while Detective Joe, being cool, took the stairs.

Feeling ultra conspicuous, I walked all the way along the busy streets to the Thai takeaway without incident. At first I didn't dare to glance back to see if Joe was following. Then I decided that was unnatural. The normal thing would be to look nervously all around for the stalker, so I did.

No Neil.

It wasn't until I was on my way back with my purchases that I saw him, standing in the doorway of a shoe shop bang on my way home. I'd arranged a deeply cunning signal to Joe: as soon as I saw Neil, I would stop, look at my watch and then continue on my way.

So with difficulty, considering I was carrying a plastic bag full of sloppy dishes of oriental food, I duly checked the time. As I drew level with Neil, he stepped out in front of me.

'Nice to see you taking the air,' he said with a sneer.

'Excuse me, I need to get past.'

'Clio, just come and have a drink with me. We should talk this through. You owe it to me.'

A tall figure loomed behind me. I turned but it wasn't Joe. Oh my God, I've lost him. Never mind, I can cope, I told myself shakily.

'Neil, you're being totally obnoxious. Just go away before you get arrested.'

'Who's going to arrest me? I haven't done anything wrong. It isn't a crime to be attracted to a woman.' His eyes glistened peculiarly. 'Here, let me help you carry your bag.'

He tried to take it out of my hand, but I resisted and the plastic bag split, dumping silver cartons in all directions with a horrible squidgy, splattering noise.

Any moment now there's going to be Thai green curry staining the elegant pavements of Passy. I was furious and just on the point of picking up the sweet-and-sour prawns and ramming them down Neil's neck when Joe finally marched up.

'Clio, I presume this is Neil.'

'Neil, meet Joe,' I said.

Joe virtually frogmarched him away down the street. Unsteadily I gazed after them. David and Goliath, I thought, except that this time Goliath was the goody.

With unusual presence of mind, I decided I had better pick up the spoilt dinner and put it in a nearby rubbish bin before I was ticked off by a passing Parisian. I was so busy with this task that it seemed like only a few minutes later that Joe was beside me again.

'So what happened?' I asked, agog.

'Neil had to go.'

I grinned. 'Right. And?'

'And he isn't coming back.'

'So what did you say to him?'

'Simple, really. Told him if he ever came near you again, I'd put his wife in the picture, explain just what a shit he was.'

'His wife? But he told me they were separated.'

'Not true. As far as the world knows, they're a normal couple. I called Buster in Canada and he says she's a foul-mouthed bitch, Neil's old lady, but she's a rich bitch and he likes to keep her sweet.'

'So you didn't beat him up?'

He grinned. 'No.'

'Shame, really.' Some ignoble part of me had been looking forward to, if not a fight to the death, then a tough bit of physical confrontation, maybe a punch or two.

'Psychological warfare is much more effective.'

'Bet he was scared of you all the same.'

'Me? I'm a dear old pussycat.'

I laughed happily. 'So it's really over?'

'Can't say for sure, but I reckon so. Sorry it wasn't pistols at dawn. Would you have preferred that?'

'Course not. Blood would be far too messy for the *seizième*.' I took his arm. 'Come on then, let's go and buy another Thai dinner.'

He smiled down at me. 'Let me take you out to celebrate.'

'No, no. My treat. We'll eat at home. Least I can do.'

'Can I do anything to help?' asked Joe, as I laid the table, my hands shaking a little in the atmosphere of suppressed sexual tension.

'Would you light the candles?'

'Sure,' he said politely.

I was feeling pathetically awkward and girly now that the drama was over, so I took another large slurp of wine to give me courage. Scooping the egg fried rice, the chicken curry, spare ribs and sweet-and-sour prawns into separate bowls, I plonked them on the table.

'Do you want chopsticks?' I asked, sitting down opposite him.

'No, thanks.'

I smiled. 'Me neither. Anyway, the Thais don't use them.'

'Don't they?'

'No.'

'How do you know?'

'Had a Thai friend once, a girl.'

'Right.'

For a while we both ate in silence, mercifully, in view of the banality of the conversation.

'I'm quite hungry,' I said.

'Yeah, me too. This is good.' He was watching me all this time with amused approval, making me happy but still stupidly self-conscious and fluttery.

'Did Neil say how he knew I was on my own?'

'Oh, he said he got talking to the concierge.'

'Thought so. She's a classic, the busiest busybody in Paris.' After another pause I added, 'You know, I'm so relieved it's all over.'

'Good.'

We smiled at each other.

'So how's Philippe?' he asked finally.

'Not sure.'

'But you're still engaged to him?'

'I don't know. Well, I suppose I am.'

He frowned. 'What do you mean? Has it been announced to the world?'

The atmosphere had changed.

'Oh, no. It's all in the air, sort of. And how's Virginia?' About time I interrogated him, I thought.

'Virginia?' He seemed genuinely baffled.

'You can't have forgotten her. She took you on a tour of the Loire. Sex on legs.'

He smiled. 'Oh, yes. Sure I remember Virginia. Kind of fun girl.'

'She certainly found you fun too,' I said more sharply than I intended.

'Yeah, we had a good time.'

'So good that you asked her to spend Christmas with you.' Again this came out all wrong.

He raised his eyebrows, not smiling any more. 'Well, she was invited to my daughter's Christmas party.'

'Why? Who by?' I asked abruptly, then cursed myself. I had offended him and the conversation was taking a wrong turn. In fact, I was cross-examining him like a jealous harridan and he didn't look too pleased.

'I can't remember. We kind of discussed Christmas and I said my daughter was having a party and Virginia said she wanted to come.'

'You mean she invited herself?' My thoughts racing, I was desperately looking for a way out of the hole I was digging myself into when the telephone rang. I jumped out of my skin. 'Oh God, maybe it's Neil. Must say, I was surprised he backed off that easily.'

'I doubt it, but don't pick it up. Let the answerphone take it.'

Tense and ready to do battle, I listened patiently to my own voice message, but it wasn't Neil after all. It was Aunt Isabelle speaking in cracked, panic-stricken tones. 'Clio, darling—'

I snatched up the receiver. 'I'm here. What is it?'

'Clio, darling, I've had another fall. Not hurt, not really, but I'm alone, can't get up. Tried to call Rosa. She has a room upstairs, you know, on the sixth floor . . .'

'I know.' She's told me a hundred times.

'I especially had a private phone put in for her, but she didn't answer . . .' Even in this crisis, she seemed to be at pains to point out that Rosa's tiny *chambre de bonne*, or maid's room, was far more luxurious than average. 'She didn't answer,' repeated a faint-voiced Isabelle.

I was as reassuring as possible. 'I know, I know. Don't worry. Keep still. I'll come straight round.'

'Rosa must be out, but she never goes out. I can't understand. And Nicos wasn't answering his pager either.' Isabelle never could quite grasp the fact that her servants might have a life of their own.

'Be with you in ten minutes,' I said.

We both went round. A big bloke like Joe would be a great help in heaving her up. In the car, I thought of apologizing for my jealous questions about Virginia. Then I decided what the hell. I'd spent all my life apologizing to people. Anyway, I had to keep my wits about me in the evening traffic: I couldn't drive the car, bicker with Joe and worry about Aunt Isabelle all at the same time. Joe himself remained quiet. So it seemed the romantic evening had fallen apart in a big way.

Poor Isabelle, she had somehow fallen in the bathroom, tried to get up but couldn't. Then she'd managed to crawl to the hall telephone before her strength finally gave out. Shaking and exhausted, she was a pathetic sight and I realized for the first time how vulnerable the old can become and how difficult it is for them to preserve their dignity. Gigi, of course, had been no help whatsoever, though Isabelle claimed that the dog had, by 'smiling at her', encouraged her to reach the phone. I doubted it myself, especially as all Gigi ever does is bounce about and get in the way. She was doing it now, as Joe and I, having ensured that there were no broken bones, heaved Isabelle into bed.

Joe was charm itself. You might think he'd been medically trained the way he dealt so tactfully with the situation. Isabelle confirmed she was in no pain whatsoever; it was just that her limbs were weak.

Or just that she'd had a few too many glasses of Burgundy, I thought unkindly, judging by her demeanour and the whiff of alcohol on her breath.

'Let's call your doctor,' I said.

But Isabelle, unusually considerate, announced it was far too late in the day for bothering with the doctor, and anyway, she was fine and she would ring him in the morning. So I settled her down for the night and fetched her everything she wanted while Joe sat patiently in the salon.

Then there was a drama when she said she had run out of sleeping pills. That's what she had been doing in the bathroom, searching for her emergency supply, which wasn't there. She must have used them up without remembering.

'Are you sure you're OK?' I interrupted.

Of course she was, she said. Nothing was broken, nothing specific or unusual was hurting. No, she absolutely refused to go to casualty when she was perfectly all right. Casualty would be far too tiring. What she more than anything needed was a good night's rest, but without sleeping pills how could she have that?

Aunt Isabelle was pretty well hooked on narcotics and I was amazed she had allowed herself to run out of them – must be starting to lose her marbles. I also had to agree that a good night's rest would do her the power of good.

'Look,' I said, 'Philippe had sleeping pills prescribed once, temazepam. I think there are a few left. I'll go and get them.'

I told Joe what I was doing and immediately he offered to fetch them for me, but frankly, quite apart from the fact that I wasn't sure where the pills were, I didn't want Joe rifling about in the bathroom cupboard and finding sordid old tubes of make-up and dead mascaras, not to mention out-of-date lotions and potions for embarrassing conditions.

'Stay here,' I said. 'Chat to her for a while, just to make sure she is OK.'

And that's how I left them, Aunt Isabelle, her colour restored to normal, lying back in a queenly manner in her bed, while Joe sat on a pink upholstered chair entertaining her. Gigi sat between them both, wagging her tail enthusiastically and occasionally leaping up to try and kiss Joe or Isabelle. Just before I shut the door behind me, I could hear them laughing uproariously together. Joe charmed females of all ages, I reckoned, and Aunt Isabelle, still a flirt despite her seventy-nine years, would undoubtedly enjoy his company.

So I was pretty surprised – devastated, in fact – when I arrived back at Isabelle's half an hour later to find that he had gone.

Isabelle took the sleeping tablets, opened the bottle in a professional manner and swallowed a couple of them whole, taking a swig of Evian to wash them down.

'What happened to Joe?' I asked when no explanation was forthcoming.

'He had to go,' she said.

'Did he leave a message for me?'

She screwed up her face as if trying to remember. 'No, I don't think so. I am sorry, my dear, but he seemed to be in a hurry. Perhaps he had a rendezvous with a lady friend.' Her black eyes swivelled towards me, then away again.

I flushed. In the heat of the moment I hadn't had time to explain to her who Joe was.

She stared at her plum-coloured fingernails, so bright compared to her bony old hands. 'One cannot blame a red-blooded woman

like you, Clio, when faced with such an attractive man as Joe,
but I would advise you to be careful.'

'He . . . It's business. He helps me with my tourist clients.'

'I am sure he does,' she said smoothly. 'But one shouldn't allow
oneself to be distracted by the charms of one's business colleagues.'

Considering Isabelle had been distracted by blokes all her life,
this was a bit rich.

'Tante Isabelle, did you send him away?'

She closed her eyes. 'No, he seemed anxious to leave. As I said,
I suspect he had a romantic rendezvous, maybe with a married
woman. That is why he was so discreet about it . . . You know,
your pills are quite good. They are beginning to take effect already.'

'They're not mine, they're Philippe's.'

'What is his is yours, and what is yours is his. You are a couple
. . . You know, my dear, I really am very sleepy. The fall, the
shock . . . You must forgive me, but I must ask you to leave an
old woman to her dreams. You are a good girl, Clio. As I said to
Joe, I am so looking forward to having you and little Alex in the
family. I told him how fond we all are of you and how little Alex
is like a grandson to me, isn't he?'

'Yes,' I said.

'And he is such a nice friend for Marie-Clementine's boys.'

'Yes.'

'I feel so tired.'

'Goodnight, Isabelle.'

Out in the street, I tried Joe's mobile, but he had obviously turned
it off. I left a voicemail saying thank you for dealing with Neil
and with Isabelle.

But there was no reply.

Somehow or other I had made an even worse mess of things
than I thought.

Twenty-Two

Alex arrived for half-term and that made me feel a great deal better. Thank God Harry and Samantha hadn't managed to steal him this time, I thought, hugging him tight as he arrived at the barrier at Gare du Nord. Away from school, he isn't self-conscious about having a soppy mother and doesn't mind hugging me back.

Next morning I looked at my lovely son guzzling a mammoth bowl of Coco Pops (he's not keen on chewy French muesli) and decided that he was the only decent male in the world. Mustn't get possessive, said my conscience. He'll have another woman in his life sooner or later – sooner with heartbreaker looks like that.

I suppose all mothers imagine their son is a stunner, but as well as being gorgeous, Alex is also kind and sympathetic for his age. I'm sure girls will find him a wonderful listener, and a man who listens to women is halfway there. A man like Joe.

But Joe still hadn't replied to my message. I told myself not to brood, but thoughts about him kept popping to the front of my mind however hard I tried to suppress them. What had Isabelle said to him? Whatever it was, he had done a runner. Without even saying goodbye. Could he really have gone to another woman? Virginia? Surely not. Isabelle might have made up all that stuff about his secret rendezvous, but it might be true. As she said, he's a charming guy. I hadn't put him down as a philanderer, but then most men are, given half a chance.

Maybe he'd been angry about me cross-examining him about Christmas. I mean, why shouldn't Virginia have gone to his daughter's party?

Then I got an abrupt email from him:

> Clio,
> Thanks for your message. Glad to hear you had no more problems with Neil. Hope it stays that way.

Been thinking. As you said all along, I guess we should
stick to business matters in future.

Joe

That sort of confirmed everything. Our never-begun fling had
died a natural death. I stuffed my feelings about him deep into
a deep hole and tried to ignore them. Sometimes, but not often,
I almost succeeded.

And anyway, there was Philippe still. More or less. Maybe less,
these days.

And anyway, Joe was extremely unsuitable in every way. Good
thing he had gone, in fact. No reason to be heartbroken over a
bloke who lived on the other side of the Atlantic. Geography is
pretty important and . . . Anyway, he's a self-confessed gypsy, an
unemployed rolling stone who had no qualifications to be a new
father for my son.

Think about Alex, a much better subject, I told myself.

I was worried that with Philippe away, there wasn't much here
to entertain him, but we went to see Aunt Isabelle and took Gigi
for walks, and went to the cinema and bowling and generally
found enough things to do. The British Embassy wives organized a youngsters' party, but Alex didn't fancy the idea and I can't
say I blame him. He's just turned thirteen and it's a pretty self-
conscious age.

We were peacefully watching a video together one evening,
The Italian Job yet again. We had just got to my favourite point
– where Noël Coward as Mr Bridger complains to the prison
governor that someone has broken into his toilet – when the
phone rang.

It was Samantha, sounding desperate and on the verge of tears.
'Clio, we need to come and stay.'

'Are you all right, Sam?'

A sob. 'Need somewhere to stay,' she repeated.

'Of course. When will you be coming?'

'Now,' she said.

Blimey.

'That's fine . . . But what's happened? Has there been an
accident?'

'No.' More sobs. 'Tell you when I get there.'

'Right, OK. Where are you?'

'Gare du Nord.' Her voice shook. 'How do you spell the name of your street, and how do you pronounce it to the taxi man?'

I told her. It didn't seem the moment to ask any further questions.

So I left Alex glued to the goings-on of Michael Caine and raced round the flat changing Alex's sheets for Samantha and Harry, making up a bed for Flora and then cleaning the bathroom, clearing the dishes from the draining board, plus all the other things that substandard housewives do before unexpected guests arrive.

About three-quarters of an hour later Samantha arrived carrying a grizzly Flora and a huge suitcase. Sam looked ghastly, pale and podgy, and on the point of breaking down.

'Where's Harry?' I asked.

Tears welled in her eyes. She shook her head mutely without answering.

'Has something happened?'

'Tell you later,' she managed, nodding her head towards Alex as if to say, 'Not in front of the children.'

'But he's OK?'

'Oh, yes,' she said heavily. 'He's very much OK.'

Time to be bright and breezy, I thought. 'Let's all take Flora up to bed. Would you read her a story, Alex?'

'But . . .' Showing faint signs of teenage rebellion, he gestured towards the television.

'Watch it later. Bit of a crisis,' I whispered under my breath.

'Come on then, mate, let's hit the road,' he said, taking Flora by the hand.

Luckily Flora was exhausted and made no protest as between us we got her into bed. Leaving Alex to start the promised story, I bustled Samantha downstairs and gave her a large glass of wine, which she swallowed in one gulp, most unlike her.

'I lost my tickets and the bloody clerk woman at the station wouldn't believe me, wouldn't give me another one,' she began, her eyes brimming again.

'What tickets?'

'For Eurostar – trying to get back to England.'

'Eurostar tickets are just like any other train tickets – if you've lost them, you've had it.'

'That's what the woman said.' She began to cry.

I put my arm round her. 'But what are you doing here on your own?'

'Oh, Clio, he's . . . he's left me. Or rather I've left him.'

'Oh my God. What d'you mean? Can't be true. It's just Harry's way.'

'He's got someone else,' she moaned, rocking backwards and forwards.

'But he loves you – the other women don't matter.'

'Other women? It's just one, isn't it? What do you mean?'

I glanced up and saw Alex coming down the stairs. 'Oh, is Flora asleep already?' I asked brightly.

'Yep, she zonked out in a flash. We didn't even get to the end of *Where's Spot?*'

I smiled. 'Jolly good.'

He stopped and stared at his stepmother. 'What's the matter, Samantha?' he asked in a concerned, grown-up voice.

'She's not very well,' I said quickly. 'Darling, why don't you make up your bed on the sofa and you can watch the rest of the movie in bed as a treat? We'll go to the kitchen and I'll cook Samantha an omelette or something – I bet you haven't eaten, have you, Sam?'

She shook her head dolefully. 'Not hungry.'

I ushered her up to the kitchen and persuaded her to have a piece of bread and a nice gooey chunk of Brie, plus another glass of wine or two. Then, for privacy in this semi-open-plan flat, we sat in my bedroom and talked. I'd brought the wine bottle with me.

Samantha told me the long rigmarole. They'd been staying in a hotel in Paris and Harry had gone off with another woman last night – a glamorous French divorcee he'd known before. This woman had invited them both to dinner, but Sam had stayed in the hotel, not wanting to leave Flora with a strange babysitter.

'You could have asked me to babysit. I didn't even know you were in Paris. She could have come here,' I said.

'Yes, but she was so naughty last time.'

'I didn't mind a bit.'

'But Philippe did. I assumed he was here,' said Samantha. Then she stumbled on with her story. Harry had not come back last night. He'd rung and given some pathetic excuse about passing out on this woman's sofa and finding himself there next morning. Then he'd allegedly been invited to stay to lunch to meet her brother, but it wasn't worth Samantha coming because they were all going to be talking French, plus they had some financial business to discuss, and Sam wouldn't know anyone, and then she didn't speak French, and . . . 'All his excuses were obviously complete bollocks,' she said.

Unfortunate choice of word in my view.

She talked and wept and talked some more, while I filled up her glass from time to time and made soothing noises. Poor Sam, been there, done that, I thought. She was raving about separation and divorce and what should she do, how should she go about it, she didn't know any lawyers. Normally an ultra-efficient and together girl, she was sounding helpless and stupid. That's what Harry does to people.

Finally I asked, 'Do you still love him?'

She hung her head. 'Yes,' she muttered.

After a pause I said, 'You know, I've been thinking about Harry and men like him. As I was saying to my mate Mary, there are three choices: one, you rise above his occasional philandering and turn a blind eye, or as blind as possible; two, you have an open marriage and play games of your own.'

Predictably, Samantha shuddered and said she couldn't possibly do that.

'Or three,' I went on, 'you divorce and break up the family, as I did.'

She stared at me through her tears. 'Do you regret leaving him?' she asked carefully.

'No, I was too young and not confident enough to cope with the Harry type, but I think you are. Confident, I mean.'

'Am I?'

'Yes, I reckon so. He loves you, Samantha. He could have married almost any of his girlfriends, but he chose you. If he's having a fling, it doesn't mean anything. He's a seriously attractive man, and of course he's kind and generous, but he has one major flaw. You've just got to decide if you can put up with it or if his good points outweigh his bad.' Apart from his generosity,

Harry's good points weren't that hot, in my opinion, but I couldn't say that to Sam.

She looked thoughtful. 'Are you saying I should forgive and forget?'

'Could be the best way of dealing with it. Or you could challenge him, saying something like if he disappears with any more strange Frenchwomen, it will be your turn to have a fling.'

Momentarily more cheerful, she looked at me. 'He won't believe that.'

'Maybe not. But it might sow a doubt in his mind. Might make him think twice next time.'

'I could never be unfaithful,' she repeated.

'I'm sure you couldn't, Sam, but then again if you are ever tempted to have a secret fling at any stage in your life, you've got a perfect excuse. No harm in looking for a reserve if Harry is going to play the field.'

Her face cleared and she actually gave a small giggle. 'I feel a bit better, you know.'

'Alcohol therapy and a cosy chat. Does it every time,' I said cheerfully.

I jumped as the phone rang. We both stared at it. Then, with some trepidation, I picked up the receiver.

'Clio, it's Harry. I'm frightfully sorry to have to ring you so late, but I've lost Samantha. She's not answering her mobile. You haven't heard from her, have you?'

I put my hand over the receiver. 'It's him,' I hissed. 'I'm going to say you're not here. Let him stew a bit.'

'Yes, sod the bastard.' Strong language for the saintly Sam.

Pretending to have just woken up, I spoke into the phone. 'Oh, hi, Harry. Great to hear from you. What did you say about Samantha?'

'We were staying in Paris and she's disappeared, just like that.'

'How peculiar.'

'Have you heard from her?'

'No, we haven't,' I lied happily. 'Maybe she has a secret lover?'

'Don't be facetious, Clio. Sam's not like that.'

'Not like you, you mean. But what's sauce for the gander could be jolly nice for the goose, as Ma would say.'

He laughed, sounding just a tad sheepish. 'If you hear from Sam, could you give me a ring?'

'Sure.'

He changed gear into his charming social drawl. 'How's Alex? When's he coming over to Paris?'

'He's fine. He's here at the moment, actually.'

'Oh, yes, of course. I forgot. And Philippe?'

'Working in Geneva for the time being.'

'Oh.' There was a pause while his brain ticked over. 'I don't suppose I could base myself at your place while I look for Sam, could I? It's all very worrying and you're so good in a crisis.' His voice had a warm, flirtatious edge.

I groaned inwardly and put on an extra brisk tone. 'No, certainly not. Just get back home and wait for her. She's bound to show up soon. Anyway, why has she disappeared? Have you been up to something, Harry? Better behave yourself. She's a great girl. You don't want to lose her, do you?'

'No,' he said, now quite serious. 'No, I don't.'

'Well then, pull yourself together and get the first train home.' I put down the receiver firmly.

Samantha stared at me. 'What did he say? Should I ring him back?'

I persuaded her to wait until tomorrow. She could buy a new Eurostar ticket and blame the expense on Harry. (Not sure why this didn't occur to her last night, but then she was in a tizzy.) Then she should call from the train and get him to bring the car to St Pancras to meet her and make him grovel.

I didn't mention his idea about coming here.

Agreeing to my play-it-cool strategic plan, she lay back on the bed staring at the ceiling. Then like a sleepwalker she stood up and made for the door. Just before opening it, she turned and asked slowly, 'If you're so full of good ideas for handling Harry, why didn't you put them into effect when you were married to him?'

I smiled. 'Much easier to be wise after the event. I've had years and years to work out why I couldn't cope and what actions I should've taken, so you might as well benefit from my research.'

'Thanks, Clio. You're clever and sensible and very kind. Still not sure why . . .'

'I'm doing it for Alex, and Flora too.' The truth was, I'd far rather have Samantha as Alex's stepmother than Harry's usual brainless sluts.

I packed her off to bed. I hope she slept. Alex's room is small and uncomfortable. Despite the wine, I didn't sleep much myself. I kept thinking about Harry and Gerald and Philippe and Joe and wondering why, if I was so full of wisdom, I had made so many crap mistakes.

Twenty-Three

'Clio, I am thinking of making you my heir once you marry Philippe.'

I nearly fell off Aunt Isabelle's spindly dining chair. We were having lunch together in her apartment. Gigi was at our feet, staring hopefully at the table, occasionally sniffing around the carpet in case one of us had dropped a morsel of food. Nicos the nervous butler had just left the room, and the maid was clattering about in the kitchen. It didn't seem an appropriate moment to make such an earth-shattering announcement.

'You look surprised,' she said with a serene smile.

'Well, I am. Absolutely stunned. But you mustn't talk about . . .'

'This apartment will be nice for you and Philippe, far more suitable than that attic of his. And of course I know you will look after my furniture and my precious things.'

'Don't talk like that. You'll be here to look after your own precious things for years and years.'

'But the lawyer will come tomorrow to discuss my will.'

I took a deep breath. 'Well, in that case, I'm sure he'll advise you to leave it within the family – not to me. And quite right too. I mean, I am really touched and honoured, but honestly it isn't the right thing to do. They, your family would hate me, and anyway Philippe and I aren't married. He isn't even divorced, and he's in Geneva, and, well . . . to be honest, I'm not sure how things are between us.'

'I suspected as much.' She stared at me quizzically. 'Does he have another woman?'

'Not that I am aware of.'

'And you? What about Joe? Are you having an affair with him?'

'No.' I hope I managed to sound amused.

'But he has made advances?'

'I hate to be rude, Isabelle, but you go too far,' I said in a level voice.

She cackled. 'Yes, I know, I know. My friends are always telling me that. In your place, I would go to Geneva. Be there with Philippe. A man should never be left on his own. One cannot trust them.'

'You sound like my mother.'

'Well, for once I am in accord with her.'

Isabelle has never met Ma. I've talked about her in the past, but I didn't introduce them when Ma was in Paris. Unlikely to be soul mates, I thought.

'But he doesn't want me in Geneva,' I said.

'Of course he does. Take no notice of his moods. Just appear with your suitcase. Go to the *coiffeur* at my expense, have a facial with Giselle, my beautician, and maybe a full body massage . . . oh, and a session or two on the sunbed. I will buy you a new *ensemble* and, of course, some provocative new lingerie. Philippe will soon find he cannot do without you.'

I laughed. 'Oh dear, I'm not sure that—'

'But I am. I am very sure that you and he will make a charming couple.'

'But you forget he's still married to Françoise.'

Isabelle made a dismissive gesture. 'I shall have a little talk with him about that. In fact, there is no doubt that my new will should encourage him to take action to divorce her. Philippe knows what side his bread is buttered, as you Anglo-Saxons say.'

I tried not to show my irritation. 'Isabelle,' I said firmly, 'I don't wish to quarrel with you when you are being so generous, but please, I do *not* want you to buy Philippe for me. We have to work things out between us one way or the other.'

'Yes, but I find men often need a little nudge in the right direction. And I am so fond of you.'

I softened. 'Look, let's leave money out of it. I will be your friend for as long as I stay in Paris, regardless of Philippe and his family.'

'What do you mean, so long as you stay in Paris? You're not leaving, are you?' she said, with a little frail gasp. I never know if she is manipulating me when she does her old-lady act or whether she has had a genuine twinge in her chest.

I smiled. 'I thought you wanted me to go to Geneva.'

'Just temporarily, my dear, just temporarily. I'm really not sure

I can do without you. Well, maybe I have said enough for the time being.'

It was only a few days later that Philippe suddenly reappeared in Paris. He gave me only two hours' notice, so no time for beauty treatments or shopping sprees to buy exotic underwear. It was more of a question of quickly washing my hair and then blitzing the flat. By the time he arrived, I was red in the face, dishevelled and far from the vision of groomed sensual delight that Isabelle recommended.

'Look, I'm sorry everything's a mess, but let's go out to dinner,' I began in a rush, kissing him rapidly on the cheek. He looked thin and tense, but there was a happy light in his eyes.

'Yes,' he said meekly. 'I have already booked at the Plaza Athénée.'

'Blimey.' I was taken aback. The Plaza Athénée is one of the smartest and most expensive restaurants in Paris.

In a fluster I rummaged around in my wardrobe, finding my best black dress and even going to the huge effort of cleaning my shoes. I also donned the most chic and elegant pieces of jewellery I possess, including, of course, Aunt Isabelle's ring.

Maybe he is going to propose again, I thought with some trepidation. What shall I say? Can I go on and on stalling, or should I be honest with myself and him, and say that I feel I am cooling off, as he had seemed to be? I hope Isabelle hasn't got at him. I bet she has. I bet she's told him that stupid idea about me being her heir.

Philippe has probably mentally redecorated her flat prior to putting it on the market and dumping off her junk and selling the rest. He's probably priced all her fine furniture and written up the auctioneer's catalogue himself.

While I was thinking these wild thoughts, I stared in the mirror. After all that panic-stricken housework my hair, which I hadn't bothered to blow-dry, was sticking out like a bottlebrush. Not smart enough for the Plaza A, so I damped it down and began again. By which time we were late in starting, but Philippe was remarkably calm about my shilly-shallying. In fact, he poured me a glass of wine to drink while I was changing and could hardly have been more gentlemanly.

★   ★   ★

The restaurant was fantastically elegant with its tall ceilings and carefully spaced silver-laden tables with their starched pale pink tablecloths. What soft, glowing luxury! Squadrons of waiters lined the room, all ultra polite, smiling and solicitous.

'Look at that lovely garden out there – must be gorgeous in summer,' I said.

Philippe, handsome in a dark suit and pale cream shirt, agreed with me. His Geneva haircut, shorter than usual, was quite becoming, I told him.

He smiled. Blinking through his designer specs, he looked tired, I thought.

The menu was tall, wide and elaborate.

'Choose anything you want,' said Philippe with astonishing generosity. An unworthy thought entered my head: maybe Isabelle was paying for this meal. She must be. Out of professional curiosity I'd checked quickly in *The Michelin Guide* before we left. At the moment they are giving this restaurant the top three stars, plus five crosses, red ones. (Stars apply to the food of course, crossed spoons and forks apply to the comfort level, and red print as opposed to ordinary black means extra *agréable*, or pretty.) Moreover the restaurant is situated in a top-rank mega-pricey hotel in Avenue Montaigne, one of the smartest streets in Paris. Had Philippe won the lottery or what?

My journalistic persona decided to make mental notes for BB. He'll be thrilled to get a report from a place like this without having to pay a bean.

Despite his rich-man-of-the-world act, Philippe blanched a little as he studied the wine list. Tactfully I said I didn't fancy an aperitif.

With a discreet flourish two waiters presented each of us simultaneously with plates of delicious, melt-in-the-mouth *amuse-bouches*. Another low, unladylike thought popped into my head: if Aunt Isabelle isn't treating us, maybe Philippe is putting me on his expense account or entertainment allowance. Either way, I wasn't grumbling, but I was surprised he felt he needed to impress me after all this time.

The special 'Bounty of the Sea' menu didn't seem to be any more expensive than anything else, so I chose that, beginning with *langoustines rafraîchies*, after a second round of lighter-than-air *amuse-bouches*. I don't know what had refreshed the langoustines, but they tasted marvellous.

The wine was delicious, the food was out of this world, and I would have felt like a million dollars if twinges of guilt hadn't attacked me from time to time. What were we doing here? Philippe looked very much like a man with something on his mind. I prepared myself. I must be tactful. What was he going to say?

Savouring its sublime sauce, I had just put the last forkful of perfectly poached turbot into my mouth when I found out.

Across the starched tablecloth Philippe inched his hand towards me. 'In effect, Clio, I must ask you to release me from our engagement.'

Speechless, I stared at his familiar face.

He sighed heavily. 'Because I have become involved with someone else.'

Still silent, I gazed at him, my heart pounding. He's had a rapprochement with Françoise. I knew it. That time in Geneva, she was there, in her black mackintosh.

'And this person is pregnant, therefore it is my duty to marry her,' he said, attempting to sound doleful but clearly pleased as punch.

I was utterly astonished.

Unlikely to be Françoise, then. Wild emotions were swirling round my brain: hurt pride, anger, no, fury at being deceived, but underneath it all I felt a surge of freedom, which was quickly replaced by a feeling of panic. Where shall I go? What shall I do? I was being dumped. Thrown out. Oh my God.

'Congratulations. That's lovely. And who is the mother-to-be?' I asked, quite proud of my attempt at cool sophistication in the middle of the maelstrom.

He took a large swig of his wine. A waiter materialized and discreetly refilled his glass, while another whisked away our plates.

'Virginia,' he said. 'She's been staying with me in Geneva from time to time.'

I choked. 'Virginia?'

That was one revelation too many. I leapt up. An attentive waiter pulled back my chair before it fell to the ground – what a faux pas that would have been. After an embarrassing grovel around on the floor for my handbag, I found it sitting on the spare chair, where I'd plonked it when we arrived. The waiter was trying to help me again. I wish he would get out of the bloody way.

For a moment I stood glaring at Philippe. Then without a word I swept out. If ever there was a moment for a sudden exit, that was it, I reckoned. I'd never made such a dramatic gesture in my life. Rather few people storm out of the Plaza Athénée before they have eaten their three-star gourmet dessert.

An ultra-polite Frenchman at the desk called me a taxi, which appeared in a flash, and little more than ten head-whirling minutes later I was at home, grappling in the back of the cupboard for my suitcase.

Of course, unlike what happens in films on these occasions, I soon realized that it was going to take an age to sort out all my stuff and decide what to take with me wherever I was going. Where was I going?

I really couldn't face staying in a hotel and it was too late to ring Mary. Worse, Virginia might be there – that is, if she wasn't languishing cosily in Geneva – and I certainly didn't want to see her until I'd worked out exactly what I was going to say: scornful, withering phrases that would, I hope, turn her into a gibbering wreck. At least for a nanosecond.

Decamping to Isabelle's was a possibility, but I couldn't face her either. Of course, there were single girlfriends who'd take me in, but they might be having mad, passionate sex with a new lover. Even if they weren't, I didn't want to talk about my situation with anyone just yet.

I solved the problem by dumping my half-packed case by the front door to demonstrate my intentions, and then, gathering up my nightgear, I dived into Alex's room, where I jammed a chair inexpertly under the door handle.

I heard Philippe's key in the lock about half an hour later. So he had solemnly sat at the restaurant and finished his three-star meal, complete with coffee and petits fours, no doubt. Bastard. Greedy duplicitous bastard.

He came upstairs immediately. 'Clio?'

I didn't answer.

A knock. 'May one come in?'

'No.'

'I'm sorry.' After a silence he continued from behind the door, 'I still care for you, but now there is the baby to consider, a new small life.'

He seemed to be trying to make himself sound virtuous, almost religious.

'There's nothing further to say, Philippe.' I couldn't manage a sob because I was too angry. I wasn't proud of this jealousy. I should be glad Virginia had stolen him because I'd been telling myself for months that I was unsure, that I didn't really want to marry him, that I should leave. Not because of Joe, because Joe wasn't serious. He hadn't been in contact for ages.

A truly wild thought entered my head. Could Virginia be carrying Joe's child, or Paolo's, and palming it off as Philippe's?

No, that wasn't her style at all. This crisis, being dumped, was addling my brain. Maybe I wanted to be the one to do the dumping or maybe, and this was the truth of it, I was just afraid of the big, wide single world out there.

'One should talk about the future in the morning,' he said. 'I shall be here a few days before I return to Geneva.'

'I'm leaving tomorrow.'

'But where are you going? I told Virginia she must allow you a month before she moved herself in here. Of course she will live part of the time in Geneva, but we both feel it essential the baby be born in France, so it is preferable that she should have her antenatal check-ups here.'

Bloody hell. I went hot and cold at the thought of Virginia living in this flat, hanging her clothes in my cupboard, putting her knickers – if she wore them – in my drawers and, of course, sleeping in my bed.

'So you are giving me a month's notice. How thoughtful,' I said, my voice heavy with sarcasm.

'I think it is always wise to be civilized about these matters. I hope we shall always be friends, Clio. And that you will bring Alex to see us from time to time.'

Us? Words failed me.

'I hope that you will remain in Paris,' he continued smoothly, still out of sight.

The door handle rattled. To my dismay, the chair I'd wedged

tilted sideways and then fell over. Philippe stood in the threshold staring at me. I hugged my arms across my chest. Having taken off my too-tight black dress, I was in my nightie, a non-transparent one but still vaguely alluring and not the kind of thing one should be wearing on an occasion like this.

'Clio, you are a beautiful woman,' he said soupily. 'And a very desirable one.' He took another step forward. 'I still . . . I still want you. We should make love tonight, for old times' sake.'

I glared at him in disgust. 'You must be out of your mind.'

'Are you saying no?'

'Too bloody right.'

'Well, I shall be here for a few days. And if you should ever feel differently . . .'

'In your dreams, buddy boy.'

Confused by the expression, he looked up with an optimistic gleam in his eye. 'What does that mean?'

I couldn't believe he hadn't got the message. 'It means, Philippe, that I will never, *ever* in any circumstances sleep with you again. And, like I said, I'm leaving tomorrow. First thing.'

'But where will you go?'

'None of your bloody business. Now please get out of my room.'

As if he was afraid I might bash him on the head, he backed off, shutting the door smartly behind him.

I paced around, thinking it all over. Not such a problem, very good for me, really. I shall have to pull myself together and find a new life. Without men, of course. Independent and strong. Which will be totally and utterly *fine.*

A small ray of sunshine shone on my dark mood. Camille would absolutely loathe her new daughter-in-law to be.

Twenty-Four

The one-bedroomed unfurnished flat in the seventeenth arrondissement was the size of a shoebox and decorated throughout in mud-brown, but I was lucky to find somewhere within reasonable travelling distance of my old haunts, except this time north of the Arc de Triomphe, instead of the much more fashionable and desirable southern and eastern areas. It was only about forty-five minutes' walk from Philippe's, but I never went anywhere near him these days, of course.

I couldn't do much about the gloomy street and the dingy entrance hall, but I was able to get rid of the pervading brownness in the apartment by painting everything a tasteful off-white. I loathe decorating and always get paint all over myself and everything else, but needs must, as Ma would say. I had to get it ready before Alex returned for the Easter holidays.

I acquired some dodgy, ill-matched second-hand furniture, and Mary gave me some old curtains of hers – a rather scary pattern, but who cares? – and lent me her sewing machine to alter them. Everything was done as cheaply as possible except for my bed and the sofa bed for Alex. These were a huge investment and the only new items I purchased. My emergency nest egg suddenly came into its own – and I congratulated myself grimly on my foresight – but my savings had now dwindled to the point of no return.

I was in pretty low spirits at the time, but the dramas of house-moving took my mind off my problems, and after Philippe's strict views on decor, I enjoyed being able to make my own decisions about the new flat, and my own decisions about everything else for that matter. Of course it would have been more fun if I hadn't had to decorate at breakneck speed on a budget. The final result was not exactly designer-coordinated – think hotchpotch-cum-junk shop – but I reckoned I could gradually improve it once I earned some money. My regular payment from BB just about covered the rent plus subsistence-level food, so in order to pay

for the phone or treats, or eat anything much more exotic than
spag bol, I'd have to do well with my tour-guiding or sell some
extra travel articles or something. Harry was still coughing up
child-support money, thank heavens. I suppose I could ask him
for more, since when Alex is here, he eats like about five horses,
but I didn't want to involve Harry further in my life.

Independence was the name of my new game.

It was weird and lonely being single again, at my age. No man
bossing me about, no man in my bed. I admit I missed sex and
a warm body snoring next to me at night. One or two married
Frenchmen made discreet passes, which I smartly discouraged.
Definitely not the direction I wanted to go, though it was faintly
cheering someone, anyone fancied me.

As for the wives, I found I had fewer friends than I thought.
I just wasn't invited out as much as before by couples. Now that
I was blokeless, I had been excluded from their circles. Never
mind – the people who mattered stuck by me, people like Mary
and Aunt Isabelle, and bachelor girlfriends made a kind effort to
welcome me back to the singles world. Singles world? The whole
idea of it gave me a strange sick feeling. I was just too insecure
and, let's face it, too old to start again with all that jazz. Anyway,
I obviously wasn't any good at Relationships with a capital R.

Fortunately I didn't have much time to brood about my lack
of social life as I had to concentrate on making money. The tour-
guide business was still frighteningly slack, with few bookings for
the new season. I was worried that, despite Joe's assurances, Neil
had somehow damaged my chances by spreading rumours and
complaints about me. To drum up some more clients, I emailed
all last year's Canadians asking them to recommend me to their
friends. And of course I also sent all my friends and acquain-
tances a change-of-address card. Including Joe.

He mailed back with a list of new tourist clients, a very short
list, but better than none at all. At first I couldn't make out
whether he realized I'd left Philippe or not. Since my mail merely
stated a change of address, nothing else, Joe could have presumed
that Philippe and I had moved together, or that I'd hired new
office space. But then, blinking, I read Joe's postscript: 'By the
way, congratulations on the baby.'

I flinched. Bloody insensitive. Not funny at all. Miss Manners

would not recommend sending a dumpee congratulations on her
ex-fiancé's new girlfriend's pregnancy. I suppose he must have
heard it on the grapevine, or more likely the Virginia creeper,
come to think of it.

Joe did not suggest resuming our non-relationship. He couldn't
have made it much clearer that he was no longer interested in
me. That suited me just fine. I was far too busy earning my daily
bread to bother about men.

Especially Joe.

Quickly I typed a not-altogether-truthful email:

> Hi, Joe,
>
> I'm busy with my journalism, and my travel business is
> picking up now. Clients from last year have recommended
> me to friends, so I don't need any more input from you.
> I'm very grateful for your help in the past, but I'd rather
> be completely independent now. So no need for you to
> bother with the hassle of roping in tourists for me. In fact,
> we won't need to contact each other again. Anyway, many
> thanks for everything.
>
> Regards,
> Clio

I sent it off there and then.

He did not reply. Which again was fine by me. If only I didn't
lie awake thinking about him half the night, I'd be perfectly happy.
Time heals all wounds, as my mother would say. And she's always
right in the end. But the wounds hurt like hell at the moment.

In need of a small gesture of revenge, I'd written to sack Virginia
from my agency, but I didn't know how I was going to juggle
Alex and tourist clients without her. Fortunately Mary had offered
to help when she could. Apparently she was gradually dropping
out of Insider Tours these days, as Elaine was in a major tizzy
due to reorganization at the top and didn't seem to know her
arse from her elbow, not that the ladylike Mary put it that way,
of course.

I was also worried about how Alex was going to react to not
having a room of his own, not having any space at all, in fact.
At least this flat was in a safe area and pretty central. I might

have found something bigger further out of Paris, but I couldn't face being sad and lonely in the suburbs.

I'd written to Alex about the drama and we'd had a long phone call. I couldn't make out how upset he was that I'd left Philippe. Not very, according to Samantha, who had taken him out to lunch. But who can tell with a child of that age? I thought he might mind rather a lot, but I had planned a surprise. Just before he returned for Easter, I was going to buy us a kitten or preferably a young house-trained cat. That was one advantage of getting rid of men: one can do what one likes.

She is gorgeous, the cat. She's marmalade with a white chest, and I've named her Simba. She doesn't look much like a lion, but it seems to suit her huntress personality. I'm very fond of her already, and as for Alex, it will be love at first sight, I know. It was Marie-Clementine who acquired her for me from a neighbour in Saint-Cloud.

Surprisingly Marie-Clementine has come up trumps since Philippe and I split. She has even offered to help look after Alex in the holidays. We met for lunch one day and discussed, in veiled terms, our mutual disapproval of Virginia. Her only advantage, according to Marie-C, is that she is 'of good family'.

'What does your mother think of her?' I asked, against my better judgement.

'My mother sees virtue in Virginia,' said Marie-Clementine sanctimoniously. Then she grinned. 'But she iz not sure where.'

Aunt Isabelle seemed devastated by the turn of events and spoke of cutting off Philippe without a sou, but she admitted that Virginia's ace, her unborn child, would win every trick, making her position pretty well impregnable.

'Anyway, I don't mind. Basically it was already over between Philippe and me,' I told Isabelle endlessly, but she wasn't convinced.

'You won't leave me, will you?' she begged. 'You won't leave France?'

'No, no, I love it here,' I said, unwilling to expand on my financial problems in case she thought I was asking for help. 'But I feel you should have this back. It's a family ring, after all,' and I produced from my pocket the box containing the pink sapphire.

She was most upset. 'No, no, it is yours. It was for you. The ring was a present to me from Monsieur, the great love of my life, nothing to do with the family, so naturally I was free to dispose of it as I please and it pleases me that you should keep it in memory of me. You can give it to the eventual wife of Alexander if you approve of her. If not, then leave it to a cats' home.' She cackled. 'But of course since you love that boy so much, you will detest his wife, therefore it is likely the cats will be in luck.'

Smiling, I let that one pass, and thanked her profusely for the ring.

Me, jealous of Alex's future wife? Ridiculous. On second thoughts, if by any remote chance I am jealous, I'm damn well not going to show it. I don't want to turn into Camille.

Isabelle cleared her throat and then went on in that pragmatic French way to tell me that she could not after all leave her money to me, now that I was not to be of the family. In fact, she had more or less decided on Marie-Clementine as her heir, or maybe she would divide it equally between the nieces. Either way, Philippe was Out.

I smiled and said it was for the best, that I'd never wanted or expected anything. She looked relieved, I thought.

Having disposed of business, she then said, 'You should take another lover. That would be the best thing.'

'No, that would be the worst thing,' I said. 'I'm far too busy.'

'In your place, then, I would select a man happily married to a dull woman. An arrangement such as that guarantees delightfully exciting romantic encounters that can continue for years and years, all without having to wash socks, or entertain tiresome business colleagues.'

Followed by a lonely old age, but of course I didn't voice that thought aloud.

Suddenly she said, 'Joe resides in Canada, I presume?'

'Yes, why do you mention him?'

A strange expression flitted across her face. Then she turned to stare out of the window. 'No reason, except that it is such a long way away, Canada. I wondered if you will see him again.'

'Definitely not,' I said grimly.

She seemed on the point of saying something. Then she

shrugged her shoulders and murmured, 'These brief *affaires* of the heart.'

'It was not an affair,' I snapped. Then before she could wring any more confessions out of me, I changed the subject and talked about the cat. I was explaining that, with Gigi's dislike of the feline world, I would be unable to have the dog to stay in future. Much as I love Gigi, I didn't fancy the thought of her leaping around my micro-mini apartment while the cat was cowering on the curtain rail.

Aunt Isabelle launched into a friendly diatribe against cats and, laughing, we agreed to differ. It's funny how minor differences of opinion with friends don't matter, whereas if I'd been having the same discussion with Camille, I'd probably be in a rage by now. I said as much to Isabelle.

She sighed. 'But one would love to be a fly on the wall during the encounters between Virginia and Camille. I shall invite myself to lunch with my sister so I may report on the scene.'

'Don't bother,' I said firmly. 'I don't mind if I never hear another word about Virginia – I don't care two hoots.'

Not entirely true, I thought, once I was back at home. I minded about Virginia's betrayal just as much as Philippe's. I've always worked on the principle that my girlfriends' husbands and partners were totally out of bounds, and I naively believed that, despite her vampish pose, Virginia and I had the same ideas on that one. Of course she did shag Joe, but Joe was not and never had been my official man. It hadn't occurred to me that she'd make a play for Philippe.

It was months before I discovered she did have a conscience and that Camille was right. There was some good in Virginia after all.

Twenty-Five

Meanwhile my financial situation was becoming precarious. The few Canadian clients who'd booked began to cancel their reservations. Whether this was due to Neil in particular – he must want some kind of revenge – or to the general fear of international terrorism, I don't know. It dawned on me that unless I could find tourists from another source, my business was going to stumble to a halt. I tried advertising in the UK, but the market there had been cornered by several specialist companies. I even applied for a part-time job with one or two of these, but they said snootily that they preferred to employ ex-army officers, people with genuine battle-field experience. I've fought plenty of battles, I thought wearily.

As for French companies, I attended a few scary and humiliating interviews, but inevitably they only wanted new guides who were prepared to work full-time during weekends and school holidays. No good. I had to think of Alex.

He did his best to be nice about the flat when he arrived for Easter, but I could see he was dismayed about our new lifestyle. He adored the kitten, of course, but even animal-loving Alex couldn't play with Simba all day. Between researching for travel articles, I found myself pressed to entertain him without Philippe to help with the masculine stuff. Last holidays was tricky enough, but now all of a sudden Alex has become too sophisticated for what he considers childish pursuits and it's difficult for a foreigner to play sport in Paris on a limited budget. Again we went to the cinema, we bowled, we window-shopped, and Mary and Marie-Clementine helped as promised, but it was not the easiest of holidays. I felt he was too young to roam the streets with his friends, and even roaming costs something.

We didn't actually quarrel about money, but I could see Alex thought I was being strict and prim on occasions.

'There's no Pepsi. Shall I go to the supermarket?' he'd offer.

'No, darling, we can't really afford fizzy. D'you mind just having water?'

'Oh, OK.' He wasn't overtly grumpy, but now and then my sensitive antennae caught a whiff of grumpiness held in check, especially when he pointed out that I still drink wine.

'It's cheaper than Coca-Cola in France,' I said gaily. But he did have a point.

We had a predictable dispute about designer trainers, which ended in Alex saying that if I wouldn't buy the latest (ludicrously overpriced) model, then he would just have to ask Samantha, but really it was a waste because they were much cheaper in France.

Then the car broke down, which put me in a terrible tizz. I can barely afford to run it as it is. 'Harry's just bought a new Audi,' Alex said tactlessly when he heard me arguing with the garage about the bill, a sum that would probably fund a Third World village for a year.

I wondered how I was going to cope in the summer without going to the seaside. My conscience told me Alex might have a better holiday if he spent more time with Harry and Samantha, but that would be an unbearable sacrifice for me.

As for the delicate matter of Philippe, I did tentatively broach the subject. 'About Philippe, he and I, as I said when I phoned you, well, we decided we didn't want to stay together. You mustn't think that it was anything to do with you. He'd really like to see you.'

'Oh.'

'It's just that he likes Virginia better than me and that's the way it is.'

'Oh.'

'I mean, you like Virginia too, I know. Do you want to pop in and see them sometime?'

'Not really.'

After a pause he said, 'I think I want it to be just us, Mum. It's . . . I get confused if there is someone and then he goes. I thought I wouldn't mind because it happens to lots of other boys at school, but I do mind, a bit.'

Full of guilt, I hugged him. 'OK, just us. Us against the world.' He was absolutely right.

Soon after he returned to school, disaster struck.

BB rang to say he was deeply saddened but he was gonna have

to sell or close down *French Fantasia*, the dear little magazine that paid me my daily bread. He had to have an urgent heart operation, a bypass in fact. He would give me a month's salary in lieu of notice.

Only a month's pay? Horrors. I pulled myself together. 'BB, I am so sorry to hear about your operation.'

'I too, my dear.'

'When is it?'

'Tooesday next. My time is nigh,' he added darkly.

Did I mention BB had a poetic streak?

So I wished him the very best, and then I asked him why he couldn't go on with the mag once he'd recovered. I could probably edit it myself for a month or two.

'I have promised my dear wife I will give up all stressful activity. It's sad for my beloved readers, but she is very firm on this one.'

'But, BB—'

'My mind is made up.'

A wild impulse popped into my normally cautious and unbusiness-minded head. 'Maybe I could buy the magazine from you.'

'Gee, I don't know. I was kind of negotiating with a big publishing company who want to amalgamate it with another journal.'

'But I would keep *French Fantasia* more or less the way it is. The same sort of articles.' But with a little less poetry, I thought.

'It's an idea. Well, of course, you wouldn't be able to give the same polish I do, but you are a kind of nice little writer. I'll talk to Arlene and get back to you.'

He came back with $20,000. Of course I didn't have $200, let $20,000 and told him so.

'OK, honey. But I have been offered much more than that by these big publishing guys who want my circulation list. I fear Arlene will demand I take it.'

Yikes. 'BB, look, I'll think about it.'

'Think quickly because the sands of time run swiftly.'

Madame Claude was elderly but sharp-eyed and chic in the inevitable black. I held my breath as she scrutinized Aunt Isabelle's ring with one of those funny little spyglasses that jewellers stick in their eye. I felt sick and traitorous even being here. I was

attempting to sell a close friend's present. How could I ever face
her again? And yet there seemed no alternative. I had to pay the
rent, I had to eat, and *French Fantasia* should provide me with
the regular means to do so. That was what I was counting on.

I prayed that Madame Claude, one of the gem dealers that
Isabelle used to frequent, wouldn't recognize me or, for that
matter, the ring. It was crazy to come here and yet I couldn't
just walk into any jewellers to sell it in case I was cheated. I'd
probably be cheated, anyway.

Madame Claude cleared her throat and smiled like a weasel
about to bite into a rabbit's throat. 'Does madame want to know
the price in US dollars or in euros?'

'Euros,' I said haughtily in French. 'I am not American.'

She looked down her sharp nose at me. I returned her gaze
as steadily as I could. Even shoe sales staff condescend in Paris,
so Madame Claude, as the owner of a serious jewellery store, was
doubly intimidating.

I felt she was about to call the police, to question if I was the
rightful owner of the ring. Perhaps I shouldn't sell it after all.
Maybe I should find the money from another source, but what
source?

After a long silence she drawled, 'One might offer twelve thousand euros.'

Digging my fingers into my palms, I blurted out, 'But, madame,
it's antique, of course, and it's been valued at more than twice
that.'

'Twice? The valuation for insurance is not the same as the
selling price, madame,' she explained slowly as if to an educa-
tionally subnormal child.

'I know, but . . . if that is all it's worth, then I shall not sell it.'

She scrutinized me again, no doubt assessing my badly concealed
state of desperation. Then she picked up the ring and said, 'I will
consult my colleague. If you return tomorrow morning, I will inform
you of our final decision.'

I didn't want to wait until tomorrow, but what alternative did
I have? Meekly I agreed.

I was awake all night worrying as to whether or not I was
doing the right thing. My choices were limited. It seemed I had
to buy *French Fantasia*, starve or go home to Mother. Come to

think of it, they probably didn't accept people of my age in Ma's retirement complex, let alone children.

There wasn't time for me to borrow the money via a bank loan, always assuming a French bank would give me one. I couldn't ask Harry for the money, and I certainly couldn't ask Isabelle. So to raise funds quickly, selling the ring seemed the obvious thing to do, particularly as I couldn't afford to insure it.

Next day Madame Claude informed me, even more haughtily, that her partner would offer €13,000 for the ring, so, full of guilt, I accepted on the spot. To buy BB out, I might have to go into the red for the balance, but I was becoming braver about financial matters these days.

I phoned BB that weekend before the Tuesday deadline and then again, in a last-minute panic, on the Monday to say the money was on its way. Exhausting faxes flew to and fro, followed by excruciatingly complicated arrangements about cash transfers to America, which took hours of hanging around in the bank making polite noises to officious clerks. BB said he could not email the magazine circulation list or sign the final documents of sale until he received the money. Not very trusting for an elderly Southern gentleman, I thought, but I guess he had Arlene's best interests at heart.

Agonizingly, by the day of his operation I still hadn't received any kind of confirmation from him that the deal was going through. I phoned and left a message with Arlene to wish him all the medical best, but she didn't reply. I couldn't ring again and say, 'What about the contract?' when her husband was under the knife, so I faxed him a get-well-soon card and hoped for the best.

Though we've only met once face to face, I really was worried about the poor old boy – I'm not entirely self-centred.

Three whole days after the operation, Arlene called to say that BB had come through OK but was very weak. I listened to all she had to say on the subject and sympathized – genuinely – with her every word. Then finally desperate, I forced myself to say I was sorry to talk business at this difficult time but I just wanted to be sure BB had received my money for the magazine, as the bank here assured me he had. Was I to go ahead and edit the next issue, one way or another?

At that Arlene became understandably upset and said tearfully she just didn't know and we left it at that. I decided I had better assemble a mag even if it never saw the light of day. I hadn't experimented with the desktop publishing program on my computer before and it turned out to be a devil. Either that or my ancient laptop was frightened of it because it kept freezing or shutting down. I cursed the machine, the program and myself, deciding that old BB must have more skills than I credited him with. It was all taking much more time than I had anticipated.

During that fingernail-biting week I managed to sell two articles to London magazines, so all this desperation and hard work were good for me. Not that the pay was that great, but it might keep me alive when or if the cheques eventually arrived.

Finally I heard from BB.

He emailed:

> Clio,
>
> I have survived. But my brush with death has made me realize I wish to leave a small mark on the world. Arlene, my dear beloved wife, agrees that you, Clio, rather than big business, should take over the helm of my little barque and sail away with it. *French Fantasia* is sold to you with our blessing. But you must include the phrase 'founded by Batsford Berryman' in every issue. Legal documents follow.
>
> *Bon voyage.*

Phew. Clio survives again. To flog BB's metaphor still further, I was still afloat, just, but there were some heavy seas to navigate.

Twenty-Six

It was hard work, but *French Fantasia* sailed, or rather chugged on with a few near capsizes, and most of the subscribers stayed with me. I was still keen to sell more articles to the British magazine and newspaper market and I'd managed to achieve one decent commission. Just after the Easter holidays, I was slaving away researching details for this boringly detailed and factual piece about the forthcoming attractions in Paris when out of the blue I received an email from Joe.

Holding my breath, I stared at his name on the screen. Then slowly I read his matter-of-fact message about a new client who wanted an instant two-day tour. Was I free?

I ought to have said, 'Don't bother, Joe. I'm not speaking to you,' but I needed the money and I far prefer getting out and about to typing about prices for concerts and exhibition opening hours. Maybe this client would recommend me to others and give the kiss of life to my guiding business. After a pretty short struggle with myself, I swallowed my pride and accepted the assignment in a brief, businesslike manner.

The new client wanted to be picked up at a country house somewhere near Chantilly, which was a bore because I always seem to get lost when I go there, shades of my first trip with Melvin and Kay. Fortunately I didn't have to collect him until noon, so there was some chance I would be on time.

Joe had given me the directions via email and they seemed pretty obscure. I was hoping to find myself somewhere near the chateau or the racecourse, but no, I was deep in surprisingly rural roads miles from anywhere I recognized.

I kept glancing down at the directions: left, then right, yew hedge, iron railings, green gate, another larger entrance, no name, but small lodge with blue door. Hurray. At last. As I drove through, the gates closed automatically behind me. With some trepidation I manoeuvred slowly down the long drive. What if this wasn't the right place? Would some grand French landowner set his Dobermanns on me?

To my relief, when I turned the corner by an old cedar tree I saw a medium-sized house rather than a huge chateau. Maybe six bedrooms, I reckoned, though there might be other rooms in the attic. Surprisingly far south for its Normandy style, the villa had a black timber frame and white rendering, with pointed gables and dormer windows in the roof – an attractive mishmash. Large informal gardens swept down to a stream at the bottom of the hill. The owners must be English, I decided, to have created such a garden. The spring flowers were flourishing in wild drifts, quite different from French plants, which have to mind their Ps and Qs in neat straight rows.

I rang the iron bell-pull beside the massive door. No answer. Hell, I've come to the wrong place. I knew it.

Footsteps scrunched on the gravel behind me. I spun round.

'Hi there, Ms Tour Guide.'

I flushed. 'Joe! What are you doing here?' I looked wildly about. 'Where's the client?'

Unbelievable. There he was, his eyes twinkling down at me as if nothing had ever gone wrong between us. I tried to glare at him, but my mouth kept smiling.

'The client had to go. He's thinking of buying this house and he wants your professional opinion.'

My brain cleared momentarily. Professional. Right. I can do professional if I want. I took out my notebook. 'Oh, I see. He wants to develop it as a hotel or something, does he?'

'Something like that. Or maybe just a family home.'

'Well, looks pretty big for a family home. Is he rich, this client? He needs to be. Look at this garden, swimming pool, tennis court. Quite a lot of work. What are those outbuildings over there?'

'Stables, or used to be.'

'Well, if he wants to go the whole hog, he could convert the stables into hotel bedrooms, but he needs an opinion from an architect or a surveyor, not me. If he doesn't, there are all kinds of grants you can get from the French government to preserve old houses as long as you open them to the public now and then. Or he could just have a few rooms for guests on a bed-and-breakfast basis as *chambres d'hôte*. I really don't know a huge amount about it except from the consumer point of view. Often it's good value staying in a chateau. Some can be pretty damp and awful, but some can be lovely. You have to be careful which you choose. Not that this is exactly a chateau.' I paused for breath and saw that Joe seemed to be laughing at me. 'Am I talking too much?' I enquired lamely.

'Not at all. I love the way you talk.'

Hm, I thought. Might be hard to stay cross with him.

'D'you wanna see round the house?' he asked. 'You're not too tired, are you?'

'Of course not. Why should I be?'

'Lovely.' I kept gasping at every room in a star-struck fashion. Whoever was selling the place had wonderful taste. Either that or the house had just grown around them. Here on the outskirts of Paris, they'd achieved English country-house charm, with worn, comfortable sofas, tatty Persian rugs and old chintz curtains, with good but equally faded antique furniture that looks as if it had never been near a showroom. Formal-cosy-decaying-muddle, I call the style – a kind of shabby-chic – and I love it. It all sat well in the French setting with the wooden floors and stone fireplaces, magnificent panelling and fine plaster-work.

'The guy who buys it, tell him not to change a thing,' I gushed. 'Hotel guests would adore it. Anyone would. I certainly do.'

He smiled down at me. 'Good. How about a glass of champagne?'

'Don't they mind, the owners?'

'No, no, they're not here. They're friends, anyway. I'm borrowing it.'

'Right,' I said. 'Well, a small glass.'

'Of course. I guess you have to be careful.'

'Yes, I'm driving . . . But what about this tour? Is the client coming tomorrow or what?'

'Not sure,' said Joe.

Damn, I thought. Maybe another fee down the drain. Never mind. It was a great house and interesting to see round it. And, I admit, very nice to see Joe. Even though I'm not speaking to him.

The central heating wasn't bad, but he insisted on lighting a fire in the drawing room. Presumptuous, I thought, but then his friends probably wouldn't mind.

I followed him through to have another look at the kitchen, which was untidy but full of higgledy-piggledy charm too. Except that the stove was modern and there were other touches to show that a serious cook wouldn't be unhappy there. Pity it would have to be brought up to date with wall-to-wall stainless steel if the place were converted into a hotel.

'Shall we eat lunch in here?' he suggested.

I don't know why this simple invitation sounded so erotic.

'Lunch?'

'Sure, sit down and talk to me while I cook. Are you OK about food at the moment?'

Strange thing to say. 'Lovely, yes. Gave up my diet ages ago, I'm afraid.'

'Of course you did. Are you OK? You still look surprisingly slim, all things considered. Maybe I got the timing wrong,' he said.

What did he mean? I smiled anyway. 'Thanks for those few kind words.'

He turned to the stove and rattled pans around. This was a new side to his character. Joe the chef. Actually, all he cooked were two fillet steaks and some pasta, making a glorious mess in the process. I didn't like to interfere.

I was about to say, 'Men who cook are very sexy,' but then thought better of it. Actually, I find Joe sexy whatever he does. Today he'd rolled up his sleeves and his arms were still faintly tanned.

Very nice arms.

'Plates and stuff over there,' he said, indicating the dresser. Pulling myself together, I found some white china and laid the table, enjoying the domesticity.

He plonked the blackened steak, plus a salad and some soggy-looking pasta in front of me, and then produced a bottle of red wine.

'Joe, I'm driving. I really can't drink any more.'

'OK, I understand. You're right to be careful. But you don't have to rush back, do you? Stay for dinner. I'll take you to a restaurant.' He took a mouthful of pasta. 'Sorry, I'm not a terrific cook, but it's normally kind of better than this.'

'But . . .'

'Eat your steak before it gets cold. It may be kind of overdone too. Something distracted me, I guess.'

Suddenly I couldn't eat a thing. What the hell was I doing here with Joe? This was totally nuts.

I stood up. 'You know, I really think I should be getting back.'

'Don't go,' he said softly, a flirtatious edge to his voice.

I caught my breath.

Help. It must be the champagne. Or the way he was looking at me.

'I mean, what are you doing here, anyway?' I blurted out. 'Why aren't you in Canada or London or somewhere? That's the thing about you. You're always somewhere else.'

'Like I said, I am, or was, an international sort of guy, with business to do all over. But I've kind of tied up most of the loose ends now. Reckon I've done with travelling.'

'Right, so what are you doing here in France?' I asked again.

'Came to see you, of course.'

I flushed. 'Why now? Why now after all this time?'

'Just before I contacted you last time, Virginia sent me a two-line mail. She said she forgot to tell me you and Philippe had broken up and that she'd kind of taken him over.'

Polite way of phrasing it, I thought. 'I see. But you already knew all that.'

He looked puzzled. 'No, I didn't. So what happened?'

'But you knew,' I repeated.

'Knew what? I don't know anything.'

Is he thick or what?

I shook my head. 'I'm confused. OK. Well, to cut a long story short, Virginia had an affair with Philippe and got pregnant, so he decided to marry her instead of me. I didn't mind too much.' I was quite proud of how calm I sounded.

'Hey, *Virginia* is pregnant too. So you both are. That's incredible.' A grim expression flitted across his face. 'Philippe must be even more of a bastard than I thought. I just don't know how he could treat you that way.'

I stared at him. 'No, no, it's just Virginia. *I'm* not pregnant. Never have been. Apart from Alex, of course.'

He sat back, scraping his chair loudly on the kitchen floor. 'Say that again – you're *not* having a baby?'

'No, of course not. Why did you think I was . . . ?'

'That old French lady, Aunt Isabelle, she told me.'

My jaw dropped. 'When?'

'Last time I saw you.'

'You mean that night she had a fall and you disappeared in a puff of smoke, without even saying goodbye?'

'Sorry. I was angry, mad as a snake, and as jealous, I guess, very jealous.' He was watching me, his eyes fixed on my face.

'Were you?' I exhaled slowly.

'Of course I was. You'd decided to have a child with Philippe, and you didn't even have the courtesy to mention it to me. Not a damn word.'

There was a silence. Then I said, 'Bloody Aunt Isabelle. What the hell was she playing at?'

'Maybe she wanted to warn me off. If so, she did a great job.'

I stared at my steak, which was now congealing on the plate. Then a thought crystallized in my mind. 'So if you were under the impression I was expecting his child, why did you come to Paris? Why did you invite me here?'

'When I heard you'd split with him, I thought you'd need someone to take care of you and the baby, so I came to find you,' he said tenderly.

Flushing, I gazed at him in wonder. 'Joe . . .'

Then I was in his arms and we were kissing and laughing and I was half crying in a stupid sentimental manner because no man had ever done or said such a lovely, amazing thing before.

I don't remember how we found ourselves upstairs in one of the grand bedrooms. I remember protesting half-heartedly that the owners might return, but he silenced me by beginning to undress me and kissing every part of me that he undressed with a loving, desperate haste. All the time he was telling me that I was beautiful and desirable and that he had wanted me for so long.

And I was kissing him too and pulling back the heavy bedspread as we sank down together on to the blank white sheets.

It was a miracle. I was full of joy and happiness and lust, with a man who felt exactly the same. I can't tell why it was so utterly fantastic, this love-making with Joe. Maybe it was because I'd been crazy about him for ages – a fact that I now rashly admitted to him, whispering in his ear between kisses. Maybe it was his passionate generosity, his patience, his subtle approach, the tantalizing pauses that had me desperately longing for more and more. And more.

Maybe I had never known what it was like to make grownup, uninhibited love with someone I was head over heels about, a man I really trusted. Who, astonishingly, seemed to feel the same about me.

As we lay holding each other afterwards, I felt sated, fulfilled and deliriously happy. And I know I made him happy too.

We spent all afternoon in bed, finally coming down to the kitchen around six to finish up the champagne and clear away the lunch we hadn't eaten. Then Joe cooked me dinner – leathery tomato omelettes. Ravenous, I wolfed them down. No question of my driving back to Paris, he said. I had better stay. So I rang up a neighbour and asked her to feed the cat, and without thinking about anything else at all, I spent a lovely night entwined with Joe.

Next morning he made coffee and then announced he was going to fetch a baguette from the bakery. I approved of this French-style behaviour and went upstairs for a languid bath in the old-fashioned bathroom. Sadly the buyer would probably have to update it, I reckoned. Hotel guests wouldn't put up with the iron stains on the bath or the scratched old tiles.

It would need a massive clean-up in general, not helped by the modified chaos that Joe and I had created. We must tidy before the prospective buyers arrived, whenever that was.

I wondered if Joe was getting a commission from the seller. Maybe he was looking for a new business in real estate. Whatever, I didn't care. Maybe when he said he'd 'tied up loose ends' that meant he was now out of work. I didn't care about that either. However little money we had we could survive.

He was so great-looking, I thought fondly, as I gazed across the breakfast table at him when he returned from the boulangerie. I love his intelligent, crinkly eyes and his rugged face. He reminds me of this house, large and classic, lived in. A bit messy but relaxed and sure of himself and where he's at. Perfect, really. Perfect for me, anyway.

And then there's something very sexy about his mouth. He always looks as if he wants to smile, or to kiss me, or both . . .

'I don't know how long you're allowed to use this place, but you can come and stay with me for a while in Paris, if you like,' I offered bashfully. 'Mind you, my flat is rather small for someone of your size.' I'd had the awful thought that he might have cooled off overnight, but that didn't appear to be the case. In fact, he was still staring at me as if I were the fairy on top of the Christmas tree.

'I have some other ideas,' he said. Then we were in each other's arms again and, not long after, back in bed.

It was some time later that he whispered that we had various things to decide and that he had stuff to confess to me.

Oh dear, I thought, here we go again. He isn't divorced after all.

But it wasn't that.

'I am thinking of buying this house if you approve of it,' he said.

'You? But . . .'

'Yep, I reckon it would be a fine place to bring up your son. Like, there's the swimming pool and the tennis court.'

'Yes, but, Joe, it must be terribly expensive. I wouldn't want you to get a huge mortgage you couldn't afford.'

He smiled. 'It's within my budget.'

'Right. But at one point you said you were trying to set up a new business.'

'Oh, I have a few small business interests all over, but I'm semi-retiring now. I thought you could keep me.'

'You're kidding. I mean, I could keep you if we lived in my flat, but not here.'

He laughed. 'Yep, I am kidding. It's all right, my darling. I can afford this house, and you and Alex. I've been winding up my affairs in Canada, like I told you. I wanted to settle in England near my daughters, but now, if it's what you want, I'm happy to be in France. Besides, I fell in love with you in France, in Chantilly, in fact.'

That caused a few more kisses, but when there was a pause, I took a deep breath. 'Joe . . . I'll have to check all this with Alex. It isn't just me. I've made so many mistakes in life and I can't go on messing him around. If he . . . Well, it has to work out between you and him too.'

'Of course it does. Now where can we go buy some animals for him?'

My feet hardly touched the ground for weeks. I stayed on in Chantilly with Joe, only going home to fetch my cat and my clothes. True to his word, he arrived back a few days later with the most gorgeous Labrador puppy. Fortunately the cat was not in the least fazed and terrorized the poor little dog by hissing and spitting every time it came within a couple of feet of her.

'Alex is going to adore them both,' I said happily.

'I bought you a present too a couple of days ago,' said Joe.

'What?'

'Insider Tours.'

'What do you mean?'

'I bought the company, the firm, from your friend Melvin. Well, I guess I made a kind of takeover bid. He wasn't pleased, but that's business.'

I was stunned. 'Blimey.'

'So you can be president and managing director if you want.'

'Me? I couldn't possibly run a big business.'

'Why not? You'd be great.'

'No, I wouldn't. I'd hate it.'

'OK, then just run the Paris branch to start with. Won't you enjoy telling that Elaine person not to wear such short skirts?'

I began to laugh. 'You are amazing, Joe, totally amazing. Are you a millionaire tycoon or something?'

'Not exactly,' he said modestly. 'But you don't have to work if you don't want to. We won't need the money. On second thoughts, maybe it's better if you don't. Then we can spend all day in bed.'

I grinned. 'You bet I want to work. Otherwise I'll be totally exhausted.'

It wasn't politically correct for a modern heroine, but that's how I became a tiny tycoonette, running two mini-businesses, more by good luck than good management or any kind of amazing entrepreneurial ability. I already owned *French Fantasia* and I didn't want to rule the world, or even Insider Tours, but I agreed to take charge of the Paris branch and I have to admit I rather enjoyed sauntering in that first day. Elaine was obviously quaking in her Piggy trotters, but I was magnanimous: I kept her on to run the office. She is efficient, and yes, I was still going to be a tour guide. Otherwise my man might get sick of me if we're always together. Not that he shows any signs of boredom yet, I'm glad to say. In fact, he seems to be as much in love as I am – which is a lot.

Joe gives me confidence, not just in bed. Even in the office I became a new, more powerful woman, thanks to him. Because he had faith in me, I had faith in myself, and I even thought about expanding and taking on extra staff. I'd probably only do it in a small way, because I wanted time for my menfolk, old-fashioned though that may be.

Of course, Joe isn't perfect. I discovered he was pretty untidy and that burnt steak and leathery omelettes were, in fact, the only things he could cook, but these minor drawbacks hardly matter when you're mad about someone. What else? Well, he can be a bit bossy and masterful, but I can be bossy too. And he likes to watch a lot of sport on the television, but that, too, seems healthy enough. And he's a news junkie, so he reads the paper for hours, deaf to the world. If I ever interrupt him, he doesn't mind, though. Even when he's doing his great financial deals on the computer, he says I can interrupt him anytime – he doesn't know how endearing that is. That and the fact that he listens to me and laughs at my jokes. And makes love to me so deliciously. Or have I mentioned that already?

'You're looking very well,' said Mary. 'Joe suits you.'

'He does,' I said smugly. 'But you look great too.' She did look very relaxed.

She told me she was overjoyed to have got rid of Virginia. Then we talked about Joe again – it was hard to stay off my favourite subject – and I was raving on about how it seemed wrong that I'd made a success of my business mostly because of a bloke rather than through girl power and my own efforts.

She smiled and said it was the way of the world and always had been. 'Besides, you've had a hard life, worked your socks off for years, and you'd actually built up your editing and tour-guiding on your own. You jolly well deserve this extra bit of luck.'

'Maybe I jolly well do,' I said.

'We all need a little help from our friends – even old Virginia came good in the end.'

Yes, indeed. I had forgiven Virginia because, thanks to her last remorseful email to Joe, he had reappeared in my life. And she did me a huge favour in nabbing Philippe.

She even said that to me.

Virginia had invited me to lunch at a fashionable restaurant, so gracefully I accepted. Glowing and flaunting her bump in an electric-pink number, she greeted me like a favourite sister and sat me down with lots of flattering remarks about my clothes and how great I looked.

'I can see you're radiantly happy, Clio. It's written all over your face, that wildly-in-love-and-never-out-of-bed look. Amazing that you managed to spare shagging-time to have lunch with me.' These last remarks were made in a penetrating whisper that must have been audible to half the restaurant.

Not sounding all that repentant, she then went on to ask my forgiveness. She'd got to the age and stage where she wanted a baby and a husband (note the order) and she fancied Philippe, so why not? She knew I didn't really love him, and anyway, she would handle him better than I did, she reckoned.

I had to laugh. 'You're such a classic bitch, Virginia.'

'Better a bitch than a dog in the manger like you were.'

There was no answer to that one. I certainly wasn't going to discuss my ex-relationship with her.

'So how's St Camille?' I asked innocently.

She grinned. 'Doesn't appear to be hugely crazy about me, but she'll come round. Bloody well better if she wants to see her new grandchild. Got to stand up to people like her, snobbish old bat.'

One has to hand it to Virginia. Her don't-give-a-damn attitude may be just what that family needs.

She's a terrible liar, though. Joe denied that he'd had sex with her on that trip to the Loire or any other time, for that matter. When I tackled her on the subject, she laughed and said yes, she'd made a pass but Joe had turned her down. To pay me back for being such a prig at the time, she'd invented a hot affair. She'd just been teasing. Might as well be hung for a sheep as a lamb, she thought.

Mixing the animal metaphors even further, I told her she was a shameless cow. She took it as a compliment.

As for that other terrible liar, Isabelle, I forgave her too because I was so happy, and I promised to stay in touch and visit her often. We talked for about an hour that first time I rang and then another two hours when I went to see her. She sounded genuinely thrilled for me, and said she liked Joe, especially when she heard that he wanted us all to set up home in France.

She didn't apologize for her machinations, but then regrets aren't Aunt Isabelle's scene. She did have a peace offering up her sleeve, though.

'Apropos Madame Claude,' she said suddenly.

I blushed scarlet. All this time I had avoided telling Isabelle I'd sold the precious ring. I know her lie was worse than my sin, but I've always majored in guilt.

'Do you have anything to say on the matter?'

'Which Madame Claude?'

'The jeweller, of course.'

I stammered out an abject apology and an explanation of my precarious financial situation at the time.

'But why didn't you come to me? What are friends for?'

'I'm really sorry, but it didn't seem right,' I said lamely.

'I understand. You wanted no involvement with Philippe's family, but I am a person apart, remember that.' She patted my hand. 'It so happens that Madame Claude thought she recognized the ring and telephoned me. For the sake of my memories, I bought it back, though she drives a hard bargain, that woman. If she is not careful, she will lose my custom.'

'Oh, I'm glad. That's marvellous. What a relief. I felt so guilty.'

She fished into her pocket. 'You are a nice girl, my Clio, and that is why I am returning it to you.'

I gasped. There it was, the lovely pink sapphire, safe in its box. 'But I can't . . .'

'Take it, my dear. You never know when you may need it again. A girl should always have something to fall back on. Tell me, does Monsieur Joe have money? He is not well dressed, but then Anglo-Saxons are often rich but scruffy.'

I grinned. 'He's very generous, and as far as I can tell, he's quite well off.'

'Excellent, excellent. Does he pay his ex-wife a large sum?'

'Isabelle, I haven't a clue. Besides, I can support myself, you know.'

'One must inform oneself of these matters.'

After more financial advice, she asked if we were getting married.

'Well, he hasn't actually asked me. I don't know if I'm any good at marriage . . . Anyway, we have to see how Alex and Joe take to each other.' I was quite anxious about this.

'Ah, yes, dear Alex. I wonder what he will think about it all. But I am sure he will like your charming Joe.'

Fingers crossed.

Alex and I were standing by the pool in Chantilly. Simba the cat was patiently stalking field mice by the flower bed, and Alex was playing with the Labrador bitch, now christened Toffee. Joe had been buying him animals ever since he arrived for the school holidays: rabbits, fish, hens, you name it, we had it. I didn't know who was going to look after this great zoo eventually, but it was an ideal way to get into Alex's good books.

'How do you feel about Joe, Alex?'

Alex stroked the puppy's velvet ears, causing her to shake her head and nip gently at him. 'So is he sort of your new boyfriend?'

'Mm.'

'He's OK,' said Alex gravely.

It sounded like a positive sort of OK. Hoping he wasn't just being polite, I sighed with relief. 'Good.'

There was a pause while we both stared over at the distant sheep.

'Sorry, I know that I promised we'd be on our own, but you see, Joe's so nice and . . .'

Screwing up his face, he said, 'It's all right, Mum. I'm older now, and lots of boys at school, well, their parents have problems and get divorced and stuff. Or they aren't married, but they change to another partner. Like, don't worry.' He seemed to be trying to put me at my ease.

I smiled. He was a month or two older at least. 'Thing is, Joe and I are very happy here, and I hope you are too.'

Alex looked thoughtful. 'Yes, he's great at tennis, and he does have a court and a swimming pool, which is pretty cool.'

Thank God children are pragmatic.

'And a brilliant car,' continued Alex, waving at the sleek new Mercedes Sports number. Not our only means of transport, I'm glad to say.

'So you really do like him?' Maybe I'm pushing too hard, I thought.

'Yes, he's cool, funnier than Philippe. Quite funny, really. And he doesn't shout about mess.'

'So you don't mind if we stay here?'

'Chill out, Mum. Course not. It's great. As long as you are happy.'

I smiled again at this grown-up statement, but should a child of his age have to cope with adult problems? 'I'm very happy,' I said. 'But I don't want to move here permanently yet if you would really hate it.'

'Honestly, like I said five times, the house is fantastic, Joe is fine, and I'm cool about it. Anyway, Granny thinks you need someone to look after you.'

I went on with my prepared speech. 'I know it's a bit of a way out of Paris, but we can still see Marie-Clementine and the cousins and your other friends.'

'Just as long as we don't ever have to go to lunch with old Camille again,' said Alex with a grin. Then he suddenly turned and said, 'I forgot something. Joe told me he wanted to marry you and he asked for my permission. Kind of weird, wasn't it?'

I stood rooted to the spot, speechless for a moment.

'So I said I didn't mind,' Alex continued. 'Is that OK with you, Mum? I mean, you don't have to. Unless you want to.'

'Yessss!' I said.

Then I saw his anxious face and spluttered, 'Maybe I'll wait and see for a while.'

He looked relieved, I thought.

I was too much in love to wait and see for very long. It was only a few months later that I phoned my mother to inform her I was getting married again.

She took it on the chin. 'Who to this time, dear?'

I grinned wryly. 'Joe Dryden, the Canadian. You met him at the museum.'

'I remember. Well, well, well.' After a pause she asked, 'It's not on the rebound, is it?'

'No, no. Well, it was extremely rocky, my relationship with Philippe, even before we broke up.' It would sound both gushy and girly and flighty to confess that I now realize I'd fallen in love with Joe almost at first sight, so I just added, 'Anyway, Joe's much nicer. We're really happy.'

'Quite right.' She was almost effusive by her standards. 'He's not a bad chap at all, that Joe.'

'So you're pleased. Thought you would be.'

She hesitated. 'Yes, dear, I think so. I never really cared for that Frenchman. Too much of a fusser.'

I smiled. Talk about the pot calling the kettle black.

She went on, 'I hope you're not rushing into anything.'

'No, Mum, not rushing at all.'

'What does Alex think?'

'He's fine about it. Especially as Joe has tactfully bought him a whole menagerie of animals.'

'That's good.' I could hear a deep breath. 'So where will you live?'

'Near Paris. Chantilly.'

'Oh, that's a relief. Now I really am pleased. I was afraid you were going to say he was whisking you both off to Canada, which would have been such a terribly long way away.'

Amazing. She's pleased. I've done something she approves of. And she cares where I live. I was touched. Any moment I was expecting her to discuss what hat my sister might wear for the wedding, but for once Roz didn't get a mention, even in passing.

'I think he will be a good influence on you, that Joe,' said Ma. 'About time you settled down at your age. Third time lucky, eh?'

'Definitely,' I said with a happy smile.